Danny Ray crossed his arms and his spurs rang lightly as he shifted his weight from one foot to the other. King Krystal looked intently into Danny Ray's eyes. "You've been through a great deal already during your present stay with us, have you not, Danny Ray?"

The cowboy grinned. "It was nothin', sir!"

Tweeeeeeeeeeeeeel! A high piercing whistle called everyone to attention. *Serpentine*'s elegant upper works were busy with hectic figures getting ready to sail.

Danny Ray glanced at the prince and the hellwain devil. He took a deep breath. Yep. Rescuing *Winter Queen* was one thing. Going up against the King of Fantasms and his cronies, well, that would be something else.

In a flash, the cowboy remembered Princess Amber's gray eyes, her laughter. The princess had been the only one in Elidor who had truly believed in Danny Ray as he had set out so long ago to rescue *Winter Queen*. And she had been the last person to bid him farewell as he had stepped back through the magic doorway to return home to Oklahoma. Now, she was out there somewhere, held prisoner by the fantasms. And he aimed to find her.

Starscape Books by Len Bailey

Clabbernappers
Fantasms

Fantasms

❧ LEN BAILEY ❧

A TOM DOHERTY ASSOCIATES BOOK
NEW YORK

This is a work of fiction. All of the characters, organizations, and events portrayed in this novel are either products of the author's imagination or are used fictitiously.

FANTASMS

Map by Ellisa Mitchell

A Starscape Book
Published by Tom Doherty Associates, LLC
175 Fifth Avenue
New York, NY 10010

www.tor.com

ISBN-13: 978-0-7653-4864-7
ISBN-10: 0-7653-4864-0

First Edition: February 2007
First Mass Market Edition: February 2008

Printed in the United States of America

0 9 8 7 6 5 4 3 2 1

Always for Denise

❖ Contents ❖

Buckholly
Harbor

FANTASMS

Port
Palnacky

Three Sisters

Hazelrigg
New
Capablanca

Islandum
Giganticum

Cricket Mill

Ockberry

Dragonfly Bay

Dumzil-
Daz

Checkered
Sea

Islandum
Magicum

Elidor

Wild are the winds
Of the Checkered Sea
Circling the world
In tranquility

Seasons come
Seasons go
Marching in time
In a timeless flow

Strong and sure
The hinges of day
Weak in their turn
Of black, blue, and gray

Ponder the center
Of any chessboard
The battle pieces
The unsceptered horde

This riddle flows
Like hourglass sand
Grain by grain
Let the hearer understand.

❧ 1 ❧

Cowboys and Clowns

"You all right, cowboy?" said a light, musical voice.

Danny Ray sat atop a cattle gate in his rodeo outfit: blue and white checkered shirt, black cowboy hat and matching leather chaps over his jeans. Even in the darkness of the hay shelter, his blue eyes shone brightly.

"Howdy, Caroline!" he said happily, his face immediately brightening up, his heart fluttering like a jar full of butterflies as he looked down into the face of an angel. Caroline Robertson's shoulder-length hair was as yellow as the shiny sun, and her twinkling eyes matched the clear blue sky around that sun. Her fancy leather top sparkled with rhinestones. He took off his gloves and left them on the gate, climbing painfully down and respectfully taking off his hat. He tasted dusty grit between his teeth and said, "Well, I got thrown in the arena, but I'm all right!"

"You want a second opinion?" she asked, smirking.

"Hey, Caroline! Saw you at the opening ceremony riding with the flag—mighty fine you looked, too!"

"Thanks, Danny." She smiled, noticing how he took in her

glittering red cowboy hat, the only one of its kind at the rodeo. She raised her nose up in the air and turned her head sideways: Caroline Robertson was this year's rodeo queen. Danny Ray sure liked her, except for that perky thing she did with her nose when she knew someone was looking at her.

"Hey! What d'ye say we go get a soda?" His head was swimming with the sweet scent of her perfume, overriding the rich, heady smell of alfalfa hay.

"Maybe some other time, Danny," she said, hesitating, and placed her small white hand on his shoulder. A flush of red passed over her cheeks.

"She's gonna get a soda with me," butted in a new voice. Here came Billy Whitehorse walking up, grinning like a possum eating a sweet potato. "After I ride Commodore, that is. He was my draw."

Danny Ray just shrugged.

"Real sorry you drew Tomahawk, Danny." But Billy Whitehorse didn't sound sorry. Instead, he spit on the ground and said, "Rode him last year and he slammed me into the panels pretty hard."

Danny Ray didn't say anything.

"Sure you're all right, dairy boy?" Billy laughed. It was more of a joke than a question. Billy prided himself on living on a real ranch, with horses and bulls, while Danny Ray worked a dairy farm. And Billy loved rubbing it in.

"Say, dairy boy!" Billy said. "You should get them blotchy black-and-white chaps for sale in the front window of Jackson's Rodeo Store—they're made outta Holstein cowhide. Then you'd be a real cow boy—get it? Ha, ha! Perfect for a dairy milker boy like you! You'd look like one of them fire engine Dalmatian dogs! Never seen a dog ride a bull before! Ha, ha!" Billy snorted and Caroline tried not to smile at the ridiculous picture in her mind.

Danny Ray was feeling pretty low. He reached up, grabbed his gloves, and plopped them together.

Billy Whitehorse stopped smiling and stepped forward, his spurs jingling. The two boys were the same height, the front rim of Billy's white hat rasping against the front rim of Danny's black one.

"I got your girl and next I'm gonna get your championship belt buckle." Billy's hands doubled up in fists. "Gonna try to stop me, dairy boy?"

"I ain't gonna fight you, Billy," said Danny Ray. "You got something out for me. Don't know what, but that's your problem, not mine."

"You're just chicken," Billy Whitehorse said as he cast an amused look over at Caroline. He came right up in Danny Ray's face, their noses just inches apart, and waved his elbows up and down clucking, *Blaaaawk! Blaaaawk! Blaaaawk!*

"Danny Ray don't have to give you no excuses!" Leaning back against the shed was a rodeo clown with a painted face, bright red and white striped shirt, purple suspenders, and blue shorts. Yellow knee-length socks stood proudly above a pair of red sneakers. "He figures you can't ride old Commodore with a black eye and a fat lip!"

Billy studied the clown a moment and then turned back to Danny Ray. "Nah, I don't think so. He's just chicken! Ain't that right, dairy boy?"

The distant PA system announced the name of Bobby Lee Henderson, Danny Ray's brother.

"Billy James Whitehorse!" Caroline stated, tugging at his hand. "Stop talking silly! It's almost time for your ride! Let's go!"

Billy looked Danny Ray up and down one more time and, with mock respect, touched the front rim of his hat in farewell.

"Danny," said Caroline apologetically, a strand of her blond hair straying to the corner of her mouth. "Maybe I'll see you later, huh?"

"But probably not!" said Billy over his shoulder, laughing. He jerked Caroline around by the hand and led her away toward the arena.

The rodeo clown sauntered over, sniffed with his painted red nose and sighed. "Bad day, eh, Danny Ray? Well, just goes to show: some days you're a cowboy, some day's you're a clown."

"What d'ye mean by that?" Danny Ray frowned.

"Oh," said the clown, "you'll understand someday. But hey! I'll bet ol' Billy Whitehorse gets thrown off in three seconds—get that nice white hat of his all covered with dirt and manure! Yessir! And then we'd have to call him Billy Brownhorse!"

"I don't need your help," muttered Danny Ray. "I can take care of myself."

"But you needed me in the arena a few minutes ago, huh?" replied the clown with a grin. His teeth looked yellow against his stark white face paint.

Rodeo clowns commanded a whole lot of respect. Once a cowboy hit the ground, it was their job to run straight at the bull and wave their arms and legs to draw the bull away from the rider. It was a dangerous job wearing bright colors and clapping and waving, shouting and running in front of an angry, frustrated bull.

"So, it was you that got ol' Tomahawk off my tail?"

"Yep. Only me—Hanky the Clown!"

"Obliged to you." Danny Ray touched the rim of his hat. "Where'd you get a name like Hanky?"

"Don't rightly know." He smiled with a twinkle in his eye as he pulled and pulled a polka-dot handkerchief from his pocket, and it got bigger and bigger until it was nearly the size of a tablecloth! *HONK!* He blew his nose and Danny Ray chuckled out loud.

But then the cowboy grew serious and leaned back against the gate and lowered his head. He and the clown were alone, the other riders and workers crowding around the corral to witness the next ride. The PA system blared and garbled out something incoherent.

"Thinking about quitting, are you, cowboy?"

Danny Ray took off his hat and ran his fingers through his chestnut hair.

Hanky continued: "Don't worry none 'bout Billy Whitehorse. Commodore'll give him what's coming to him. Too bad, though," he added with a special gleam in his eye. "If only Billy had to ride a real commodore, eh, Danny Ray? Huh? A *real* commodore!"

Danny Ray's backbone tingled as memories of the magical kingdom of Elidor flooded his brain. Riding atop the Sarksa Commodore, a stick-thin, immensely tall pirate with a head like a praying mantis and a long whip tail with a razor-sharp stinger on the end, is an experience quickly burned into one's memory bank. Danny Ray had ridden the savage pirate, his bright blue rope looped tightly around the creature's neck. He tensed, re-membering the excruciating pain when the commodore had plunged its stinger into the small of his back.

Danny Ray snapped out of the whirling memory to find that he had dropped his gloves and was in danger of crushing the rim of his cowboy hat in his fist. He flipped out a red handker-chief and wiped the sweat from his forehead. His threatening encounter with the Sarksa commodore hadn't been of this world—so how could this rodeo clown know about it?

Danny Ray moved out from behind the gate. "Who the heck are you?"

"Question is," answered Hanky, stuffing his handkerchief back into his pocket, "who are you?"

The clown pointed his orange-gloved hand into the shadows across the barn where bales of hay were stacked twenty feet high. Just beyond, a shiny doorway glimmered mysteriously.

"The magic doorway!" breathed Danny Ray, putting on his hat.

"Recognize it, do you?" asked Hanky softly. "Takes a special feller to walk through that doorway once—but an even more special feller to do it twice. Are you that sort of feller?"

Danny Ray studied the doorway. Sure enough, it was the same door as before, shimmering, glimmering, popping with sparks. He wiped his mouth with the back of his blue and white checkered sleeve. He recalled what had happened before when he had stepped through that door: falling, twirling, whipping dizzily through the air until arriving in the Kingdom of Elidor and surviving an unforgettable string of hair-raising adventures. The faces of friends from that strange world flashed through his mind: beautiful Princess Amber, Captain Quigglewigg with his orange face and green whiskers, Prince Blue, the elegant Sultana Sumferi Sar, Hoodie Crow and Piper the master gunner.

There followed images of the monsters he had battled: GrimmAx the gargoyle, the Sarksa pirates, devils, bollhockers, and skull-mungers, and the Ghost of Buckholly Harbor. Danny Ray had been stung nearly to death, had almost plummeted to certain death hundreds of feet off the back of the red bat, was nearly eaten by a Sarksa queen and then again by an ol' nasty ghosty. But, shoot! Looking back on it, he had had a hoot-hollerin' fun time! And Prince Blue had found his true color and that fair, wondrous kingdom of Elidor had been saved from the grip of the tyrant, King Dru-Mordeloch of Trowland.

Danny Ray snapped his head around as cheering erupted from over near the corral. Bobby Lee had ridden his steer the full six seconds. There'd be no living with his bragging for the next few months.

He looked back at the sparkling door.

"What's on the other side of the door this time?" Danny Ray thought he'd ask, just in case.

"Could be anything." Hanky shrugged, reaching down to retrieve the cowboy's gloves off the dusty ground. "Could be anywheres."

"Last time I walked through that door I had a real neat magic blue rope given to me," said Danny Ray.

"Well," said the clown. He went to rub his chin but checked himself: he didn't want to smudge his makeup. "You go walkin' through that there door and I'll sure as sugar see what I can do for you."

Hmmm, thought the cowboy. Why was he being chosen . . . again?

Danny Ray walked cautiously toward the door. He could feel its power, he could see his wavering reflection in its liquidlike surface.

"I know you're hurt right now, Danny Ray, and you might not be up fer an adventure. Your tailbone feels like someone got a hot poker up it, right?"

"You rid bulls before?"

"Ridden most everything," said Hanky, shaking his head as his yellow mop hair twirled from side to side underneath a tall, black stovepipe hat. "And had most everything ride me, too. But the rodeo's the place for me. Yup. Even if I can't ride no more, well, I can still help out. Anything's better than quittin'."

"Well, I ain't no quitter," said Danny Ray. "Somebody, or a whole bunch of somebodys, on the other side of this doorway needs help real bad, right?"

The clown smiled and made an orange thumbs-up.

A drop of sweat tickled Danny Ray's cheek. Just then, Billy Whitehorse's name was announced, blaring out over the arena along with the name of Commodore, the bull he was about to ride.

"Well," said Danny Ray. "I ain't accomplishing much on this side of the door, am I?"

He pressed his hat down firmly on his head, hitched up his belt, and checked his chaps.

"So long, Hanky," he said. "Watch my gloves for me."

After a deep breath and an ever so slight hesitation, Danny Ray leaped through the flashing liquid door!

❧ 2 ❧

Mumpokers!

The swirling, howling darkness roared about Danny Ray, pushing him head over heels and spinning him around like a top. The Storm Demon shrieked, nearly deafening him as it wrapped its bitter cold wings about the cowboy. Danny Ray had ridden the storm once before, but not one this hauntingly dark, not one so cruelly intent on harming him. The screaming and the howling increased in intensity. Danny Ray clamped his eyes shut. He grabbed on to his cowboy hat and held on for dear life as he continued falling into oblivion.

He felt the Storm Demon lick the side of his face with a cold blast of wind, heard the sound of heaving wings, and the tempest began to subside.

And then, silence.

The bottom of Danny Ray's boots touched against something solid. He waited for the darkness to dissipate, but instead it deepened. Stars appeared overhead in the still, watchful silence of night. He stood on the bank of a sleepy, gurgling creek spanned by a small bridge. Its stonework, long ago encrusted with moss and creeping vines, was the sort of bridge that might inspire tales of terrible trolls hiding in the shadows beneath its hoary arches, or nasty creatures bent on malice and mischief to little boys.

Where the heck am I? he thought.

His cowboy boots made hollow sounds as he took uncertain steps across the bridge into a meadow, quiet and peaceful with a star-dusted sky overhead. He walked easily along, hemmed in on either side by a dark forest.

Up ahead, a huge temple with large white pillars dominated the landscape. It seemed forlorn and tired in the darkness. Its pale dome glowed like the moon above the surrounding trees.

Danny Ray opened a tall iron gate that honked like a goose and led into the temple's manicured gardens. Hedges appeared out of the night like sculpted monsters, while even dainty fruit trees took on uncharacteristically menacing forms.

The sound of crunching gravel beneath the cowboy's boots stopped. He studied the temple's four pillars, each fashioned in the likeness of a graceful, robed woman, each of whom grasped her robe with one hand and beckoned out toward the garden with the other.

But then Danny Ray's eyes widened. He gasped aloud, striding quickly to a long, heavy table of marble draped in black ribbon. There lay the silent, still body of Princess Amber, King Krystal's daughter, peaceful in death. She was arranged beautifully in a glimmering golden robe, a circlet of fine gold practically invisible amid her radiant blond hair that framed her perfect face. Tiny silver slippers peeked out from her robe.

Never again would they carry the small feet of the princess down the garden paths, never again twinkle brightly as she skipped up the palace stairs, never again bear her lightly around the dance floor.

Danny Ray slowly removed his hat. His blue eyes overflowed with tears as he remembered Princess Amber's warm, coy smile when he had returned after recapturing *Winter Queen*. Danny Ray had saved her from being forced to marry the evil King Dru-Mordeloch.

"So, I'm back in Elidor after all," he half whispered to himself. "And things are a whole lot worse than when I left!"

He edged a hand toward Princess Amber's lifeless fingers, adorned with costly rings. "Ouch!" he said and jerked back his hand.

"Ouch!" he yelled again, but this time from a sharp, stabbing pain right smack-dab in the seat of his pants.

"Who are you, peeking and sneaking around here?"

Danny Ray turned and looked down to see a small golden-haired girl in a white dress holding a spear.

"I ain't peekin' and sneakin' nowhere," he said, bending down to look her full in the face. "Who the heck do you think you are with that silly spear?"

"I'm Cherry Quiggs—Princess Amber's Traveling Maiden!" she replied proudly. "I'm supposed to stand guard here at the Temple of the Dead until Princess Amber passes into the Vale of the Moon!"

"You're just an ornery little girl! Go ahead and point that pig-sticker somewhere else!" He guided the sharp point of the spear away from his face. "Seems like every time I come to this doggone world I get poked in the rear!" He turned from the tiny girl. A sad look passed over his face as he studied the princess. "Well, I knew her. She was a real nice girl."

"I loved Princess Amber with all my heart." The corners of Cherry's mouth dropped. But she lifted the spear again. "And I'll stick any thief—"

"I ain't no thief. I can't hardly believe you haven't heard of me: my name's Danny Ray," he said, doffing his hat.

"You have funny clothes."

"I'm a rodeo cowboy from Oklahoma, from the Otherworld. I was here in Elidor a while back."

"Which star is Oklahoma?" asked Cherry, looking up into the night sky.

"I think it's on the backside of them stars," he said, pointing up into the heavens, "or on this side under beneath, sort of. Shoot—I guess I don't rightly know!"

"What's that sticking out of your back pocket?"

Danny Ray felt around behind him and exclaimed, "What the heck—a slingshot! So, this is the shining friend Hanky promised me!" exclaimed Danny Ray. It glowed with a red, glittery light.

"Your friend to help you steal the princess's ring!" Cherry scolded.

"I ain't stealing nothing!" scoffed Danny Ray.

From out of the temple, a group of little men, dark in the starlight, waddled down the stairs toward them.

"Great," said Danny Ray, sighing. "Mumpokers! King

Krystal's palace guards!" He rubbed his rear end, remembering his very first encounter with their sharp barbed spears. "They ain't grown a whole lot since I saw them last, neither."

They were shorter than short, meaner than mean, and quickly surrounded the cowboy. Their helmets were black bowls, each with a hole in the top where sprigs of blond hair jutted out sharply. Their armor glittered black in the candlelight and they each carried long black lances tipped with sharp hooks.

"Ouch!" cried Danny Ray as the captain of the mumpokers jabbed him in the seat of the pants. "Dang it! That hurts!"

"Quiet!" said the captain. The mumpokers broke out in this chant:

"The word is Mum!
The word is Mum!
If you babble as such
We'll poke yer bum!
If you yabble too much
Your rear'll be numb!
So perk up yer ears
The word is Mum!

The word is Mum!
The word is Mum!
Don't care who you are
Or where you're from!
If you're a star
Or if you're a bum!

Just shut yer yap
The word is Mum!

The word is Mum!
The word is Mum!
For yackity-yack
We'll poke you some!
For clackity-clack
We'll beat yer drum!
We'll smash yer thumb!
We'll squash yer plum!
So knackity-knack
The word is Mum!"

3

The Wooden Princess

"I am Lord Red!" said a stocky stump of a man robed in crimson with bright medals on his chest.

The mumpokers parted as he broke through their circle. "What in the blooming blubbering blasted blazes is going on here?"

Cherry pointed at the cowboy. "He tried to take a ring off Princess Amber's finger!"

"Why you little—I didn't do no such thing!" countered Danny Ray.

"A thief!" Lord Red's black mustachio slanted in a sneer across his face.

"Lord Red, you know I ain't no thief!" exclaimed Danny Ray, crossing his arms in a defiant gesture.

"Shut up!" snapped the captain of the mumpokers. Yellow eyes peered out from his round black helmet pulled too far down over his forehead. He only stood as high as the boy's silver-studded belt, but he motioned menacingly with his lance.

"Wait a moment," said a tall man, robed in green, coming to

stand by Cherry's side. He looked Danny Ray up and down. "It's that young cowboy fellow from Yokyhama!"

"Oklahoma, Lord Green!" corrected Danny Ray. "You guys forgotten already what I did for you—rescuing *Winter Queen* and all?"

Lord Green's eyes glittered on either side of a sharp, beaklike nose as he asked, "Tell me your name?"

"Danny Ray!" replied the exasperated cowboy. "Stop foolin' around. It ain't been that long since I was here last."

Another fellow in a yellow robe pointed a trembling finger at him. "Just because you saved Elidor doesn't mean you can swagger up here on our terrible day of grief, and hope to steal jewels from the princess. Foul deed—you thieving thief!"

"Crooked crook!" agreed Cherry Quiggs.

"Robbing robber!" croaked the captain of the mumpokers last of all.

"Who dares to disturb my daughter's rest?" came a new voice, a soft voice, and an old voice all in one. "Who is interrupting her tranquil journey to the Vale of the Moon? And where, where is her Journey Maiden?"

The new voice belonged to a white-haired man robed in gold and wearing a crystal crown. He tapped his cane along the gravel path, followed by members of his court. Little Cherry met him and hugged the folds of his robe.

Immediately, the mumpokers bowed, as did Lords Red, Green, and Yellow, but the cowboy remained standing, blinking in the dim torchlight.

"Cherry, my dear," said the king, reaching down and stroking her hair. "What is wrong?" But before she could answer the old king's eyes settled on the cowboy. "I am King Krystal. There lies my daughter, Princess Amber, fair flower of Elidor, dead. Young man, what trouble are you causing that the mumpokers and Lord Red, Lord Yellow and Lord Green should speak so harshly to you—should seek to arrest you? Speak!"

"It's me, Danny Ray!" cried the cowboy. He started toward the king but the mumpokers barred his way. "Danny Ray— from Oklahoma, sir! From the Otherworld! Don't you remember me?"

King Krystal hobbled next to the bier where Danny Ray stood. The mumpokers, mumbling and grumbling, reluctantly parted. The king tapped his cane on the ground and the tip began to glow brightly. He held it up near the cowboy's face and his own grief-torn face brightened.

"Danny Ray!" he cried.

"Do you know him, Your Majesty?" asked Cherry, still clutching the king's garment.

"Know him? Why Danny Ray rescued *Winter Queen*!"

"What is a Winter Queen?"

"*Winter Queen* is my huge, twenty-five-story queen ship that was stolen from me. Danny Ray came into our world and voyaged across the dangerous Checkered Sea and rescued *Winter Queen* just in time for the Great Chess Game against evil King Dru-Mordeloch. And he saved Princess Amber from marrying that evil villain!"

The old man paused and looked down on Princess Amber's still form.

"But remembering those glad days brings me much pain, much pain, indeed. A few of my subjects," he continued, with a sidelong glance at Lord Red, Lord Green, and the cowering Lord Yellow, "wonder if I have succumbed to hopelessness. My eyes are red from weeping and from sleeplessness. I walk slowly and stumble from being pressed down with grief. And my memory, as you can testify, is somewhat scattered because of dreadful fears of the future. My eldest daughter, Elidor's princess, is gone forever!"

The king reached toward her cold, white hand.

"Wouldn't do that if I were you, sir," warned the cowboy.

"Wouldn't caress my beloved daughter's hand before she leaves for the Vale of the Moon?" asked the king crossly.

"Well, sir, when I touched your daughter's hand a moment ago, I got this splinter." Danny Ray held up his finger. "Don't know about Elidor, sir, but where I come from, a princess ought not to have splinters."

Danny Ray continued. "This ain't your daughter, sir. Seems to me it's just a block of wood—as prime and seasoned a cut of birch wood as I ever seen! Someone must have whittled long and hard to make it look like the princess. Nice paint job, too!"

"A wooden princess?" scoffed Cherry.

"Utterly unbelievable!" cried Lord Red, stepping up next to the king.

"Palpably preposterous!" declared Lord Green.

"Beyond belief!" Lord Yellow exclaimed.

Danny Ray gestured to King Krystal: "Go ahead, sir, see for yourself!"

Everyone held their breath and leaned in, watching intently as King Krystal laid his knuckles against his daughter's hand, then gently, ever so gently, knocked.

There came a hollow sound.

"This is most alarming!" said King Krystal. "Where, then, is my daughter? But—but then this is also heartening! For it means—oh, be still, my rapidly beating heart—that my daughter is alive! Perhaps she is in danger, but she is not dead!"

"Someone has absconded with the princess?" asked Lord Red, changing his mind and his tone.

"And has made it appear as though she's dead!" remarked Lord Green, brushing a hand beneath his chin.

"Oh!" cried Lord Yellow, on the verge of fainting.

"Yes! But for the first time, I have hope! Princess Amber is alive!" exclaimed the king, taking a deep breath and knocking gleefully on the beautifully carved block of wood. "Ha! Oh, Danny Ray, how blessed we are that the Lord Advocate has sent you to us once again!"

⇒ 4 ⇐

Fantasms!

"Something's wrong!" Cherry cried, and hugged the king's robes tighter.

Danny Ray felt it, the heavy air pressing in with an ominous weight, like a storm was brewing, but strangely there was no thunder, no lightning. The candles around Princess Amber's bier flickered while their larger cousins, the torches held high by the mumpokers, waved and sputtered.

The wind sighed sorrowfully.

New hope that his daughter was alive made King Krystal's eyes sparkle. He studied the starry heavens as if the form of Princess Amber might appear in one of the far-off constellations. But the mumpokers—oh, that was a different story! They were afraid that the princess might appear and they hunched and scrunched and bunched together. Much to the consternation of the king, they began to chant this song in low voices:

"What if we see a ghost, a ghost?
What if we see a ghost?

Who will she scare the most, the most?
Who will she scare the most?

Down from the stars or up from the ground
She's ironbound, she's flower-crowned
And till the sun has called up the day
We'll sing, we'll sing, we'll sing away!

But what if the ghost sees me, sees me?
What if the ghost sees me?
It'll be time to flee, to flee!
It'll be time to flee!

Down in the ground or up to the stars
We'll sit in our holes and smoke our cigars!
And till the sun has called up the day
We'll sing until she flies away!"

"Some palace guards you are," King Krystal snorted, "putting fear, cowardice, and running away to song! Cigars, indeed!"

"Yeah," snickered the cowboy, jumping at his chance to jab back at them. "Maybe you should call 'em mum-*smokers*!"

The king chuckled, but then caught himself as the air became even more charged with energy. Danny Ray felt it; a slight humming emanating from the ground up through his boots.

The cowboy looked toward the temple and his heart skipped a beat. The statuesque women of the pillars shimmered with a translucent inner glow. One of the women came to life and began to move her arms and her head while the pillar's capstone of flowers and berries became her crown.

She stepped out onto the front stairs of the temple.

The captain of the mumpokers trembled, his kettlelike helmet bobbing up and down on his head. With a chorus of yells and shrieks, he and his men broke and ran, yelling and yammering through the garden gate and out into the meadow. Lord Yellow could contain his fear no longer and went shrieking into the darkness after them.

The figure's eyes opened and cast a ghastly stare down upon them out of a fair face belonging to a princess or a queen, crowned with a diadem decorated with dragonflies and flowers. The folds of her exquisite robe waved slowly, as if in an underwater dance.

Lord Red and Lord Green were pale and shaking but Danny Ray reached in his back pocket for his trusty slingshot.

"Princess Amber!" whispered King Krystal. His mouth opened in wonderment as he perceived her white, marblelike shine replaced by a soft inner light. "Amber the Golden—my precious child!"

"Father?" said the mouth of the ghost. Her voice was sorrowful, unnatural, deep. Her horrible eyes changed to gray, then became as flesh, turning this way and that, searching. Danny Ray felt his legs shaking and his mouth became as dry as cotton.

"My dear!" King Krystal made a move toward her.

"Father! Stay where you are if you value your life!" Her voice was urgent, commanding. "I am not alone. I am held prisoner."

A further transformation took place, no less amazing than the first. Each of the other sculptures of the remaining three pillars transformed into black-draped figures. Within the hooded shadows of their faces there glowed orange slits for eyes. They stood tall, imposing, surrounding the princess and whispering threats, curses, and murderous imaginings. Upon their robes gleamed crawling, slithering images of foul creatures, designs of perdition, and filth runes.

Danny Ray broke out in a cold sweat. It seemed that the foul creatures were focusing their eyes, their hate, directly at him.

"Are you among the living?" asked the king. "Or have you drifted forever beyond the moon?"

"I am living, Father, but barely so." The ghost of Amber mouthed the words. "As fragile as a butterfly's breath, so is my life. As the delicate butterfly's wing, so is the thin plane upon which my life rests."

She continued: "These dark enemies who have abducted me from the land of sunlight, of pleasures, of warmth and green hills, are most powerful." On her upraised arms, Danny Ray saw cuffs of iron connected by thin, fiery chains. "These who hold fast my chains are called 'fantasms'!"

Lord Red covered his mouth and quickly held up a medallion as protection. Lord Green gasped the dreaded name: "Fantasms! Heavens help us!"

"At the coming of the new moon, when the moon is not in the sky," said Amber, her fair and yet horrible face turned down upon the king, "then shall the cup of my life tip over, and my spirit wing its way to the Dark Vale of the Moon."

"No! Not there!" King Krystal raised his silver cane threateningly at his daughter's abductors, and he trembled with fury as he barked out harsh words of reproof. But the fantasms only laughed, their eyes glowing an even sharper orange, and then to demonstrate the futility of the king's warning, they pulled viciously on her chains.

"Hold on there!" Danny Ray heard himself call out. The princess directed her eyes toward the cowboy. There was a hesitation, a brief questioning in her glance—did she remember him? Just as the cowboy went to challenge the fantasms, her image and those of her tormentors shimmered and trembled and began to waver and fade.

"Father!" she said. "Do not risk your life or that of any other person. Consider me beyond reach, already beyond the moon." She pointed northward. "Grieve and wail only briefly for my passing. Remember me when you frequent my garden, this fair place where I will never walk again!"

"Amber!" cried King Krystal, and it saddened Danny Ray to hear the anguish in his plea. "Don't go! Most precious, most beautiful flower in all of Elidor—do not leave!"

"Fare you well, my king. Fare you well," she said, and raised her hand, "my father!"

"Amber!" he cried once more. He dropped his cane and stumbled forward—if he could grasp just the hem of her robe! But the vision vanished and the pillars turned back to cold stone. But where her vision had been, another took its place: the daunting image of King Dru-Mordeloch of Trowland.

"Watch out, sir!" cautioned Danny Ray.

The cowboy reached down, grabbed a stone and fitted it to the slingshot. Faster than you could say Willamy Womp-Wrider, he shot at the dark horned figure, who uttered a malicious laugh as the stone passed through him and clattered against the temple door's moon dial.

"Well, finally we meet, Danny Ray rodeo cowboy!" Dru-Mordeloch's red eyes swiveled over to the king. "Did I not warn you, King Krystal, of my power in magical arts, and of my coming season of retribution, that I would be revenged of you and your insults, and that your kingdom would someday be mine?"

"I should have known it was you who stood behind the disappearance of my daughter," said King Krystal harshly, "as it was you who had also plotted to kidnap *Winter Queen*."

"But you ain't gonna get away with kidnapping Princess Amber!" put in Danny Ray. "We beat you last time and we'll beat you again!"

Dru-Mordeloch laughed. "Ah! Your threats against me, Danny Ray, are as useless as that red contraption you hold in your hand. The fantasms are not mere Sarksa pirates, and believe me, you will learn the difference!" His image began to shimmer and fade. "Farewell for now, Danny Ray! But be assured that I will exact my revenge on you—personally!"

"What will we do now?" asked the king in a soft voice.

"Shoot, sir!" exclaimed the cowboy. "There ain't no need for a long face! Your daughter's alive!"

"Why, yes!" said a spirited King Krystal. "Yes! Amber is indeed alive! Ha, ha!" He breathed deeply and smiled. "Elidor will be a happy place again as it was when I danced with her as *Winter Queen* sailed into Birdwhistle Bay!" The king slapped the cowboy on the back.

"What's a new moon, sir?" asked Danny Ray.

Lord Green answered from his depth of knowledge of all things celestial. "The full moon slowly dwindles, night after night, until it is completely gone from the night sky. A new moon happens once a month: it is a night of complete darkness—a night without a moon."

"Wherever Amber is, you'll find her, won't you, Danny Ray?" pleaded the king. "But we must hurry! After the new moon, the princess will be beyond our help!"

"I'm going, too!" exclaimed Cherry.

"I'm sorry, my dear," the king replied, shaking his head. "This rescue will be far too dangerous for a little girl."

"Especially for one as ornery as you!" added the cowboy.

"But I'm Princess Amber's Traveling Maiden!" she responded, raising a defiant nose in the air, just like Caroline Robertson, Danny Ray thought.

"Your Majesty," said the cowboy. "Last time I was here I learned that I can't go it alone. I'll need some help."

King Krystal, ignoring Cherry's hugging and tugging on his robe, addressed the whole group: "Luck is on our side—Danny Ray, the rodeo cowboy from Oklahoma, has returned to us! Danny Ray, name your companion!"

"Where is Prince Blue? Can I take him with me?"

"Oh, my goodness!" cried King Krystal as embarrassment spread over his wrinkled face. "When I thought Amber was killed, I wrongly suspected that the same strange magic that had transformed the prince into Prince Blue was somehow to blame."

"You blamed Prince Blue for what happened to Princess Amber?" asked the cowboy. "Well, where is he now?"

"The dungeon!" gasped Cherry. She pointed to a nearby group of gnarled trees that shadowed a walkway lined with tall iron posts joined together with heavy chains. They led up to an immense rusty door standing in deep shadow.

King Krystal shook his head. "I've made a terrible, terrible mistake!"

⇥ 5 ⇤

Electric Cockroach

 Danny Ray stood directly in front of the iron door leading into the dungeon. Large figures of armored knights decorated the door, each standing with weapons drawn to warn trespassers. But the cowboy wondered who could break into such a place?

Lord Red took out a heavy key and fitted it in a large, ornate padlock until it went *click!* It took all of Lord Red's considerable huffing and puffing to push the door open. Damp, musty air hit the cowboy in the face.

"Prince Blue's in here?" asked Danny Ray.

King Krystal nodded dejectedly.

"An evil place!" whimpered Cherry.

"All dark and damp," said the king.

"All wet and wormy," put in Lord Red seriously.

"All clammy and creepy," finished Lord Green, flashing the cowboy a sinister smile.

Danny Ray looked at Lord Green and Lord Red. "I take it neither one of you is going in with me? Maybe you guys should be wearin' the same color as Lord Yellow: yellow for cowards!"

King Krystal held Cherry back as the cowboy entered the dungeon, alone. The door slammed shut behind him—pushed by a fuming Lord Red probably.

As he walked along the tunnel it became darker and darker. He felt a cold wall and that seemed to steady him as he began coaxing himself along, one foot in front of the other, like a tightrope walker. Overhead, something flickered with a yellow iridescence and then winked out in an instant.

"Hello!" Danny Ray called. The void was silent. He was alone, with only his echo to keep him company.

"Lookee there!" Danny Ray muttered for only himself to hear.

The pinprick of light reappeared. Danny Ray sniffed and put his hands on his hips.

ZZZzzzZZZ, buzzed the tiny light.

"Gosh!" cried Danny Ray with delight as it came to rest on his forefinger. "It's—it's an electric cockroach!" he declared.

It didn't just glow in the tail like fireflies back home in Oklahoma. Nosiree, the whole cockroach, from head to tail, was lit up with a bright, yellow light. Danny Ray held it aloft like a lamp in the darkness and saw that the tunnel had opened up into a cave.

The cockroach took off and buzzed in circles around his head and then landed on the front rim of his cowboy hat, shining out like the light on a miner's helmet. Danny Ray reached out to either side and felt only cool, damp air.

"Gosh!" he said as a large purple spider with white and black stripes scurried onto a high ledge of rock and disappeared into a crack where veins of glittering minerals streaked the walls like frozen lightning.

As he ventured deeper and deeper into the earth, the air

became heavy. Something on the ground moved, something shiny, metallic, like a hefty centipede or maybe a silver serpent. Its red glowing eyes looked his way. It paused, as it rose on its multiple squirming hind legs and spread open its sharp jaws, making an awful clicking, whining noise.

CLANG!

Something long and red struck at the worm, and it jumped to one side. As his eyes adjusted to the darkness, Danny Ray could see the short red spear, poising for another strike. No—it was a tail!—the tail of a tall, red devil with black horns and an evil scar down the side of his face. The devil was shackled to the rocky wall at the wrists and ankles with heavy, iron chains, but his tail was free, coiling, waiting for another opportunity to strike out at the worm.

CLANG! CLANG!

"Stalker-tracker!" growled the devil, intent on the vicious worm trying to force its way around him.

Danny Ray backed away to the opposite wall. He felt something in his back pocket and reached around. That's right—he had a slingshot! It glowed with a red, glittery light—just what the doctor ordered!

"Ha!" shouted the devil, taking another sideways swing at the worm—a "stalker-tracker" the devil had called it, pinning one of its legs against the wall with his pointed red tail. The silver creature squirmed, squealed, and screamed. The devil winced, a deep growl wrenching from his throat as the serpent-thing writhed violently back and forth. Sweat beaded up on the devil's shiny red face. It wouldn't be long before the stalker-tracker wriggled free.

Danny Ray reached down to the dark floor with frantic

fingers. The glowing cockroach shed the light he needed as his hand closed down on a jagged rock—lucky find! He fitted it in the slingshot's cradle, pulled back—*whack!* The stone merely ricocheted off the thing's shiny, hard shell.

The cowboy grabbed another stone. He crept closer and pulled back the arms of the slingshot farther, farther. He waited, feeling the icy pain building up in his forearm. Still, he waited. The devil let out an agonizing growl—the stalker-tracker was beginning to wrestle free!

"C'mon," whispered Danny Ray, holding the slingshot dead still. There! The worm raised its hideous head, poised up on its back legs, its mouth opening to reveal its vulnerable white innards, surrounded by fangs, sharp and curved, dripping with thick, oozing poison.

WHACK!

Danny Ray's aim was true. The sharp stone shot down the worm's throat with a sickening, wet smacking sound.

The stalker-tracker rolled back and forth violently on the stone floor, screeching horribly. The cowboy covered his ears. But now the devil's angle was lethal. It poised its sharp tail above the worm and stabbed down viciously, piercing deeply into the worm's protective armor. The devil snarled, jabbing its tail in deeper, deeper.

Then the screeching stopped. The nightmare thing lay still. The devil laid his head back against the cave wall, breathing heavily as the electric cockroach buzzed along the length of the lifeless creature, circling around its head, around its blank eyes.

Danny Ray glanced about him. "This place is worse than any jail I ever seen!" He shivered and looked back to make sure the dreadful worm was really dead.

"D'ye hear that, boys?" came a voice. "Hey, Jonesy! This young feller ain't never been here before! Ha, ha!"

There, chained against a nearby wall, sat a group of sullen, grimy men.

"He'll find out soon enough, Chipper, when the gorimuth finds him down here!" answered another voice. "Let's tell 'im where he is, fellas!"

Then they all joined to sing in unison:

"Have you not heard of Dumbledown Dungeon?
It's of great renown, you know!
If you lie or steal or gripe and complain
It's where you're bound to go—
Oh, yes!
It's where you're bound to go!

Have you not slept with rats and snakes?
You'll be wide awake, you know!
With spiders and bats and flies and worms
And cockroaches that glow—
Ha, ha!
And cockroaches that glow!

Have you not dined where it's dark and damp?
It's a sickening thing, you know!
What plops in your soup bowl, sings on your spoon
May go down your throat kinda slow—
Yum—yummy!
May go down your throat kinda slow!

Have you not played in Dumbledown Dungeon?
It's a frightening thing, you know!
With ghosts and bogies that yell "peek-a-boo!"
And it's waiting for you here below—
Watch out!
And it's waiting for you here below!

So, if you've not heard of Dumbledown Dungeon
You should watch what you do, you know!
If you lie or steal or gripe and complain
It's where you're bound to go—
Oh, yes!
It's where you're bound to go!"

"Gosh! You guys know that song pretty well," replied Danny Ray.

"Got lots o' time to practice, ain't we?" snorted the one called Jonesy.

"Just a croakin' choir in chains, are we!" said Chipper bitterly, spitting on the ground from a space between his front teeth.

"So, what in tarnation landed you guys in jail?"

"To be answering your question, young fella," interjected Jonesy, "we'm over here be in prison for stealin' *Winter Queen*! Ain't you remembered of us?"

Danny Ray's misty memory began to clear. He recognized the tall hellwain devil as the leader of the crew of thieves that had stolen the queen ship *Winter Queen*. The devil's yellow eyes glowed as he looked up from cleaning the stalker-tracker's white blood off his tail; presumably, he remembered the humiliation of surrendering the ship and his sword.

"But what we done don't stack up to what that little sprig of royalty done!" added Chipper, jutting his chin toward a disheveled boy in blue tattered clothes sitting next to the devil.

Danny Ray knelt in front of him. "Prince Blue! Holy cow— I barely recognize you!"

"Do I look that bad, Danny Ray?" The prince smiled grimly. "They don't have mirrors down here, or lights for that matter." Danny Ray could see that his hands were bound by iron cuffs and chains that clinked and clanked as the prince rubbed some patch of horrid, sticky, gummy stuff sticking to his robe. "I certainly don't feel like Prince Blue anymore."

"Prince Grungy Stinky Slimeball is more like it!" The cowboy reached out and took hold of his chained wrist.

"Let the prince tell you what evil he done!" piped up one of the prisoners.

The devil shuffled protectively next to the prince and growled: "Shut yer stinking gobs!"

"You don't scare us, Tûk!" jeered Jonesy. "You're wearin' the same chains like'n us!"

"Well," said the prince gloomily, "does my good friend from Oklahoma have a magical way of getting me out of here?"

"You're being set free. Princess Amber's alive!"

"Alive? But how—"

"WHO YOU?????" boomed a frightful voice. "HOW YOU GET HERE?"

Danny Ray nearly jumped clean out of his boots. There stood one of the ugliest, meanest creatures he had ever seen.

"Ain't you never seen a gorimuth before, boy?" cackled one of the prisoners.

The stocky, black-scaled gorimuth strode toward them. It looked like a huge mound of shiny slick slime. Its large, glassy-red eyes took in the cowboy, and from its forehead dangled a thin fingerlike appendage with a small, bulbous light shining on the end, for lighting up the deep caverns of the dungeon. It had two sets of arms, two protruding from each side of its neck and two from near its hips, presumably to hold a prisoner, slap him in the face, and lock him in irons, all at the same time.

"The gorimuth's got you now," snickered Chipper, looking Danny Ray's way. "Now you're one o' us!"

"You'll come to like it down here, cowboy," said Jonesy. "The scruff-rats is real polite—genteel, you might say."

"Hush down!" gurgled the gorimuth, his thick black lips plopping one over the other. "Or like a sausage I eat you! M'm?"

"My name's Danny Ray," said the cowboy, not waiting to be asked. "I'm a rodeo cowboy from Oklahoma."

The gorimuth's lips vibrated as he stepped toward the cowboy. As quick as lightning, Danny Ray scooped up a stone, fitted it in the cradle of the slingshot, and aimed it straight at the hideous, oozing beast.

"C'mon, you big scaly squid-fish!" He pulled back the rubber arms of the slingshot. "You lay a hand on me and you'll get what's coming to you!"

The gorimuth considered the unfamiliar weapon.

"His Maj'sty, King Krystal, sent me down here to spring this fella free," said the cowboy and motioned with his head toward Prince Blue.

"He's lyin'!" insisted the one called Chipper.

The massive gorimuth shook his head with a disapproving grunt, a crease slicing through his jellylike forehead.

"No I ain't," assured the cowboy. "Besides, you got enough hands to grab us both if we try something stupid, right?"

"You're trying something stupid now," commented Jonesy, jerking on his chains with a clink. "He ain't gonna take you nowheres!"

"You have my word of honor on it!" said the cowboy, lowering his weapon. "And I'm sorry for pointing this here slingshot at you!"

"Blub—a—blubba," blubbered the gorimuth with his thick lips, and considered Danny Ray again. He produced a large iron ring from which dangled crude, odd-shaped keys along with the shrunken head of a vicious rat. He unfastened the prince's heavy chains from the wall and locked them onto his thick iron belt.

"UP!" he commanded. With his lower set of thick black hands he lifted Prince Blue bodily to his feet and jerked on his chains to lead him away.

The devil called out to the departing prince: "Farewell, Beesa Blue! Much good luck!"

"I'll be back for you, Tûk!" said Prince Blue.

The dangler angler lamp on the gorimuth's forehead glowed brighter to show the way out of the dungeon. "Leg it! Both n' you!"

The bright electric cockroach flitted in circles, buzzing a farewell. Danny Ray tipped his hat goodbye. He was a little sad to leave his glowing friend behind.

⋆ 6 ⋆

Serpentine and *Wasp*

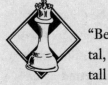 "Behold, *Serpentine* and *Wasp*!" cried King Krystal, gesturing upward with his silver cane. Two tall bishop ships, each nearly two hundred feet high, were tied to the pier in Birdwhistle Bay. Danny Ray eyed the graceful curves of *Serpentine*, all the way up to her upper deck where green and yellow lights twinkled on and off. Next to her stood her twin bishop, *Wasp*, fashioned of purple masonry.

A ray of sunlight shot over the eastern mountains and smote *Serpentine*'s top knob, the dark green stonework glowing with a rosy hue. *Wasp*'s glowed with a strange orange halo.

"Those are a neat pair of ships!" said Danny Ray happily. Prince Blue blinked in the morning sunlight, newly freed from Dumbledown Dungeon and his chains. Lord Green and Lord Red stood nearby, fuming.

"Yes!" the king proclaimed. "I am exercising my authority as King of Elidor, Cherrydale, Birdwhistle Bay, and of Ironwood: I have chartered these two bishops, *Serpentine*, commanded by Captain Mumblefub, and *Wasp*, by Captain Giddyfickle."

But then Danny Ray's expression changed. Wait a minute—he

had experience with bishop ships. On his first adventure, he had sailed with the prince, Lord Green, and Lord Red from this very harbor, noisy with cheering multitudes of people waving colorful flags in the noonday sun, sending them off. They had boarded a bishop ship at that time, the *Anabella*, and she had broken down not long after they had reached the open sea. He and the prince had been picked up shortly thereafter, walking on the Checkered Sea, by *Hog*, an old garbage hauler rook commanded by one Captain Quigglewigg.

Near the pier stood the Tree of Wisdom, the greatest of the old trees in Elidor. King Krystal sat down beneath its massive limbs. A flurry of yellow and brown leaves fell despondently to the ground from its drooping branches, silhouetted against a nearby glow globe. The king watched the cowboy's skeptical expression.

"Thinking about the old *Anabella*, Danny Ray?" he guessed. "But *Serpentine* and *Wasp* are sound ships! True, they're bishops and can only sail diagonally, but they're two of the fastest bishops on the Checkered Sea—and reliable!"

The cowboy nodded. He recalled the Sarksa pirate ships *Vulture* and *Black Widow*. Both of them had been bishops, and both had been formidable enemies.

"Where is *Hog*?" asked Danny Ray. "And Captain Quigglewigg?

"I honored your request for him before you departed last time—he has a new rook ship now. He could be anywhere on the Checkered Sea. But these two bishops will suffice beautifully, eh?"

"Last time I was in Birdwhistle Bay, sir, it was a real cheerful place," remembered Danny Ray. "Birds flyin' all over a-squawkin' and chirpin'. Shoot! I don't see or hear a danged songbird anywhere!"

The cowboy looked up. A large blood buzzard winged its way across the bay, its dark red wings outlined against the whiteness of Mount Featherfrost rising majestically in the pale blue sky.

"Alas!" said King Krystal, "the songbirds have gone for the same reason that the trees are sorrowful. The birds will return and sing their melodies once again and the trees will lift their weary arms only when Princess Amber returns to Elidor! A wise leader must listen to all of his subjects, but especially to the trees and birds! They have voices, too, and sense danger to which we mortals are blind. I only hope," he continued thoughtfully, "that there are trees where she is now."

There came a rumbling sound. A rook ship, high as a tall building, sailed into Birdwhistle Bay from the Checkered Sea, heading toward a nearby pier to unload her cargo. The harbor's black-and-white-checkered surface was as polished and hard as the open sea beyond, never a wave, never a ripple.

"Wow!" mouthed Danny Ray. "I'd forgotten how big a rook really is!"

Rook ships were a little shorter than bishops, but wider, heavier, and more powerful. This rook's stern bore the name NORTH STAR, and her crew, odd-looking blue-skinned fellows with hooked noses and fur balls for hats, waved from high up on the deck.

"Where do you think Princess Amber is now, Your Majesty?" Prince Blue asked.

"Amber gestured to the north, a slight clue with a reference to her whereabouts," replied the king. "That rook that sailed by just now is named the *North Star!*—perhaps that is a favorable omen!"

Lord Green leaned down and whispered something to Lord Red who nodded and chuckled softly.

King Krystal beamed. "You are our returning champion: the one and only Danny Ray. You and Prince Blue must choose your quest companions."

"I'm not a champion anymore, sir," muttered the cowboy. He nudged the ground with the toe of his boot. "I got thrown during my last ride before the six seconds were up."

"The lad is unsure of himself, Your Majesty!" Lord Green said. "The fantasms are beings from a time before time and they served an evil before evil!"

"How can you have a time before time?" Danny Ray frowned. "Or an evil before evil? You're nuts!"

Lord Red jumped in. "Deception is the fantasms' main weapon, and they are able to take on new and ghastly shapes at will!" His voice sank to a whisper. "They are said to feed on the stolen souls of the innocent and beautiful. What is known of them are fragments of myth and legend. Until now. I shudder to think what evil has stirred them to action. Legend holds that they live in the dark regions where none who have gone have returned."

"If no one's ever returned, how do you know all this stuff?" countered the cowboy.

"Fantasms are too dangerous for a mere cowboy!" shot Lord Red, ignoring him. "They are not tangible like the Sarksa pirates. Why, a rodeo cowboy won't have a, a—" Lord Red's temper had so choked him that all his words clogged up together in his throat.

"A snowflake on a hot griddle's chance?" suggested Danny Ray.

"Well, yes!" Lord Red's beefy jowls champed together in frustration. "Yes! A snowflake on a hot, well—whatever a griddle is, yes, I suppose. But Your Majesty, you get my point, don't you?" Lord Red looked to the king for help. "Lord Green and I must be allowed to accompany this—this cowboy!"

Lord Green, with images of the sun and moon glimmering in his green cone hat, stepped forward, spreading his hands out solemnly. "Every thousand years, the King of Fantasms is released from his dark prison and wanders to and fro across the unsuspecting world with his lesser kings. And why? He must bring the number of fantasms to five, for then he can revolt from his eternal chains and usher in the return of the Age of Stars, when there will be no sun, no moon. There are now but three fantasms—we all saw them, did we not? So we must stop him from gaining two more kings!"

Lord Red spoke up: "The fantasms will spin Danny Ray around until he won't know left from right, up from down. My prowess in fighting and Lord Green's magic is what is needed here! Just think of the other creatures that await him! Dunnies and feapers, gnomes and creepers, whiners, pinkets, giants and leapers, brags, bogey-beasts." Lord Red exhaled, his black mustachio wiggling back and forth at the corners of his mouth. "Spunkies, pipsqueaks, spriggans, gnomes—"

"You already mentioned gnomes," pointed out Lord Green.

"Well, then," Lord Red said, frowning, "if that is not enough, there's black fians, scrags, selkies, and pookas!"

Lord Green's eyes sparkled with emerald flashes as he stated: "And what of magical herbs, of plants and fantastic flora?" He opened his hand. A green flash revealed both scraggly purple leaves and sparkling stems with thorny flowers. "Can Danny Ray reveal the powers of Mucklefinn weed, or of Tinsel-leaf, or of the Harlequin flower? Indeed, not! Your Majesty, I think Danny Ray will want Lord Red and myself to go along to rescue the princess."

"What a hoot!" Danny Ray laughed. "When the fantasms showed up last night with their spooky orange eyes, you and Lord Red almost wet your pants! But listen to you now—all brave and ready to go sailing across the Checkered Sea to rescue the princess! Nosiree. Prince Blue and me—we'll find Amber wherever she is!"

Two figures appeared on the roadway—the gorimuth jailer, reappearing from Dumbledown Dungeon, and behind him, in chains, came a most fascinating red prisoner.

"What is the meaning of this?" shouted Lord Red, his black mustachios quivering with temper.

"The hellwain devil!" exclaimed Lord Green, peering at the sharp black barbs along the inside of the hellwain's forearms. "He's supposed to be in jail!"

The gorimuth brought him to the king and unlocked his chains. Danny Ray looked up at the red devil. He stood seven feet tall and bared his fangs, but there was an unmistakable sign of amusement in that grimace. He wore only a black loincloth and a thick leather belt with a small pouch.

"This is Tûk," announced Prince Blue proudly, placing one hand on his hip, the other gesturing proudly toward the crimson-skinned creature. "He will be accompanying me and Danny Ray to rescue the princess."

"We insist on going, too!" broke in Lord Red.

"Lord Red and I were left behind last time!" added Lord Green.

"Bah!" spit out Tûk.

"Be still!" cried King Krystal testily. "Lord Red—hold your tongue—and you as well, Lord Green!"

The cowboy crossed his arms and his spurs rang lightly as he shifted his weight from one foot to the other. King Krystal looked intently into Danny Ray's eyes. "You've been through a great deal already during your present stay with us, have you not, Danny Ray? A short stint in Dumbledown Dungeon; squaring off with our jailer; poked in the seat of your pants again by the mumpokers; scared to death by fantasms; and finally—oh, blessed Danny Ray!—discovering that my dear daughter's dead body is actually a fake!"

The cowboy grinned. "It was nothin', sir!"

Tweeeeeeeeeeeeeel! A high piercing whistle called everyone to attention. *Serpentine*'s elegant upper works were busy with hectic figures getting ready to sail.

Danny Ray glanced at the prince and the hellwain devil. He took a deep breath. Yep. Rescuing *Winter Queen* was one thing. Going up against the King of Fantasms and his cronies, well, that would be something else.

In a flash, the cowboy remembered Princess Amber's gray eyes, her laughter. The princess had been the only one in Elidor who had truly believed in Danny Ray as he had set out so long ago to rescue *Winter Queen*. And she had been the last person to bid him farewell as he had stepped back through the magical doorway to return home to Oklahoma. Now, she was out there somewhere, held prisoner by the fantasms. And he aimed to find her.

❖ 7 ❖

Commodore Mumblefub

 "The Tower of the Rose!" cried Prince Blue; standing on *Serpentine*'s upper deck. The tall, majestic tower glowed with a rosy hue as *Serpentine* slowly glided by. "See how it reflects pink in the morning sun."

Danny Ray removed his hat in reverence to the mighty tower. Its top, shining with a white beacon, stood out beautifully against the sky.

Tûk loomed nearby like a silent bodyguard. The black pitchfork that he leaned on must have been eight feet tall, while the golden hilt of his sword winkled and twinkled from its scabbard. Oh! How the devil must have hooted to be reacquainted with the gallant weapon that he had given up when *Winter Queen* had surrendered!

He scrunched up his long hook nose, and Danny Ray wondered if it was because Prince Blue still smelled like a caravan of camels. Maybe it was because the last time Tûk had seen this tower was as a prisoner aboard *Lady Amethyst* as she had sailed into the bay.

Prince Blue snapped his fingers, a mighty rude thing to do, and Tûk handed him a telescope as they approached yet another tower looming ahead, guarding the western approach to the harbor.

"What is that tower?" asked Danny Ray.

"The Tower of Fire. Its walls glow with a fiery orange flame when the sun sets. As you can see, these two towers stand as sentinels to Birdwhistle Bay's entrance. When we pass between them, we will be out on the open sea."

Prince Blue became distracted. The cowboy followed his gaze upward to the ramparts of the mighty structure. Outlined against the orange light of the tower stood a cloaked figure.

"Princess Ruby," said Prince Blue. "She is Princess Amber's older sister. She has lived alone atop the Tower of Fire since her husband, Lord Purple, died."

The prince handed the telescope back to Tûk, whose slick black tongue licked his upper fangs as he refocused the glass and handed it to over Danny Ray.

Princess Ruby's image leaped large into the lens. Somehow, the cowboy had expected her to be gazing down upon *Serpentine* as she sailed slowly out of Birdwhistle Bay. Instead, she looked out to sea. Her profile was delicate and breathtaking, her black hair and cloak waving wildly in the brisk morning breeze. He could guess at her eyes, dark and cold like deep wells, and her red lips, in sharp contrast with her pale, white skin. Danny Ray was struck by her presence, even at this great distance, so much loneliness, so much heartache.

Serpentine's impressively high deck was dominated by a huge globe jutting up from the center, creased downward from near the top by a wide slit, and topped with a small knob. Danny Ray thought it looked like a grinning seal balancing a small egg on its nose. Across the middle of the globe stretched another horizontal deck, where he could see sailors lined along the perimeter, and near the top knob yet another deck. What a vantage point they must have! Danny Ray thought, as the bishop turned and headed northeast on the long diagonal.

"Many pardons, Beesa Blue," said the hellwain softly. Tûk had quietly slipped away and reappeared with two cups of steaming honeysin.

The sweet fragrance of the mug's contents wafted into the cowboy's nostrils. He touched his lips to the warm cup, sipping cautiously at first, like a cat, and then like a dog, gulping down the whole rich, spicy concoction. He wiped his mouth with the back of his sleeve and nodded his thanks to the devil, handing him the empty cup.

"Hmmm, that's good!" the prince said, nodding, still sipping his. "But make it hotter next time, eh, Tûk?"

What happened next nearly popped the eyes right out of the cowboy's head. Tûk took the mug, and from the hellwain's mouth shot a blue flame that licked around the open mouth of the cup. The honeysin began to swirl and steam.

"My lands!" exclaimed Danny Ray. "That's the darnedest thing I ever saw!"

"That's enough, Tûk!" said the prince, tapping the hellwain on the shoulder.

"You'd be a hoot in Oklahoma, Tûk!" remarked Danny. "The most popular fella at the church barbecue!"

The hellwain grimaced. Satisfied that the prince was satisfied, he stood back out of the way.

"What's with him callin' you Beesa Blue?" Danny Ray inquired.

"Well," replied the prince, catching a drop of the golden drink with his forefinger and then licking it off. " 'Beesa' means 'strong friend.' I got him out of prison, remember?"

"Yeah, but don't that just make you even? I kinda remember he saved your bacon in the dungeon—"

"With your help, Danny Ray, yes, I know. So, anyway, Tûk is now my personal bodyguard—sort of."

"Your butler, more like it," commented the cowboy.

"Now, now. Tûk has loyalty, and I simply could not argue him out of his decision."

"I didn't hear you try very hard," said the cowboy wryly. Danny Ray glowered at the prince, thinking back on how scary Tûk had appeared as a warrior aboard *Winter Queen*. The devil looked absolutely preposterous serving drinks. "In fact, I didn't hear you try at all!"

The prince waved him off while Tûk, oblivious to their conversation, was happy to bring up his long red tail with its barbed tip and scratch behind his ear.

Danny Ray narrowed his eyes at the prince. He noticed that he hadn't bothered thanking Tûk.

THUD!

"Belay there!" came a shout.

A swarm of sailors parted to reveal a chest lying a-kilter on the deck with a mound of gold coins cascading out its lid. One sailor screamed as a huge gargoyle raised a whip of knotted ropes called a cat. Down came the whip, *WHACK!*, and down again, *WHACK! WHACK!*

"My dear prince!" coldly announced a tall, thin man, uniformed in dark green to match *Serpentine*'s general color scheme. Ribbons and a single gold star adorned his chest. His matching half-moon hat, worn sideways, made the cowboy think of Napoleon Bonaparte, had Bonaparte been tall and skinny.

"Although your dirty robes prohibit me from calling you Prince Blue, I have berthed you and your servants below in the State Cabin, along with your dunnage."

"Thank you, Captain Mumblefub," the prince said, glancing up at his medals.

"Aha, not captain," Mumblefub said, his thin fingers flicking beneath a long thin nose. The dark eyes residing under wispy black eyebrows appraised Danny Ray as he corrected the prince, touching the gold star on his chest. "With two vessels under my command, the *Serpentine* and *Wasp*, I now rate a commodore."

WHACK! WHACK! The bosun continued to beat the poor sailor, and Danny Ray wondered if the commodore even noticed. Tûk widened his nostrils, trying to catch a scent of Mumblefub. Evident dislike played across the hellwain's red face.

"Many pardons, Commodore Mumblefub," said Prince Blue, bowing. "And many congratulations."

The commodore made a weak attempt at returning the bow, with a slight nod of his head, continuing all the while to look Danny Ray over: the cowboy hat, the blue-and-white checked shirt, the chaps and boots. The commodore's eyes reflected what could only be interpreted as haughty amusement.

"*Serpentine* and *Wasp* are handy ships, very fast," said Mumblefub. "We can run any pirate top-knob-under in just a few hours."

"Allow me to introduce Danny Ray," offered the prince, "and Tûk."

The commodore turned his back on the cowboy to view the bosun continue to beat the hapless sailor.

Danny Ray spoke up: "When's that gargoyle gonna stop whipping him?"

"That is my bosun, KinKill," said the commodore casually. He clasped his hands behind his back and mused: "Discipline is the key to success in any venture, is it not? Especially on such a dangerous voyage as this—nasty fantasms, and whatever else awaits us! I simply cannot insult such a fantastically wealthy monarch as King Krystal, by allowing his generous payment to be strewn all over the deck. M'm?"

The screaming ceased, but not the beating with the cat, as the sailor fell unconscious. The bosun seemed to loose interest, tucking the bloody cat back in his belt and directing the body to be dragged away and the trail of blood swabbed from the deck.

"Now, let me return your congratulations, Prince Blue," said Commodore Mumblefub, displaying a beautiful gem-studded gold watch on a dazzling golden chain. "On the occasion of your being released from Dumbledown Dungeon and having your royal title of prince returned to you!"

Prince Blue's face lit up. "Why, thank you!"

He carefully opened the watch cover, and to his amazement there was no hour, minute, or second hand but a round smiling face with emerald-green eyes. "Nine o'clock of the morning it is!" said a musical, lilting voice. Just then, the ship's bells struck twice.

Mumblefub went to walk away but turned on his heel and said, "Kindly step back from the front edge, young sirs, and your devil servant, too. Grab hold, if you please!"

"Nice meeting you, too," said Danny Ray under his breath when the commodore was a safe distance away.

"Ha! But overjoyed to be a commodore is he!" The hellwain smiled, uttering his first real sentence since coming aboard *Serpentine*.

The commodore reminded the cowboy of Lord Green, the way they both spoke in that musical, indifferent tone, along with their uncanny ability to smile with their mouth while their eyes remained hard and unfeeling.

As the two bishops sailed out from the shadows of Mount Featherfrost's arms, the sparkling expanse of the marbled Checkered Sea opened up, stretching out before them as far as the eye could see.

Orders were shouted and sailors scurried back and forth across the deck in a sort of organized chaos, preparing the bishop for fast sailing. The bishop would be picking up speed soon.

Tûk said: "Take a grip-hold of the hand ring, Danny Ray. Here!"

Danny Ray grabbed onto the ring and with his free hand took off his cowboy hat, letting the fresh wind tousle his chestnut hair. He murmured, "I'd forgotten how the Checkered Sea glitters!"

"Thousands of miles across," replied Prince Blue. "*Serpentine*'s a bishop, so we must sail diagonally northeast toward the

Islands of Magic and then diagonally back northwest. If we had been lucky enough to charter a rook, like the old *Hog*, then we could have sailed straight north. But, like Mumblefub said, *Serpentine* and *Wasp* are extremely fast."

The hellwain looked to the distant horizon, perhaps thinking of home, wherever home was for a pirate.

A white seagull wheeled overhead, balancing perfectly on the wind's edge, squawking harshly at them. It dove playfully over their heads, and for that split second, the cowboy let go of the hand ring—

"Danny Ray!" shouted the prince.

As *Serpentine* lurched forward, the cowboy was jerked violently backward and his feet flew up into the air! A cascade of color flashed before his eyes, of sky blue and dark green, wind whistling in his ears, and then a collision with the deck and a crushing pain in his shoulder. Danny Ray lay still then rolled over onto his side and found himself nose to nose with a pair of black boots. He followed the boots up above the dark green leggings, above the dark green officer's coat adorned with ribbons and a gold star, upward into the stern face of Commodore Mumblefub.

"You did that on purpose!" Danny Ray sat up and found he was near the steerage wheel—he had flown halfway across the deck! Tûk ran up and helped him to his feet, and then glowered at the commodore and gripped his pitchfork menacingly.

Commodore Mumblefub's chin jutted down toward the cowboy. "Young sir, I ordered you to grab hold—that means to *keep* hold, as well! Prince Blue, you heard me warn him, did you not?" The commodore's stern eyes shifted to the cowboy, who was still rubbing his sore shoulder. "Hmmm. I take it, young sir, that you feel you should receive special treatment—that you are not required to thoroughly obey my orders. For instance, Prince Blue had the sense—"

"Yeah, but you saw me let go!" Danny Ray winced in pain.

"Young sir, discipline is the order of the day, hm? I was busily engaged in preparing this ship for a hasty departure, which contributes greatly to my standing orders from King Krystal. I do not have the time or the inclination to double-check the diligence of each person aboard this ship in obeying my instructions. No doubt you'll gain your sea legs soon enough and stand on the deck with the best of my sailors!"

Tûk handed Danny Ray his slingshot and his cowboy hat that had blown into the scuppers near the edge of the deck. Danny Ray continued to work his shoulder and then began straightening out a dent in the crown of his hat.

"Course east by n'east, sir!" called out the helmsman, wooden faced, keeping his eyes straight ahead.

"Keep it at that." Mumblefub turned back to the cowboy. "*Serpentine* was to sail a light voyage into the south seas, visit Spice Mountain with their dancing camels, singing snakes, and the warm air filled with cinnamon rogue spices. Hm, but no matter. I can't pass up this much money." The commodore waved his hand toward more iron chests of gold being carried across the deck and down below. "*Serpentine* may not be your first choice but you are not mine, either."

The towers of Birdwhistle Bay had dwindled beneath the horizon as the two bishops sped along, leaving Elidor far, far behind.

"Our time together has started off rather unhappily," mused the commodore, without much conviction. "So then, young sir. Rule one: I am the commander of this vessel. Rule two: Listen to the commander. Rule three: Obey the commander—or you will be miserable."

"I'm already miserable," said Danny Ray curtly.

The sailors who were congregated around the massive steerage wheel held their collective breaths as the commodore cleared his throat with a gurgling sound that at first sounded to Danny Ray like nervousness, but from the terrible glow in the commodore's eyes, could only be interpreted as cold, furious rage.

"You will address me as commodore, if you please," said Mumblefub, touching his badge with shaking fingers. "Or even if you don't please, young sir—or should I say Danny Ray, the wonder boy! Oh, yes! I've heard about you—your former exploits and what a fine hero you are, how you abandoned the *Anabella*, a bishop like ours, when she became disabled. But I personally find you discourteous, even disrespectful."

KinKill, the bosun, the bloodstained tips of his whip grazing the deck, came to stand at the commodore's elbow. His fearsome eyes, shining with undimmed malevolence, took in the cowboy and his strange clothes. Up close, Danny Ray could see that the large dark spots on KinKill's hide were actually tufts of coarse hair. The horns atop his head were longer and sharper than those of other gargoyles Danny Ray had seen. KinKill apparently represented a very dangerous species.

But then the bosun caught the piercing stare of the hellwain devil towering behind Danny Ray and the needle-sharp prongs of his pitchfork, and his left eye flickered with a nervous twitch.

Prince Blue placed his arm around the cowboy to guide him away, but Danny Ray pushed him away in a huff of anger and muttered, "Leave me alone!"

"Enough, Danny Ray!" the prince said under his breath. "For goodness' sake, keep your temper!"

"Aha. Enough, indeed," Mumblefub said, flicking at his nose in a contrived, nonchalant manner that galled Danny Ray. The commodore looked up and down at Prince Blue's grimy robe and at the filthy hellwain devil. He turned to a nearby lieutenant and nodded with his head. "One of my officers will show you below to your cabin. Enjoy a hot bath. Change clothes."

Mumblefub considered the frowning cowboy, and coldness closed like a curtain across the commodore's features. "Aha," he concluded, with a curt nod of his head to the cowboy. "But we shall draw a very, very cold bath for you, Danny Ray, my young hotheaded sir!"

❋ 8 ❋

The Horrible Cat!

The next morning boasted a fresh, clean gusting wind in the bright sunshine—just what Danny Ray needed! He stood at *Serpentine*'s front rim, the wind long ago having blown back his hat that fluttered like a butterfly against his shoulders, secured around his neck by the rawhide chinstrap.

He shivered, not from the cold, but from a memory of yesterday in the bath quarters—of looking in Prince Blue's tub and seeing wicked little black bugs and beetles and centipedes swimming and struggling in circles in the soapy water. Yep, Dumbledown Dungeon must really be a downright filthy hole.

After his bath, the cowboy had slept uneasily all night, a dark, fitful time of toss 'n' tug, rolling and muttering, with fantastic dreams of hideous monsters wearing Holstein chaps chasing him over the whole length and breadth of Cherokee County. One episode had seemed particularly real, that of a fantasm peering in through the sleeping-cabin window, but when the cowboy had rubbed his sleepy eyes it had disappeared.

Danny Ray snapped out of his daydream as the ship's bell

sounded out eight times. Feet scampered up from below as the watch changed. The cowboy glanced around: no commodore in sight. The crew went about their duties; some making, some mending, some scrubbing, some polishing. *Serpentine* was a spit-and-polish ship, everything in its place and everything dazzling, glinting like fire.

A storm was brewing, with a deep rumbling of thunder like distant cannon fire. The breeze freshened, strengthening into a strong crosswind. Up the signal halyard scurried several colorful flags, arriving at *Serpentine*'s top knob and flapping maddeningly.

"First lieutenant's signaling Cap'n Giddyfickle," said a likable sailor standing nearby, his face splitting into a toothless grin. He was dressed in nankeen trousers and a red and white striped shirt, his gangly, candy-striped form dwarfed by the massive black and green center ball of the bishop. He gestured back to *Wasp*. "Cap'n Giddy's a drunky, mind it mate—drinks too much! Never was a cap'n better named. And he's a bit loose wid his line o' sailin'—perturbs the Commodore Mums somethin' fierce! Look how ol' *Wasp* sails off kilter like, off her station proper!"

But even after the lieutenant's signal, *Wasp* continued to wander back and forth in her diagonal path. The officer snapped shut his telescope and pointed to a gun crew. Danny Ray flinched as a signal cannon banged out, an angry retort matching exactly the lieutenant's mood and meant as a warning for *Wasp* to pay attention to the signal flags. The acrid smell of gunpowder wafted across the deck—and sure enough, answering flags from the dark purple *Wasp* flew up into the wind.

Someone aboard *Wasp* was restoring order to her helm. She began steering true, in the exact middle of her diagonal path.

"So, what were ye a-thinking of just now, mate?" asked the sailor.

"Those clouds." Danny Ray pointed to the dark band of storm clouds marching up from the south, threatening to cancel out the sun. "I saw Princess Amber's face. But then it changed, boiled and swarmed over into a weird shape, like a fantasm."

"All o' that in one cloud?" said the sailor. "Well, don't you worry none, Mr. Cowboy. We'll find yer princess fer you!"

But how? thought the cowboy. Where is she now, this lovely princess? And when the fantasms attack, will they do so all at once or one at a time?

A whistling woodwind tone sounded over the deck as the bishop's center ball turned, lining up its enormous slit to the change of the mounting wind. The cowboy felt an immediate surge in speed as the bishop offered less resistance to the elements.

The sailor laughed and said, "You ain't used to bishop ships, is you?"

"Nope," he replied, placing his hat firmly on his head. "Last time I sailed, it was on a rook called the *Hog*."

"Bishops ain't like rooks, nosiree!" said the sailor as a small company of his buddies gathered around them, one of them producing a small accordion.

"We seen how you was cruelly knocked about yesterday," said the accordion player. "And we have us a song as to put *Serpentine*'s finer manners for'ard. My name's Tipsy from up Scalawag Shoals way, and we'm fittin' to play you this song, Danny Ray."

Tipsy smacked his foot down in time, the accordion whining like a complaining cat, and the crew joined in with this chorus:

"A rook is a pig
And a pig is a hog!
The knight is heavy
And jumps like a frog!
Yes! The knight is heavy
And jumps like a frog!

Ship there! Deck there!
O'er the sparkling sea-o!
If they're thieves or scum or pirates or thugs,
They're just like you and me-o!

A bishop is fast,
A graceful tower
But compared to the rook
Has a little less power.
Oh! Compared to the rook
Has a little less power.

Ship there! Deck there!
O'er the sparkling sea-o!
I kissed the captain's daughter twice,
Just between you and me-o!

But in beauty and speed
And power supreme
All pieces and pawns
Must bow to the queen!

All pieces and pawns
Must bow to the queen!

Ship there! Deck there!
O'er the sparkling sea-o!
If you can swab the deck and lay a gun,
Come sail along with me-o!
So swab the deck and lay your gun,
And sail along with me-o!"

"Deck there!"

The singing abruptly stopped as a call came from the lookout perched high atop the bishop's top knob.

The singing band of sailors scattered, jostling to their stations, leaving Danny Ray alone with the accordion player who continued to play softly, his attention being drawn out westward over the sea to where the strange ship had been spotted.

The cowboy strode over to a polished wooden rack holding a large green telescope embossed with gold and fine writing. The image of two distant bishops sailing southwest toward Elidor sprang sharply into the lens. His experience aboard *Hog* quickly reasserted itself as he focused the glass in a flash, their details sharp and defined in the magnificent telescope. The cowboy was still surprised at how motionless he was able to hold the telescope. In his own world, how a ship might pitch and roll to the heaving back of the ocean, a rodeo on water!

"What d'ye think you're doin'?" came a shout, and Danny Ray felt the telescope wrenched from his hands. There stood the bosun, KinKill, towering over him, and the gargoyle's horns rose up in anger. His eyes rolled over red with unmitigated fury and he held the telescope like a weapon, as if he were about to clobber the cowboy on the head with it.

The sailor, eyes closed, continued to play his accordion softly, serenely, unaware of the danger.

"Stuff it, you stupid bird!" whispered Tipsy, nudging the sailor and then nodding to where Commodore Mumblefub's hat had just appeared above the deck. "God is in his heaven!"

The accordion whined down to a wailing whisper and the two sailors shuffled away with a terror-filled glance over their shoulders. Abruptly, the gargoyle raised the beautiful telescope over his head and dashed it to pieces on the deck.

"Aha," said the commodore, coming up and teetering forward and back—heel to toe while balancing his weight ever so precisely with his hands clasped behind his back. He glanced down at the shattered glass lying like a shimmering pool beneath the remains of the battered and bent telescope.

"Found this scrub a-lookin' through yer glass, sir!" growled the bosun, never once taking his eyes off the cowboy. "Told 'im to hand it over, it belonged to you, sir, and flung it full down, he did, full down on the deck!"

"He's lying!" shot back Danny Ray.

"Still, you refuse to address me as commodore, or sir," said Mumblefub to the cowboy, visibly struggling to control his temper.

"I didn't rightly know the telescope belonged to you," answered Danny Ray, "sir."

"But you knew it wasn't yours," Mumblefub replied and

picked up the broken telescope, shards of glass tinkling onto the deck. He traced a long finger around the telescope's battered housing. "Do you see this gold leaf? The silver scrolling along the length of it? The emeralds set upon the edge of the eyepiece? Does this look like an ordinary telescope to you?"

He tilted his head and leveled glowing eyes at the cowboy. He continued snippily, "I suspect that the code of the sea, even in your own world, is that a captain, much less a full-fledged commodore, is God on his ship. This part of the upper deck is my personal, my sacred space. No one is allowed to walk here, much less to even touch my telescope! At our first meeting I called you discourteous and disrespectful. To that I add an impudent, disobliging, contemptuous, supercilious tuft-hunting little spark of a sprig."

Danny Ray crossed his arms and stared unblinking at the commodore until Mumblefub sniffed with satisfaction at the momentary truce of silence.

"I suppose you've never been flogged, Danny Ray?" asked the commodore, throwing the ruined telescope into the scuppers.

At Mumblefub's mention of flogging, KinKill unfastened the cruel-looking cat from his belt and added, "I strips off yer shirt and hoists you up, spread-eagle-like, on the grating. Then I whips you, with this here cat, to within an inch of yer life!"

A deep, gurgling laughter issued out of the bosun's mouth, and the patches of hair on his hide rose up in excitement.

"A dozen lashes won't kill you, young sir," added the commodore, "but they will make you wish you were dead. And I'll wager you will reconsider ever touching what does not belong to you or setting foot on this part of the deck again!"

A savage hand grabbed Danny Ray's collar from behind and
he felt claws biting into his neck as the snaps of his shirt gave
way, exposing his back. The bosun spun him around and pressed
him down on the cold barrel of a cannon. Danny Ray's cowboy
hat flew off his head. KinKill brought his blackened fangs to
within inches of the cowboy's ear. "Been wantin' to crisscross
your back wid the cat since I first laid eyes on you!"

"Stop!" came a deep shout from somewhere behind. It was
Tûk—he was saved!

The cowboy heard the sailors grumbling, shuffling aside for
the devil.

Suddenly the cat whistled through the air.

WHACK!

Danny saw a flash of light. A split second of unbelief flashed
through his mind before a rushing train of pain roared down
his back. He sputtered and then gulped air, his face screwing up
in agony.

Now, the cowboy had been stung by wasps before, even
Sarksa pirates, and he had been hit by barbed wire snapping like
a whip when he stretched fence with his dad. But nothing,
nothing at all compared to the pain of the cat.

"What d'ye think you're doing?" came Prince Blue's distant
shout, and Danny Ray felt Tûk's hands raising him gently.

"Aha. I merely wanted to frighten the boy," mused the commodore.

"The king's charter protects us against this sort of savagery!"
said the prince.

"I ordered KinKill to stop—surely you heard me, Prince?
But it isn't the first time an order of mine has been hidden and

confused in the heat of passion. I'm sure KinKill, here, is disastrously disappointed over any discomfort brought upon the cowboy. KinKill?"

"Indeed, I am," the bosun said, bowing his head, his upper lip still drawn back in a snarl. The hellwain devil bared his fangs at the gargoyle and laid his horns back.

Danny Ray flinched as the commodore's hand jerked, revealing a swift glint of silver. Then Mumblefub replaced his dagger in his belt.

But a change had come over the bosun. KinKill trembled all over. He made a choking noise, fell to his knees, and rolled over on the deck, displaying an ever so small slit in his side from which trickled a stream of yellow blood.

"You see, young sir, how I deal with the slightest disobedience?" said the commodore coldly, reaching down and retrieving the cat from the bosun's twitching claw. "Discipline is always the order of the day, is it not? Commands not heard are identical to those not heeded, not obeyed, hm?"

In response to the cowboy's stony silence, the commodore touched the rim of his hat and said curtly, "Exactly so. Let my steward know of any need on your part."

The commodore spun on his heel and walked away, his heavy boots thudding on the deck like a drum, matching exactly the ominous and distant thunder of the storm.

The heaving of KinKill's chest stopped. The dark spots on his back turned a lighter, ashen gray as his death throes ceased.

The prince reached down and picked up the cowboy's hat. As he draped the cowboy's shirt back over his shoulders, Danny Ray felt as if salt were being poured down his back. He put one foot in front of the other, staggering toward the stairs leading to the lower decks. And then his feet left the deck entirely as Tûk lifted him and cradled him protectively in his arms. Even in his condition of pain, Danny Ray was surprised at the coolness of the hellwain's arms. He looked up, considered Tûk's strong red jawbone as the devil did a most remarkable thing: he lowered his face and sniffed the cowboy, catching his scent. He carried him down into the dark regions of the ship, into the comfortable confines of their cabin.

An unexpected wave of loneliness swept over the boy from Tahlequah, Oklahoma. He missed his mom and dad, and his brothers. And when his dog Diesel's sniffing face flashed into his thoughts, he was on the verge of crying. Why had he come back to this strange, dangerous world?

He closed his eyes as Tûk laid him down on his bed. He wanted to be far away from Commodore Mumblefub, the dark green ship named *Serpentine*, but most of all, as far away as possible from that horrible, horrible cat.

✦ 9 ✦

Drawing Blood

Nighttime.

Danny Ray opened his eyes. He tried to move and felt a searing pain down his back. The cat had not been just an ugly dream.

He had slept fitfully on his stomach throughout the storm-ridden afternoon and evening. But neither the storm nor the raw welts on his back were responsible for his grim mood. He felt a foreboding sense of danger. Disconcerting warnings had raged in his dreams.

The cowboy lay still, sensing that someone else was in the sleeping cabin.

"How do you feel?" asked the prince.

Danny Ray raised himself up on his elbows. In the dim light of their cabin, Prince Blue was the picture of comfort, dressed in a purple robe and reclining in a large puffy chair backed up against the great windows of the State Cabin. His feet were propped up on Danny Ray's bed while his arm lay on the cold iron breech of a large cannon firmly secured with tackles and breechings, its large muzzle nudged against the upper part of the port lid. His garment shimmered in the light of an over-head lantern that was swinging to the movement of the ship. Danny Ray noticed he wore the large gold ring that had been given to him by the sultana on their return voyage to Elidor aboard *Winter Queen*.

Nearby, Tûk stood looking out of the dark stern windows that reflected his powerful physique. He must have been think-ing of home again, for his bestial mouth worked up and down, mouthing words in his savage native tongue.

Danny Ray spied the golden watch, dull and dim, hanging by its fine chain on a peg, turning back and forth slowly, rocking to the easy motion of the ship.

"Don't much trust that commodore guy," he muttered, just loud enough for the prince to hear. "I'd get rid of that watch if I was you."

"And insult the commodore?" Prince Blue's brown eyes set-tled on the cowboy. "Believe me, Danny Ray, it's going to be a long voyage if you and the commodore can't become friends."

"Friends?" countered the cowboy. "You saw how Mumble-fubble—"

"Mumblefub!" corrected Prince Blue with surprising temper.

"Whatever. You saw how he dumped me on my rear end. How he had me whipped. Shoot, there's some folks you just can't be friends with!"

Danny Ray studied the prince's new robe. The prince waved his hand irritatingly and explained: "I'm afraid I must endure this garment, for now." He gazed over to a heap of dirty blue cloth piled on a nearby chair. "Oh! How I loved my dear blue robe! It will never come clean! Is that what you were thinking?"

"I was thinkin' about when you became Prince Blue for the first time, how you brought me back to life—from my stinger wounds, remember?"

"And so you were wondering if I can heal your back right now?"

"Something like that." The cowboy winced.

"Well, Danny Ray, I hate to say it, but those amazing powers seemed to last only during the precise moment of my changing into Prince Blue. I couldn't even free myself from prison, right?"

"So, with you wearin' that new purple robe, do I have to call you Lord Purple?" asked the cowboy. "Or Lord Grape or Lord Eggplant? What a hoot!"

The prince went quiet and then said thoughtfully, "You must not call me Lord Purple. He's dead now."

"Well, I'm sorry," said Danny Ray in a solemn voice. Something caught his eye. He gently eased himself out of bed and made his way over to Prince Blue's massive trunk.

"I found it half empty—the lock's missing," the prince said, playing with the black tassel on his belt. "A lot of my clothes are gone—that's why I'm wearing this absurd purple thing!"

Danny Ray opened the heavy lid and rummaged through the contents, which consisted of some books and a pile of shirts.

"Your blue rope isn't in the trunk, if that's what you're looking for," Prince Blue confirmed.

"Dang it!" said the cowboy when he reached the bottom of the trunk. "Dang it!" he said again.

"What is meant, 'dang it'?" asked Tûk, turning from the stern windows.

Danny Ray just shook his head. The magical rope of thrillium had been the cowboy's dazzling companion when he rescued *Winter Queen*. It had seemed to have a mind of its own, shortening or lengthening to suit Danny Ray's needs, or unfastening itself from a knot at just the right time. He had used the rope to lasso pirates and a Sarksa commodore, as well as snag the huge ship *Winter Queen*, and then ride through the air pursued by a hungry ghost! Before he had left to go back to Oklahoma, the cowboy had entrusted the care of it to Prince Blue.

But now the rope was gone.

"Wow! Look at this!" said Danny Ray with a soft whistle, as he retrieved a silver dagger with designs of intertwining serpents and sharp-toothed dragons. He pulled it from its sheath and tapped the flat of the blade against his hand.

"You remember Princess Ruby?" Prince Blue asked. "The dark, lonely woman we saw as we left Birdwhistle Bay? I told you that sorrow over Lord Purple's death drove her to live mournful and isolated in the Tower of Fire. What I didn't tell you was that Lord Purple was my oldest brother. No one will be named Lord Purple ever again."

Danny Ray's foreboding dreams of that night, muddled and vague upon his awakening, now called out loud and clear. And it terrified him.

Danny Ray, clearly shaken, asked Prince Blue, "Is it the same with ships? I mean, can two ships have the same name?"

"No," replied Prince Blue. "Only when a ship is destroyed or broken up can the name be used again."

Danny Ray's stomach tightened at the thought of what he

knew he had to do. His shaking hand held the dagger behind his back as he approached Prince Blue.

Tûk instinctively sensed danger. He quickly turned from the window, hissed, and lunged at the cowboy—too late! Danny Ray poised the sharp dagger against Prince Blue's neck.

"Weapon, drop!" said Tûk in a deadly tone. "Now!"

Danny Ray could feel the hellwain's yellow eyes scrutinizing him, his sharp, pointed tail within inches of his head. The devil's scar pulsated, keeping rhythm with his mounting rage.

Prince Blue froze. He looked up into the furious face of the cowboy, who forcefully whispered through a clenched jaw. "Tell your big, red devil dude to back down. Right now. If I feel his tail even so much as graze me, or if even one little spark from his mouth touches me—you get this dagger. I ain't foolin'."

"Tûk, step back," breathed the prince, now clearly shaken. "Danny Ray, this isn't funny—"

"Don't try no tricks!" The cowboy said. "This ain't your grandma's butter knife—ah! Don't even move a muscle—don't even twitch cricketlike, or you'll be sorry. I mean it!"

"The flogging has made you lose your mind!" the prince said shakily. "But I'm not the one who whipped you!"

"If I am crazy then you best be real, real still-like—got it?" The cowboy moved his face close to Prince Blue's, studying his eyes. "You're all in this together—ain't you, you and Tûk . . . and Mumblefub? That's why my rope's missing."

"What?"

"I can put up with a lot of guff, like ol' Billy Whitehorse coming up in my face." Danny Ray smiled a terrible smile. "But when someone's out to really hurt me, or even kill me, then all bets are off."

"Who is Billy Whitehorse?" the prince asked desperately. "And who's trying to kill you?"

"Nice try." Danny Ray licked his lips. Then he spoke the words: "You're one of the fantasms!"

There, he had said it. His grip tightened on the dagger.

"You had me almost believing that sob story about your so-called brother. You lying dog, you had me feeling sorry for you, whoever you are. But you made a mistake: you slipped up when you told me no two ships could have the same name."

The frightened eyes of the prince looked away from the fierce gaze of Danny Ray.

"Them two bishop ships I saw through the telescope earlier today, the ones heading toward Elidor," said the cowboy, "they were named *Serpentine* and *Wasp*, just like these two ships! Now, fancy that! Not just one ship, but two, with the same names as us. Mighty suspicious, ain't it?"

"Maybe you saw a mirrorlike reflection of our ships," suggested the shaken prince. "Sometimes storms can play—"

"You think I'm downright stupid?"

"At present, yes I do!" the prince retorted in defiance. "Why didn't you tell me this before?" His mind was working quickly even with the point of the dagger still pressed against his soft neck. "Do you know what this means?"

"Sure do. Means that the *Serpentine* and *Wasp* we're sailing on are fakes. Means that I gotta get off this ship pronto. For you it means this dagger!"

A low threatening growl emanated from Tûk's throat.

"You're right about these ships," said Prince Blue, thinking quickly. "Yes, of course you're right. But that doesn't mean I'm a fantasm!"

"You're not the Prince Blue I knew," said Danny Ray. "He wasn't the kind of feller that would have his own personal slave, or take gifts from the likes of the commodore. Not the kind of feller who'd let his friend get whipped by the cat!"

"You've changed too, Danny Ray—"

"You just hush up," interrupted the cowboy as he readjusted his grip on the dagger. "Lord Green tried to warn me that the fantasms were a real tricky enemy. I just had no idea how tricky. I can't believe I was fooled from the very start—a fantasm posing as my old friend Prince Blue!"

Danny Ray took a quick look at Tûk and then over to the cabin door and back again. "I should have known all of you were in it together—ah! You just hold still!"

"I have a question for you, Danny Ray," said Prince Blue. "If I am a fantasm—which I most certainly am not—why didn't I just let KinKill flog you to death? And then just hang you from the top knob of the ship?"

"Don't know—you tell me. Maybe you want to have some fun with me first—you know, play with me a little before you decide to do me in, just like the Sarksa pirates."

Danny Ray shivered a little to recall how the tall, sinister pirates had stung him with just enough poison so that they might torture him at a later time.

"So, how you're going to kill me?" Prince Blue asked, frozen in his sitting posture. "Are you going to stab me or slit my throat? And furthermore—can you really kill a fantasm?"

"You just hush up," Danny Ray said, breathing deeply. He was calm now, holding the dagger dead steady. "I ain't gonna tell you again." The decorated handle of the dagger was beginning to press deep grooves in the palm of his hand.

Out of the corner of his eye—a white blur—*WHAAAM!* Something hit him hard!

The room whirled around him as he tried to keep his balance, the dagger waving around in his hand, and then he fell into the open trunk. *THUD!*—the lid slammed down on top of him.

Danny Ray managed to twist onto on his back—oh! the pain as the welts on his back rubbed against the rough wooden bottom. He waited, switching the dagger to his other hand. Sweat beaded up on his forehead and he wiped his mouth with the back of his arm.

He could just make out the muffled voices in the room. So, he was right about Prince Blue, or whatever his name was. Then he thought he heard a new voice, high-pitched, and then laughing. Well, he thought, we'll see how they laugh when they open this lid and get stabbed. Then the awful realization hit him: they might just lock the trunk shut, drag it over to the window, and throw him off! That would sure fix his wagon for good!

The cowboy took a deep breath. What to do—what to do? He would have to act soon. He heard footsteps. Whispering. Someone drawing close. Danny Ray braced himself to spring upward, dagger at the ready.

There—a crack of light appeared—the end of a broom handle being shoved into the trunk. This was his chance! With a violent rush he bolted upright—his head crashing against the wooden lid as it flew open!

Blinding light. Then laughter. More laughter.

The cowboy blinked like an owl, swishing the dagger back and forth across the room. His eyes adjusted. There was Tûk on the other side of the room, a mouth full of fangs as he cackled, and Prince Blue, still sitting in his chair. And just above him stood a little blond girl, broom in hand.

"Cherry!" exclaimed Danny Ray. "He ain't Prince Blue—"

"Oh, stop it, Danny Ray!" said the prince testily.

"You stabbed him!" said Cherry angrily, getting ready to swat the cowboy again with the broom.

Danny Ray took a long, even look at the prince.

"Enough of that talk about my being a fantasm!" Prince Blue stretched his neck to reveal a red spot from where a crimson drop had made its way down his neck. "I'm afraid you've drawn blood—and fantasms don't bleed!"

Danny Ray sheepishly lowered the dagger. He felt really dumb as he stepped out of the trunk. Tûk handed Prince Blue a cloth and then turned, giving the cowboy a particularly evil scowl.

"Sorry," said the cowboy.

The prince dabbed at his neck and then motioned at Cherry. "As you can see, we have a stowaway."

Danny Ray's temper returned. "What the heck are you doing here, Cherry?"

"No one would let me come along—just because I'm a girl!" exclaimed Cherry. "King Krystal said no, so I made my own way!"

"At least I know why my sword, my hat, my best shoes are missing," mused the prince, "and half my clothes! And your rope, too, Danny Ray!"

"I had to make room for myself in the trunk somehow," said the little blond girl angrily. "But I threw a rope under that bed! It was digging into my back!" She stooped and rummaged under the prince's bed, pulling out the shimmering blue coil.

"Cool!" said Danny Ray, grabbing it away from her.

"Blue rope, new hope!" cried the prince.

"Who cares about that rotten old rope!" she snapped.

Danny Ray shook his head. "You've landed yourself in a real fix, Cherry—this ain't just a walk in the park. I didn't come all the way from the Otherworld for a fun-filled adventure: we're out here trying to rescue the princess and there's folks that want to really kill us."

"Danny Ray's right," said Prince Blue. "We're in real trouble, Cherry. And he's right in thinking we have to get off this ship. I saw a map near the binnacle lantern up on the main deck. Tonight we happen to be sailing near the only land we'll see for a long time."

"What land?" said Cherry.

"Islandum Magicum," said the prince.

Tûk gnashed his fangs and frowned.

Cherry gasped, "The Magical Islands!"

"I take it that's bad?" said Danny Ray.

Cherry looked over to Prince Blue and Tûk, and then back to the cowboy. Her lower lip began to quiver.

The cowboy snapped up the front of his shirt, tucked it in, and put on his boots. He cast a longing eye at his bed, so warm, so inviting. He glanced at his three companions and then beyond them at the blackness of night showing through the cabin windows.

"I got a plan," stated Danny Ray. "The first part is finding a way off this here bishop ship. Second part is gonna be running across the Checkered Sea."

"In the middle of the night?" whined Cherry. "Running to where?"

Danny Ray put on his cowboy hat. "That's the part you really ain't gonna like!"

✦ 10 ✦

Pipsqueaks and Unicorns

 The ship's bells chimed four times. The last candle in the State Cabin puffed out, a long tendril of silver smoke curling up into the darkness, and ever so slowly, one of the large stern windows opened with a creak. Danny Ray tiptoed out onto the balcony. The storm had passed, leaving the heavens strangely tranquil. Overhead, the night stars glittered like a handful of sugar crystals spread over a dome of black velvet.

He tied the end of a shimmering coil of blue rope to the balcony railing and let the thin strand fall silently over the stern of *Serpentine* into the darkness. He made a hand signal and the others scampered across the balcony.

"Cherry!" whispered Danny Ray. Her bright blond bangs were peeking out the front of her hood and ruffling in the breeze. "Get up on Tûk's back!"

She hesitated. She glanced down wide-eyed, far, far below, where the squares of the Checkered Sea flowed out from beneath the bishop.

"I—I'm scared!" She looked doubtfully at the devil, who appeared black in the surrounding night.

"So am I," said the cowboy softly, "and so's the prince. Now, go on! Get up on Tûk's back."

The prince reassuringly patted her on the shoulder. "Tûk won't let you fall, Cherry."

"I want Danny Ray to carry me," she said softly. "He knows how to handle that rope. And he's very, very strong. And he's not afraid of anything."

"Tûk's even stronger than me," explained Danny Ray. "Now crawl up on that devil's back!"

"No!" she said defiantly.

Tûk, losing his patience, put one leg over the railing, his sword flashing in the dim night. He had left his beloved pitchfork behind, and with no rope or other device, began scaling down *Serpentine*'s back wall using only his sharp claws and tail.

Danny Ray huffed and looked down at the stubborn little girl. He grasped the rope confidently, looped his chinstrap under his chin, and motioned for her. Cherry's lower lip quivered as she peered down once again over the balcony's edge. Finally, she offered her hand and then let out a soft squeal as the cowboy swung her up on his back.

Danny Ray swore under his breath as Cherry pressed herself against the sore welts on his back and wrapped her arms tightly around his neck. He took a thick belt of leather and draped it around them both and pulled tight, making him wince with pain. Only now did he understand, late at night and a world away, a little of the discomfort that Tomahawk the bull must have felt with him on his back.

"Cowboy up!" he gasped, the rodeo cowboy's age-old cry of encouragement. The balcony's railing felt cold under his shaky grip. The odds of them scaling down the back of the bishop without being spotted—or without someone falling to their death—were slim, but it was their only chance of escape.

"The time is ten o'clock of the night," said a soft voice. Prince Blue ignored the cowboy's searching look and snapped the glittering watch shut and tucked it away.

Danny Ray looked up and saw the faintest sliver of the waning moon: time was running out for the princess. In but a few nights there would be no moon in the night sky, the new moon Lord Green had warned of, and the princess would depart this world forever.

He let out a nervous huff as he put one leg over the railing. Then the other. He mulled over the terrible drop. His mouth went dry, his stomach turned flips, just like before he mounted a bull at the rodeo. He had to admit, though, he'd be a lot more scared if it weren't for his rope of thrillium. It had saved him more than once in his previous trials.

"Hold on, Cherry!" he managed to say in spite of her iron-strong arms wrapped around his neck, nearly choking him to death. He checked for his slingshot in his back pocket, confirmed his grip on the rope, and over the side he went, his cowboy boots kicking against the hard stone of the bishop's outer wall.

"If you drop me, I'll never forgive you, Danny Ray!" cried Cherry.

That made Danny Ray think of another girl, the Sultana

Sumferi Sar, ruler of Port Palnacky far to the north. She had said those same exact words to him long, long ago. He had to admit he missed her, at least as much as he was willing to miss any stinky girl. She had been a great help the first time he found himself in Elidor. He grudgingly admitted, too, that she was pretty tough—for a girl, that is. He had thought maybe he'd see her this time around, but the chances of that were looking pretty grim.

The wind gusted, swinging the rope with its desperate passengers to the left then back to the right. Next, Prince Blue climbed over the balcony, contributing his weight to the dangling tendon and making it a bit more steady. The cowboy looked up in wonder at the prince's flowing robes and beyond to the line of rope and the towering ball of the bishop, its green and yellow lights flashing against the night sky.

Down they went. Danny Ray could feel the tightness in his arms. His injured shoulder cried out under the added weight of Cherry as they scaled down the wall, lower, lower. The rope went slack as Danny Ray's feet came to rest against a ledge. He knelt down, out of breath, atop *Serpentine*'s ornately carved stern, crowded with immense statues of serpents, of fighting griffins, of unicorns and winged lions.

The prince eased down beside him and said in a low voice, "By the way, Tûk is not my slave."

"What?" asked the cowboy.

"About what you said before . . . about Tûk. He's not my slave!"

"Well, you never say 'thank you' or 'please' to him."

"Really, Danny Ray! I am the future king of Elidor. The words 'please' or 'obliged' or even 'thank you' simply are not found on the tongues of kings."

"All right," said the cowboy, wiping his sweaty forehead. "But look, can we talk about this some other time?" He gripped the rope and looked the prince straight in the face. "I'm kinda busy right now."

Tûk came out of the darkness and pressed his long gnarled forefinger against his lips. "Much quiet!" he whispered, pointing downward.

Just below was a wide balcony bathed in yellow light from the commodore's Great Cabin. The cowboy leaned back and tied the slack of the rope around the snouts of a snarling two-headed tiger.

"Don't they ever clean up here?" asked Prince Blue in a low voice, looking at his filthy hand.

PEEP! PEEP!

What was that? Something was above them, hidden in the confusion of the griffin and the monstrous lion carvings of the stern.

PEEP! Two large white eyes blinked down at them from a round, plump body about the size of a bowling ball. For all Danny Ray could tell, it had no arms or wings but only two pudgy feet.

"A pipsqueak!" whispered Tûk, motioning with his horned head. Cherry reached up to poke the gentle-looking oversized grape.

"Get down!" cautioned Danny Ray.

They hunkered down in the shadows of the statues as a group of officers and sailors appeared below on the balcony. The cowboy removed his hat and peeked sideways through the open mouth of a fierce unicorn.

"One o' our tripptoppers 'as give out, sir," said a short swarthy officer, referring to one of *Serpentine*'s engines. Danny Ray, from his last Checkered Sea voyage, was well aware of the tiny engines that powered these huge ships, such as the tantarrabobs—tiny, rust-colored shaggy-haired creatures that eat coal, and, of course, the silky, golden-haired clabbernappers that eat pearls. He wondered what tripptoppers might look like.

"Oh, aha. *Serpentine* will mend well enough," said a thin voice that the cowboy knew all too well. Commodore Mumblefub joined the officers and sailors on the balcony. "Once we sail her into Sarksa Town."

Danny Ray licked his lips. Sarksa Town? Was that on one of the Magical Islands? The Sarksa were a ruthless brood of pirates that Danny had encountered on his last adventure. They were stick thin, standing ten feet tall, with heads resembling a fly or praying mantis. They had long whip tails with poisonous stingers on the end. The cowboy had killed a whole bunch of them in sword and cannon fights, along with their commodore, not to mention three Sarksa ships destroyed by the cannon of the old garbage rook *Hog*.

"Yessir," said one of the officers, laughing evilly. "I'll like to see the face of that Otherworld cowboy when we sail into that evil place!"

So, the Sarksa must know that he and Prince Blue were back on the Checkered Sea again. But why would Mumblefub hand them over to the Sarksa to even an old score—unless there was more gold to be had.

"I'd a thought, sir," said another officer. "You'd want to personally teach that snippy, whippy little cowboy a thing or two?"

But it was what Danny Ray witnessed next that sent chills like lightning bolts down his spine. The officers and crew stepped back as the commodore's eyes fired up like orange furnace flames. His shape rose up tall and black, the hooded face looking down at the crew, who trembled and cried out in terror. A skeletonlike hand gripped the hilt of an ancient sword at its belt.

Commodore Mumblefub was one of the three fantasms! But Danny Ray realizing the fact made the transformation no less terrifying: the shimmering black of its robe like the hunched-over wings of a vulture; the hollows in its face where the merciless eyes burned.

"The cowboy and the one called Prince Blue," replied the dark-shrouded menace, with a deep, blood-chilling laugh. "Yes, I shall have my time with them before we drop anchor: first the flogging, then the cutting, the stabbing! Finally, the mending, when I sew them back together for the Sarksa to have their fun."

The prince's eyes widened and Cherry gasped.

The transformations didn't stop with the commodore. The officers to either side of the fantasm began to split open. A myriad of red glowing eyes began emerging from bulbous heads that made popping, squishing sounds, as the sailors changed into hideous creatures resembling large insects with long, needle-sharp mouths. Their skin, if skin it could be called, shone like dark red metal. Their wings, folded neatly along their sides, sheltered claws with sharp talons. It came to Danny Ray that they resembled giant, hulking mosquitoes—albeit very dangerous mosquitoes!

"Whiners!" hissed Prince Blue, just loud enough for Danny Ray to hear.

Whiners? Danny Ray thought. His aunt Nancy back in Tulsa was a whiner—and she didn't look nothing like them!

"And the one called Tûk?" gurgled one of the whiners.

"He is far too dangerous for any of you," the fantasm replied. "I'll deal with him personally."

"*Peep!*" The pipsqueak let out an ever so faint chirp of fright.

The fantasm raised a thin-fingered hand in caution. Its head turned back and forth as those ghastly eyes peered out from beneath its black hood, taking in the elaborately carved stern, and a long, drawn-out hiss escaped its mouth. One of the whiners lifted off from the deck of the balcony with an ominous humming of wings.

PEEP! PEEP!

That pipsqueak was bringing the whiner straight to them!

"Get down!" commanded the cowboy. Cherry was so terrified that the cowboy had to take her by the hand. The four of them wedged themselves tightly together in the shadow of the carved unicorn. Danny Ray looked between his boots where Prince Blue lay. A cold tremor ran down the cowboy's spine as he spotted Cherry's dress, peeking out of her cloak and glittering noticeably in the darkness. He snapped his finger softly, trying to get the prince's attention.

The whiner drew nearer and nearer. The cowboy felt a trickle of sweat roll down the side of his face. Shoot! Danny Ray snapped his fingers again and Prince Blue caught his frantic appeal, throwing a fold of his robe over Cherry. She became instantly invisible! The magic rope, as if sensing the need for secrecy, had changed from its normal shimmering blue to pitch-black—undetectable in the shadows.

PEEP!

The whiner's visage rose above the wall. Danny Ray and Tûk lay in the darkness directly beneath it. With alarmed fascination, Danny Ray studied the claws opening and closing and the sharp barb at the end of its spearlike mouth. On either side of its face where its mouth joined to its head, a set of three eyes shone like sparkling red sapphires stacked one on top of the other.

Danny Ray saw Tûk's body tense. He knew the hellwain could take care of a whiner if they were discovered, spit out fire and flame him out in midair. But then what of the rest of them, and the terrible fantasm?

A black claw gripped the rim of the carvings, just inches from Danny Ray's face as a long, thin, metallic arm with razorlike hairs extended up toward the helpless pipsqueak.

"PEEEEEEEEEEP!" it called out as claws closed around its plump body. The balcony below erupted in raucous cheering as the whiner lifted the pipsqueak off its perch and displayed it to those below. Even the sailors forgot their terror of the fantasm and joined in this hideous verse:

> *"Chug-a-lug!*
> *Bite the slug*
> *Pour his guts*
> *In a jug!*
> *Lift it up*
> *To your mug*
> *Drain it dry*
> *And chug-a-lug!*

So, chug-a-lug
Chug-a-lug
But save a sip for me!
We'll drink and smile
And burp a while
In a gory jamboree!

Chug-a-lug!
Grab the bug
Take his head
And give a tug
Hear it pop
Like a plug
Suck 'im dry
And chug-a-lug!

So, chug-a-lug
Chug-a-lug
But save a sip for me!
We'll drink and smile
And burp a while
In a gory jamboree!
Ha!
So, save a sip for me!"

Over and over they chanted, louder and louder as the whiner buzzed in midair, holding the helpless pipsqueak like a trophy and drawing it closer and closer to its mouth.

Danny Ray ventured a peek at what was happening. The

fantasm grinned wickedly, its eyes flaming all the brighter at the promise of gory nourishment. And then, with a sickening whack, the whiner drove its sharp mouth into the pipsqueak's body.

"*PEEEEEEEEEEEEEEEEEEEEEP!*" it wailed, its eyes wide with pain.

The chanting was interrupted with a chorus of cheers. Danny Ray could hear a hideous sucking noise above the drone of wings, and deep within those cold red eyes there awakened a fractured white light, like lightning bolts. The pipsqueak's beak moved feebly, as if trying to voice one last cry of pain, and then it was over. The small, delicate creature was sucked completely dry and the whiner threw the empty sack away into the night. It buzzed back down to the balcony and followed the fantasm and his minions back into the Great Cabin.

"C'mon!" cried Danny Ray, jumping up and slapping his cowboy hat back on. He untied the rope, looping it again around the trembling little girl, hauling her up on his back. "Gosh, Cherry!" he added. "You're heavier than a sack of potatoes!"

She whimpered softly and buried her face in his neck.

The natural outward curve of the bishop's walls became more pronounced, making it easier as they continued down the side of the ship, but only a little easier. Again, Tûk was out to the side with no ropes, no hooks. Once, Danny Ray thought he saw the devil slip, but in a flash he pressed the talons of his forearms against the stonework to regain his hold.

The cowboy paused once they were well below Mumblefub's cabin. He took a heavy breath and looked out into the wind and howling darkness. Yep. He had to admit, he felt sorry for the pitiful little pipsqueak.

❖ 11 ❖

Skiing Lessons

 As they continued descending the back of the bishop, the speeding surface of the marble sea loomed closer and the rumbling noise of the ship's base grew louder. Danny Ray stopped abruptly, gripping the rope, and Prince Blue nearly landed on top of him.

"Sorry," the prince called down.

"Shhhh!" The cowboy pointed below his boots to where a dull yellowish light leaked through the open ports of the lower gun deck.

Danny Ray searched frantically with his pointed boots for a foothold. He could hear voices from inside the ship, very near, accompanied by scattered laughter. Someone coughed. He caught the fragrance of fruity pipe smoke wafting out to join the night breezes. Tûk, upside down on the wall, cautiously peeked into the lighted interior of the ship, his face showing up a brilliant red against the surrounding gloom.

The devil jerked his head back. A head emerged from the gun port—then an arm as a sailor emptied his tankard over the side. Danny Ray was right above him, the heel of his boot mere inches from the back of his head. Wait! It was Tipsy! Gosh—if he turned his head the slightest little bit, he'd see them for sure. In the absence of his trusty pitchfork, Tûk drew out his sword.

There they waited, seemingly forever, hanging just above the long row of ports, as Tipsy breathed in the cool night air, unaware how close he was to death—with a curved, razor-sharp sword poised just above his neck. Danny Ray hoped to goodness Tipsy didn't have to die.

Danny Ray's shoulder burned as though someone were stabbing it with a hot poker: Cherry had turned from a sack of potatoes into a load of lead bricks. He wondered how Prince Blue was faring just above him. Ah! His hands started to slip!

A loud, piercing whistle sounded from the bishop ship's upper works. Tûk's face shot up from the light and looked overhead, his tail wiggling like a black snake. Dang it! What if their cabin had been broken into and they had been found missing? What in tarnation would they do then? It wouldn't take long for Mumblefub to search the ship or one of them whiners to find them stuck like flies on flypaper on the backside of the ship!

Tipsy spit a wad of something, watched it fall away into the darkness, and drew his head in. There came a deep rumbling sound as the cannons were drawn inside the ship and all the port lids closed. Of course! The whistle had been a signal to darken ship as they neared the Islandum Magicum! Danny Ray could hear the scraping of the cannon muzzles against the inside of the port lids as they were secured with tackles and breechings.

And then silence.

Danny Ray looked up at the prince and nodded. They continued descending until they reached the wide base of the ship, trembling and vibrating in the wild wind. Cherry seemed a whole lot lighter. The cowboy sighed with pleasure to let go of the rope to ease his aching arms.

He was used to viewing the sea from a high, remote perch. But now the speeding surface of the sea was terrifyingly near, the large squares fleeing out into the darkness. Wisps of smoke trailed from the bishop, curling in a frenzy until they were swallowed up in the black of night. The cowboy narrowed his eyes. There, barely discernible in the gloom, followed the other big bishop, *Wasp*, directly in *Serpentine*'s wake. The thought struck him that since Mumblefub was a fantasm, Captain Giddyfickle of *Wasp* probably was, too.

"*Wasp* sails on the black squares, just like *Serpentine*," said Danny Ray in a louder voice, to be heard above the fantastic rumbling from the bishop. "When we touch down on the marble sea, we're gonna have to lean and slide off to the side! You guys ever ski before?"

The shocked look on the prince's face told him he had no idea what he meant.

"What is skiing?" asked Cherry, voicing the other's unspoken question. The hellwain devil, having just strolled around the base of the bishop, scratched his head.

"Great," said Danny Ray glumly in the buffeting wind. "All right, let's say you're on a lake of water—"

"A lake of water?" Cherry said, scrunching up her nose.

Shoot! How could he explain skiing to them? And skiing on a hard surface like the Checkered Sea!

"All right, look, you guys. I'll go first with Cherry. Watch what I do—keep a good grip on the rope and just lean back on your heels as far as you can. Got it?"

Tûk had begun to guess at the cowboy's meaning. He rubbed his hands together and grinned adventurously. Prince Blue nodded, and with no further word said, the cowboy hitched up Cherry a little higher on his shoulders and gripped the rope with both hands.

"Here we go! Hold on, girl!"

The cowboy set one boot down on the speeding marble of the Checkered Sea. His leg shook and vibrated wildly as the bishop ship tugged powerfully on the rope. He set down his other foot and leaned back on his heels, letting the rope pay out, his spurs ring-ting-tinging against the marble as they moved farther and farther away from the bishop. Cherry's feet dangled just above the surface of the speeding marble.

Danny Ray had never worried about crashing while skiing on water—actually it was kinda fun! But he didn't want to find out what it would feel like to slam down on the hard surface of the marble Checkered Sea, tumbling and rolling around until the fillings in his teeth rattled out!

Cherry, wide-eyed with fright and her mouth gaping open, her blond hair flying wildly, screamed out above the deep thunder. Danny Ray puffed, felt the extra tension on the rope as Prince Blue and then Tûk stepped off from the base of the bishop ship, the prince's dark robe flapping wildly in the wind. The cowboy's arms ached more than ever. His thighs burned with fatigue as he leaned to his right, steering Prince Blue and Tûk with him. They had swung as far to the side as possible, just before their momentum might swing them back toward the center of the ship, the magical rope went slack.

"Yikes!" shouted the cowboy. Prince Blue went down in a heap right in front of him. Danny Ray did a flip in the air over him, Cherry and all, and somehow he managed to wrench around so that he landed on his side, sliding along the marble.

The cowboy's heart was in his throat as he skidded to a stop and scrambled to his feet and the rope fell limp around his boots.

He had learned from the rodeo to hit the ground and run, just in case that bull came hunting after you. Quick as lightning, he grabbed Cherry's arm and ran like the dickens—huff-puff, huff-puff—her shimmering dress flickering in the night. Prince Blue ran, too, with the curling twisting rope all tangled up around his head and neck. The sight made Danny Ray chuckle amid his terror, for out of the corner of his eye the cowboy caught sight of *Wasp*, her huge mass dividing the darkness and lumbering down on them like a blind maniac!

With a shout, and the last of his strength, Danny Ray pulled Cherry past him and shoved her forward, and they fell together, sliding, sliding, the hot wind of the passing ship rolling past them like the breath of a dragon.

The rumbling died down. Silence surrounded them as the twinkling helm lights of *Serpentine* and *Wasp* were lost in the impenetrable gloom of night.

Danny Ray raised himself up on all fours and then to his knees, breathing heavily. He felt like he'd been through a war. Prince Blue, still tangled up in the rope, lay on his back panting like a dog, mouthing prayers into the heavens between breaths and thanking his lucky stars to be alive.

Tûk brought up the rear, striding tall and black against the stars with an unmistakable smile playing across his features. "Again!" he snapped as he readjusted his sword belt.

"You're one crazy fellow, Tûk!" Danny Ray shook his head and chuckled. The devil loved living on the edge, enjoyed the thrill of danger, even if it might kill him.

Prince Blue untangled himself and Danny Ray began looping the rope around his shoulder. It shone again with that lovely, vibrant blue. He thought of how lucky he was to have such a rope, such a trusty friend!

"Hey, Prince," said Danny Ray. "Here we are again out walking on the Checkered Sea. Just like old times—brings back memories, huh?"

"Not all of them good, Danny Ray," he responded.

"Oh," said Cherry dully, "my dress, my dress. It's a mess!"

She threw herself facedown on the shiny marble and cried so pitifully that Tûk knelt beside her. He brought up his hand to pat her gently on the back, but he thought better of it and just let her sob her heart out.

At least she was alive to cry.

Tûk pointed to a deeper blackness on the horizon where the stars didn't shine and said: "Sugarwood Island, ha?"

"Land," said the prince meditatively. "Largest of the Islands of Magic."

"We have to go there?" sniffed Cherry, peeking out from her tangled hair.

"This is the part of my plan I knew you really wouldn't like," said Danny Ray in his most gentle voice. He sighed and then fastened the rope to his belt. He helped Cherry to her feet, looked toward the hump-shaped blackness in the east, and prepared for the hike. "Besides, there's nothing else we can do."

"You got us away from that fantasm, Danny Ray," the little girl said, wiping her nose with her sleeve and then arranging her messy hair as best she could. "Thank you, Danny Ray. Thank you."

Tûk, too, nodded his appreciation.

"You're mighty welcome," he said, hitching up his pants and looking sidelong at the prince. "I know kings don't dare say such things."

❖ 12 ❖

Sugarwood Island

Danny Ray awoke from a deep sleep with a loud snort. He pushed his hat back from his eyes. The eastern horizon showed a lighter gray as, overhead, the tired stars winked and blinked out with the rising of the sun.

The cowboy lay on his back on a warm, soft, moss-covered rock in a deep hollow on Sugarwood Island, sheltered from the Checkered Sea. His dreams had been strange and magical: a large bird flying overhead, its dark wings bearing the stars away; deer with strange amber eyes, their heels kicking up as they flickered and flashed into the mysterious night.

He opened his mouth and yawned so deeply that his jaw joints crackled, and then he raised up, ever so slowly, on his elbows—oh! How his shoulders and arms ached! Last night's escape down *Serpentine*'s lofty side had made him exercise muscles that, apparently, rodeo cowboys seldom use. And it had been a strange experience running across the smooth marble of the Checkered Sea in the middle of the night and then stumbling up the uneven shore of Sugarwood Island.

Tûk sat beside a small campfire, eyes half closed. Amazingly, the devil was able to sit upright, as if on a three-legged stool, balanced perfectly by his two legs with the point of his rigid tail stuck into the ground. A low, steady humming emanated from his black lips as he seemed to be meditating.

A slight snore on the other side of him announced Prince Blue's presence. He lay perfectly straight, hands on his chest, nose pointed toward the open sky, resembling the form of a king fashioned on the lid of a stone tomb—but the cowboy chuckled to think that statues didn't snore!

Danny Ray knew the prince wasn't faking sleep—fakers always frowned too much, or their eyes twitched or something. Danny Ray was the World Champion Sleep Faker—he could fool anyone, it was all in the breathing—long, regular breaths. The prince was definitely out of it. The small raw wound on his neck, the size of a pencil jab, reminded the cowboy of the incident the night before, when Tûk had been ready to kill him—

"Utu—barasa!" said Tûk urgently.

Danny Ray nearly jumped out of his skin as the devil's séance ended in this urgent pronouncement. He felt a keen flow of goose bumps down his legs as the hellwain came to stand over him. Maybe Tûk hadn't forgiven him for assaulting his master, and now, with the prince asleep, he could settle the score!

Unexpectedly, the devil reached out and touched Danny Ray's shoulder, and then the other one, leaving a smudge of ash. Then the devil leaned over the sleeping prince and performed the same brief, strange ritual.

"For protection!" he growled.

The delicious scent of something cooking brought Danny

Ray's attention back to the fire, where a spit lay suspended over the lazy flames with a small clump of charred meat. He had no idea what the devil had hunted down and cooked, but he was about to find out, for the hellwain tore off a leg piece from the carcass. His red hooked nose hovered over the meat as he sniffed at it.

"Wulver, ha?" said Tûk, displaying it to the cowboy.

Danny Ray didn't know what the heck a wulver was, and didn't give a darn, either. Right now, what the cowboy missed most was a big brawny bowl of hot oatmeal with melted butter and brown sugar. With some toast . . . and a glass of cold milk. And a doughnut, too.

Danny Ray shrugged and said: "Don't look like there's enough for both of us." He was relieved that the devil wasn't going to kill him, grill him, or boil him alive. "You jest go ahead and help yourself, Tûk."

"Not for Tûk!" snickered the devil, waving at the meat. He reached down into the fire with his bare fingers and retrieved a hot, glowing coal and popped it in his mouth.

"Wow!" exclaimed Danny Ray. "That's the darnedest thing I ever saw!"

Tûk handed the cowboy the scrap of the meat, the devil champing and crunching on the coal with smoke issuing out of his mouth. The cowboy looked at the food suspiciously, sniffed at it in hellwain fashion, and bit tentatively through the black-ened skin.

"Shucks! This is good!" said Danny Ray. "A little greasy, but good!" In a few bites—and a burp—it was gone. Tûk put back his head and laughed. Danny Ray accepted more meat from the hand of the hellwain, and gobbled that down, too.

Tack!

Danny Ray wiped his mouth on his sleeve and asked, "Hey, Tûk, what in tarnation was that noise? And where is Cherry?"

The sound had come from behind them where the trees poked their heads out of the mist.

Tack! . . . Tack!

"C'mon with me," said Danny Ray, getting up.

Tûk shook his head vehemently. "I stay with Beesa Blue."

The cowboy climbed up out of the hollow and looked between a gap in the hills out over the Checkered Sea, still dim in the morning mist. The sea was empty: no *Serpentine*; no *Wasp*.

TACK! . . . TACK! . . . TACK!

The sound grew louder as he took a path winding down into a dense patch of fog that enveloped him with foggy arms. Large trees frowned down on the cowboy, their creeping, grasping branches appearing unexpectedly, like ghosts out of the murk, letting him pass by untouched—for now. Around a small bend in the path, the woods opened up into a small clearing.

"Doggone that girl!" His hand jerked around to his empty back pocket. Yonder stood Cherry with his slingshot, shooting stones at the knot in an old, hoary oak tree. She drew back the slingshot and let it fly—*TACK!*

"Dang it, Cherry!" snapped Danny, approaching her. He tried to grab the slingshot back but the little girl gritted her teeth and wrenched it away. "A slingshot ain't no toy for a nutty little girl!"

"You take that back, Danny Ray!" she said, pointing her finger at him.

"Gosh! I can't stand having girls around!" he said, a little louder this time, and kicked at the dirt.

"You have to share!" countered Cherry. The cowboy grabbed at the slingshot again and Cherry jumped back a step.

"There's some things that ain't meant for sharing," said the cowboy, putting his hands on his hips. But then his eyes lit up with an idea: "Hey! You can borrow my rope—how's that?"

"You just hope I'll hang myself!" She took aim at the tree again, pulling back on the slingshot's elastic arms. "No, I like this better. I'm becoming a very good shot."

TACK!

Danny Ray laughed. "What a hoot! Whoever heard of a girl gettin' good with a slingshot? Girls ain't good at nothing 'cept playing with pink stuffed animals and such."

"Just you take that back, Danny Ray!" she repeated, pointing the same threatening finger at him.

"I even got a song to prove it," said the cowboy, ignoring her puffed-out cheeks and red face. He put his boot up on a rock and folded his arms. "Goes like this:

"I like bugs and spiders and lizards and frogs
Slimy things that squirm under logs
Big purple chickens and green-spotted hogs
'Cause I'm a boy, you see!

I like pickin' my nose and playin' in mud
Rolling around in the muck and the crud

Lickin' up ketchup pretendin' it's blood
'Cause I'm a boy, you see!

I eat dirt and leaves and beetles and chalk
Old bubble gum and tar on the sidewalk
I'll gnaw the varnish off a grandfather clock
'Cause I'm a boy, you see!

Now, girls are weird and smell like flowers
And play with dolls for hours and hours
Eatin' crumpets and tea and sweets not sours
'Cause they're just girls, you see!

Girls like nuzzles and kisses and cuddles
Not diggin' up things that go wiggly-wuggles
Or playin' with trucks and stompin' in puddles
'Cause they're just girls, you see!

Now, boys are the best in most every way
We make the best monsters and cars outta clay
Wherever we go we got something to say
'Cause we're boys, you see!"

"That's a stupid song!" snapped Cherry.

"It certainly is!" said a groggy voice. There stood Prince Blue rubbing the sleep out of his eyes, shadowed by Tûk. "Danny Ray, have you forgotten all that the Sultana Sumferi Sar did in helping us rescue *Winter Queen*? She was a girl."

"Yeah, but she was a regular girl—and a pretty good one at

that, not a small-fry up-in-your-face troublemaker like Cherry. And I didn't have to cart the sultana around on my back wherever we went—and she didn't take my stuff without asking!"

"I've got a song of my own!" shot back Cherry hotly. "It's called, 'I want to kick your head in!'"

But then Cherry became stock-still, like a statue, with a startled look frozen on her face. Her hand began to tremble and the slingshot fell from her limp hand.

The prince, too, looked off the way she was staring. There, beyond the tree, atop a boulder, stood a tall shadow.

A wisp of fog passed between them, but when it cleared, the shadow was still standing there.

"Stay real still, girl," said the cowboy softly. A tear trickled down Cherry's cheek. She was too terrified to even cry out.

In one quick motion, Danny Ray lunged down and grabbed the slingshot, fitted a stone in the cradle, aimed and fired.

Danny Ray felt something rush by him—it was Tûk! The devil waved his sword around his head in hellwain fashion, screaming as he ran headlong at the figure. But just as he got close, it vanished.

Danny Ray looked down. How his slingshot shook in his hand! He had half a notion to be angry with Cherry for filching it, but she was still sobbing uncontrollably. The cowboy came over and knelt in front of her, talking to her in low, soothing words and wiping her nose with his red handkerchief. He took a glance back at the boulder. The tall, willowy figure of the devil stood there, sword at the ready, looking out in all directions.

"Was that a fantasm?" she whimpered. "Look!"

Danny Ray gazed toward the eastern horizon, which had turned the light blue color of a robin's egg. There, towering over them, rose an immense purple crystal pyramid soaring into the morning sky. Its summit sparkled, catching the sunshine and reflecting out in all colors of the rainbow. At its base, dark valleys and ravines of pink, purple, and red crystal awakened, displaying haloes of color arcing through translucent cliffs and leaning geometric towers.

"Sugarwood!" exclaimed Tûk.

So that's where the island got its name, thought the cowboy. Mountains and valleys of glittering rock with forests of towering columns like sugar crystals.

"Well, as they say in Kentucky, let's get to headin' up the hollow." The rodeo cowboy checked his blue rope and hitched up his pants.

"Danny Ray," said Cherry meekly. "I have a bad feeling about this place."

"Me, too, as well" said Tûk, nodding fiercely.

"*Serpentine* and *Wasp* are gonna come lookin' for us," said the cowboy. "We can't be goofin' off out here in the open."

"I'm in charge of this rescue!" shot back Prince Blue. He stormed by the cowboy toward a steep-walled purple canyon. "Follow me!"

The cowboy watched him stride stubbornly up the hill toward the mountain. He rubbed the back of his neck and muttered, "Well, here goes nothin'."

❧ 13 ❧

The Bad Magician

Tûk's face was set in deep thought as he studied the entrance to a cave that they had happened upon while searching for the shadow man. It looked like a monster's open mouth, grimacing with stalactite teeth of pink crystal. Danny Ray hunkered down and peered in.

"Follow me, you guys," he said.

"I'm not going in there!" said Cherry, her face set in a frown.

"Wanna stay out here until *Serpentine* shows up for you?" asked Danny Ray.

"They have a lot of islands to search before they find us," countered the prince.

"Suit yourself." The cowboy shrugged as he cautiously crept into the cave.

With a collective grumble the three followed him beneath the mammoth teeth into the darkness of the cave. Prince Blue was last, grumbling loudest of all.

"Lookee here! A hole in the floor as big as a door!" The cowboy pointed.

"I forbid you to go near there!" announced Prince Blue in his best royal voice.

But Danny Ray did anyway.

"Wonder where in tarnation it leads?"

"I command you not to look in there—"

But Danny Ray knelt down and peered inside. "Walls look real smooth," he said after a low grunt. "Smooth as snot drippin' off a brass doorknob."

"I order you to stand back from that hole, Danny Ray!" the prince said firmly, joining the cowboy with Tûk, and then looking down into the deep unknown.

"What's wrong with you two?" said the cowboy, straightening up.

Sweat beaded on the prince's forehead. "What do you think, Tûk?" he asked.

The devil's eyes shone yellow in the darkness, like a jack-o'-lantern. He shook his head and sniffed. "Like Dumbledown Dungeon is this path."

So, that was it, thought Danny Ray. Prince Blue and Tûk were having flashbacks of their dreadful ordeal in the deep, damp dungeon.

Cherry peeked around the devil into the dark hole. "Oh! Things can't get any worse than this!"

Tûk stepped back as the prince's watch began vibrating on its chain. Prince Blue flipped it open. The face was dull, the eyes dead, the mechanical voice silent.

Something was wrong.

CRACK! The face of the watch broke open. Something pale

and scaly like a snake uncoiled from inside the watch and raised its sharp-beaked head.

"Stomp on it!" cried the cowboy, making a lunge for it.

Its bat wings fluttered open as it flew into the air like a tiny winged serpent.

"What in heavens—" gasped Prince Blue.

"Gossip!" gasped Tûk, snatching at the tiny dragon that deftly dodged the devil's black nails and flitted like a dart toward the light at the cave's mouth. The hellwain opened his mouth and launched a tongue of flame at the thing, which let out a high-pitched *Yoooooch!* that echoed off the stone walls.

Danny Ray went for his slingshot—too late! In a flash of scales and talons, it was gone.

"For your information, Cherry," said Danny Ray, hands on his hips, and shooting the prince a particularly angry look, "things just got a whole lot worse!"

Prince Blue's eyes were furious. "How could I have possibly known—"

"I told you to get rid of that watch!" shot back Danny Ray. "I told you not to trust Mumblefub! The commodore hid that gossip in your watch to track us if he ever lost track of us!"

"Beesa Blue is king, ha?" seethed the devil, a puff of smoke wafting from his nostrils. The black pupils of his eyes narrowed in a display of anger.

"Yeah, he's a king, so he deserves expensive gifts, don't he?" Danny Ray wiped his mouth, his voice trembling with rage. "So why don't you knuckleheads take a wild guess where that gossip is headed? To *Serpentine*—that's where—to tell ol' Mumblefub we're right here on Sugarwood Island!"

"When he said 'knuckleheads,'" put in Cherry simply, pointing at Prince Blue and the devil, "he's talking about you two—not me."

"What's the matter with you, anyway?" Danny Ray stood right in front of the prince. "Last time I was in this world, when you changed into Prince Blue and saved my life, I thought you were real cool. Now you got some kinda attitude problem!"

"I was thrown into Dumbledown Dungeon for days for something I didn't do!" retorted the prince. "And you just stuck me in the neck with a knife for being someone I'm not!"

The cowboy paced back and forth, fuming. He stopped at the hole and looked in. The cold air felt good on his hot face. Hmmm. Danny Ray noticed the sparkling walls seemed to slope downward. He put a boot on the threshold, testing it—

"Danny Ray!" yelled Cherry.

"*Yiiiiiiiiiikes!*" he called out as his feet slipped under him and he fell down the slippery, slanting, sloping slide. He twirled, whirled, swirled around, holding on to his hat with one hand and grasping thin air with the other. Down he went, the wind whistling in his ears as he picked up speed, when all of a sudden—thump, bump, and tumble! He found himself sliding across a level plain of polished crystal as he came to a complete stop.

He sat there for a moment, looking up at a translucent ceiling of purple and pink. With a groan he got to his feet and checked his rope, his slingshot, his chaps, his spurs—all there, thank goodness!

What was that? He heard a sound, barely discernible, from the direction where he had come. It was the faraway voice of Cherry, calling down the hole.

With his head still wobbling dizzily, the cowboy cupped his hands around his mouth and yelled: "I'm all right!" He listened for a moment. Nothing. Maybe they had heard him, maybe not.

"Ain't this just great!" he muttered. No way to crawl back up that shaft.

Danny Ray walked across the dark, mirror-smooth crystal floor. The domed, faceted ceiling grew steadily more lofty and the walls to either side retreated outward. The light dancing in that vast chamber was subdued and diffused, a weird, shifting kaleidoscope of color.

The cowboy stopped short. "Well, I'll be—"

Here came a dancing ballerina, toes pattering lightly, elegantly, across the floor. The only trouble was, the top half of the girl was missing! "Well, I'll be—" Danny Ray said again, as the pair of legs, frilled with a pink tutu around the waist, flittered daintily by him and danced away.

"Well, I'll be—" he said a third time, pushing his hat back off his forehead.

"You'll be what?"

Danny Ray spun around to see a pudgy little man with a floppy red hat and blue spectacles, and dressed in a yellow and orange suit; but who could be sure of any colors in this atmosphere of shifting light? As he introduced himself to the cowboy, Danny Ray thought he seemed a normal enough fellow, except for the queer presence of a knife handle protruding from his chest. "I can tell you, sir," he concluded confidently, "that you'll soon be one of us!"

"Us?" asked the cowboy, when up walked a man who, like the first, introduced himself to Danny Ray most cordially, and most extensively, except that his head was cradled in the crook of his arm.

"Nice to meet you, too," replied the cowboy, completely amazed that, even with his head cut off, this fellow could talk up a storm! Danny Ray looked at the pudgy man. "How come you got a knife sticking outta your chest? And did you know," he said to the other man, "that your head is cut clean off?"

"Yes, I do! But that doesn't mean we appreciate cutting remarks, young man!" replied the cackling head. "Did you catch my joke—cutting remarks?"

"Of course he does!" the pudgy man said. "He is, after all, a very sharp young man, is he not—ha, ha!" The knife handle jiggled up and down over his belly as he fell into a spasm of laughter.

"But seems to be rather on edge, does he not?" said the carried head, the eyes rolling over to look at the pudgy man, whose belly wiggled as he laughed again.

"What's your point?" said the pudgy man, almost out of breath, overtaken by a fresh wave of laughter.

"C'mon, you guys, knock it off," said Danny Ray.

With the utmost sincerity they began explaining their odd punctured and sliced state, when a lovely woman, dressed in a sparkling, tight-fitting outfit, floated overhead like a sky diver frozen in flight. Danny Ray reached up and gently took her hand, guiding her down to the ground. But as soon as he let go, like a helium balloon she floated back up to her original position.

"What the heck's going on here?" asked the cowboy.

"Ask her!" The woman pointed.

Here came the lovely ballerina, her black hair pulled back tightly in a bun, her long, graceful arms floating out like a swan's, but with nothing but air beneath her! She stopped in front of Danny Ray, a questioning look on her face, which prompted Danny Ray to point and say, "Your dancing legs went thataway!"

With a quick, smooth twirling motion, she glided away in the direction Danny Ray had indicated. She had not spoken a word to him, not even a thank-you. Well, he figured, missing your whole lower half might make anybody pretty grumpy.

The floating woman said, "Here he comes, the one who has caused us such distress!"

"Uh!" said the pudgy man. He grew nervous, while the headless man nearly dropped his cranium on the hard floor.

A tall, thin figure walked toward them dressed in a tuxedo and top hat. For the life of him, though, the cowboy couldn't see a thing wrong with him: no missing arms or legs, no knives sticking out of places they shouldn't, and both feet firmly planted on the ground.

"A pretty bad fellow, is he?" asked Danny Ray.

"On the contrary," spoke up the head nestled in the crook of the man's arm. "He's an extraordinarily good fellow."

"He's just not a very good magician," said the pudgy man, looking down his chest at the silver handle. "I was spread-eagle on the spinning wheel, and he missed missing me!"

The bad magician took off his tall stovetop hat and hung it unceremoniously on the pudgy man's knife handle. Danny Ray had never seen someone wearing a hat on their chest before.

The tall man stood motionless, studying the cowboy, who, in turn, studied him back. The magician's face was divided in half, right down the middle, one side of his mouth smiling, expressing happiness, the other frowning, showing displeasure. Danny Ray thought, There's something familiar about his clothes . . .

"I apologize for the errant throw I made with the knife," said the cheerful side of the magician's face as he addressed the pudgy little man. "My magic's not very . . . well, let's just say I'm working to get it right."

"And what about me?" cried the floating woman pitifully. "Am I to levitate forever and ever?"

"I'm so sorry, my dear!" the magician said, wiping his forehead. "I'll say this, that—"

"At least you can speak through a head anchored securely to your body!" said the headless man.

"Pardon me for my mistake with you, too," replied the magician earnestly. "But you, out of everyone, will be delighted to find that the magic guillotine is fixed and out of the shop!"

Danny Ray didn't like the sound of that. Guillotines cut folks' heads off.

Yup, he was on his own in this weirdest of places and filled with the unluckiest people! It was just as well his friends hadn't followed him down the slide, for as the tall magician looked him up and down again with dark, quizzical eyes, the cowboy felt pretty unlucky, too.

✦ 14 ✦

KarooKachoo

"Howdy! The name's Danny Ray," he said politely, extending his hand to the inept magician. "You the king of this here island, are you?"

The silence between them had an ominous bearing. The magician made a motion, running his hands through his long, stringy black hair, his dark eyes still taking in the cowboy. The happy side of the face spoke: "So, you're the one who finally showed up."

"Yeah, I guess so," said the cowboy, a little puzzled.

"Who are the other travelers with you?" he asked. "What do they want here?" He sniffed the ash on Danny Ray's shoulder. "Ah—the scent of devil!"

"How do you know about Tûk?" asked the cowboy.

"Last night I saw you and your companions running across the Checkered Sea to my domain. I know when anyone trespasses on Sugarwood Island!"

"Say," the cowboy muttered, his eyes narrowing, "ain't you the fellow that ran away from me this morning? Hope I didn't hit you with the stone."

"I didn't run away from you," he said, and then his voice dropped. "The sun was rising: She comes with the sun."

"She who?" blurted the cowboy, a little dumbfounded. "You mean Cherry?"

"No." The tall man looked off and cocked his head, reciting in a shaky voice:

"She haunts my steps
In full sunlight
Never on a cloudy day
Never in the hush of night

Ne'er a word She utters
In Her silent heartache
In shade my heart shudders
Like a dream in full awake

Never to return to me
She wanders in woe
My Love is gone from me
To a land dark and low."

The man turned and walked away. The pudgy man nudged Danny Ray and said, "Please! We are obliged to follow him!"

"Yes!" said the headless man. "He can turn nasty in but a second—so beware!"

So they trailed after the magician, who took one long step for every one else's two (or three in the case of the pudgy man!). Only the hovering lady, swooping gently overhead, had no difficulty in keeping up. In the distance, once or twice, Danny Ray caught a glimpse of the ballerina, still searching longingly for her runaway legs.

"Here!" said the pudgy man, waddling along beside Danny Ray. He lifted the top hat off the knife handle and handed it to the cowboy. Hmmm, thought Danny Ray, studying it curiously. "You must carry the master's hat, since you will be his assistant!" the pudgy man added.

"I don't know nothing about magic tricks and such," stated Danny Ray. "And by the looks of you guys, he doesn't, either! And where the heck is he taking us? I got friends on the outside who are gonna be worried sick over me."

But the cowboy's questions were soon to be answered, as the cave opened up into a vast kingdom of delicate diamond-like doors, of wonderfully chiseled walls, of soaring, sparkling staircases.

Nearby stood a bright green cube as big as a house, with transparent walls so that it looked to be made of glass. Danny Ray cupped his hands against the smooth emerald-colored glass and tried to peer inside. Next, he pressed his ear against it. Nothing.

"Wow!" exclaimed Danny Ray. "This is one huge square of green glass!"

Just then, the magician appeared, and something about his countenance caused the pudgy man to gasp frightfully and caused the hovering lady to cover her ears. The head in the crook of the thin man's arms grimaced, for the evil side of the magician's face began to move, to contort, and the words from out of that mouth were harsh: "Danny Ray, I overheard you state that you do not wish to be my assistant."

"Maybe some other time," said Danny Ray, placing his hands on his hips, "but right now I'm on a mission to rescue Princess Amber of Elidor. I got no time for being nobody's errand boy!"

"You're wrong," said the magician. "You've got all the time in the world."

The front of the cube swung slowly outward, slowly, ominously, although there were no visible hinges or latch.

"One more chance!" said the evil side of the magician's face, just inches from Danny Ray's.

"Forget it!" cried Danny Ray. "Hey!"

The cowboy was shoved into the box, and it closed with a muffled *THUMP*!

He was completely alone.

Time to think it over, huh? Time was one thing he couldn't afford to waste. The sooner he escaped the better. But after a few moments of examining the glass wall, of pounding his fists against it, of kicking it, he slumped down and wiped his forehead with his red handkerchief.

"You can't break out of here—no, no, no!"

Danny Ray jumped up. Coming at him from across the box was the strangest character he had ever seen.

"Hey, hey, hey!" she said, her cheeks throbbing as if her heart were pounding in her mouth. "What's that on your boots? What's that on your head? What's that on your belt? What's—"

"I'm a rodeo cowboy. These here are spurs," said Danny Ray, picking up a booted foot and spinning one of them. "This here's my cowboy hat, and this blue thing is my magic rope of thrillium. But you're the darnedest thing I ever saw!"

"I am a Dragonfly Girl!" she replied. "And you're the . . . darnedest thing I ever saw, too, whatever 'darnedest' means!"

She was just taller than Danny Ray, with streaks of green, blue, red, and yellow on her cheeks. Her frenzied hair, standing out in all directions, was purple at the roots but blond on the ends. Her shirt and pants were decked with ornaments and jewelry. Her feet had seven toes apiece, and she extended a welcoming hand to the cowboy that had seven fingers. Some inner voice, in spite of the circumstances, told the cowboy he had nothing to fear from her.

"My name's Danny Ray." He extended his hand. "I'm from Tahlequah, Oklahoma."

"I am KarooKachoo."

"Bless you!" exclaimed Danny Ray.

"No, no, no! I didn't sneeze—it's my name!" She stepped into the middle of the floor, looking off into the distance as if she were on stage, bowing low, and the strands of pearls around her neck rattled and clattered together. Danny Ray found, to his surprise, that she had a wonderfully mesmerizing voice as she recited:

"KarooKachoo is all my name
For time on end it's been the same
With fiery cheeks and a rainbow mane
KarooKachoo is all my name!

Sugarwood Island's magic is sure!
With caves of sparkling treasures pure

Of herbs that heal, of balms that cure
Sugarwood Island's magic is sure!

I need to fly back home—and quick!
The Queen of Dragonflies is sick
She may die at a second's tick
I need to fly back home—and quick!

But first I've come to steal a look
To steal an herb, to steal a book
A charm to brew, to stir, to cook
But first I've come to steal a look!

So come, my friend, and lend a hand,
We'll make a whopping, thieving band!
Your smile tells me you think it's grand,
So come, my friend, and lend a hand!"

"I ain't smiling," said the cowboy glumly. "I'm downright frowning—can't you see that with them weird eyes of yours?" Danny Ray was referring to the seven pupils in KarooKachoo's crazy eyes that would retreat far back into her head when she got excited. "Now listen, Miss Achoo, or whatever your name is, I got a ton of worries of my own. First"—Danny Ray started counting off on his fingers—"I gotta bust outta this box. Second, I gotta find my friends. Third, I gotta rescue Princess Amber."

"Fine! Fine! Yes—that's fine!" The Dragonfly Girl nodded

emphatically. "But I have tasks, as well! Where does the magician hide his magical herbs, the herb aurora?"

"Shoot, how would I know?"

"Oh! When I left Dragonfly Bay three days ago, Her Majesty, the Queen of Dragonflies, was terribly ill. That is how the magician caught me, searching the cliffs for aurora. But I must find a way to fly back home—and soon! We can help each other! Yes, yes, yes!"

"Don't know how we would," Danny Ray said flatly. "What's this aurora herb you're talkin' about?"

"Oh, aurora—with its wonderful yellow flower and petals that soar to the heavens, to the heavens where the gods do sit! Oh, aurora—like the sun and then the moon. But where on Sugarwood Island does the magic herb aurora grow? Do you know? Do you know?"

"Don't know nothin' about no magical plants, or books or spells, neither. Say," Danny Ray remarked, looking at his multi-colored cell mate, "has that magician tried to change you into something unnatural, or tried a trick on you, or tried to eat you?"

"Would you?" asked KarooKachoo. Her hair stood even more on end, and one of her eyes dropped out and sagged down on her cheek. She giggled and plugged the eye back in the socket.

"Gosh! That's the darnedest thing I ever saw!" cried the cowboy. "But, come to think on it, KarooKachoo, you don't look like a dragonfly to me."

"I am the inner being, the soul of the dragonfly!" she stated dramatically, her hand brushing against the colorful stripes on her cheek. "Red and yellow highlight my wings; blue and green adorn my head. I am the heart, the soul of the rainbow empress!"

"What is a rainbow empress?" asked Danny Ray.

"One day you shall see!" she whispered, looking over her shoulder.

"Oh," Danny Ray said gloomily. Despite his exciting companion, he felt pretty dejected. He leaned against the wall and slowly slumped down, resting his chin on his fist. He scanned the top of the box—no breathing holes. Now he knew how a captured butterfly felt. Maybe they would both suffocate in here.

"Just great," he muttered again, all of a sudden feeling very weary, and allowing his tired head to fall forward on his arms.

❖ 15 ❖

Mr. Tabbashavar

Danny Ray raised his head from his arms. He had dozed in this uncomfortable sitting position, a deep, numbing nap—but for how long? A dull ache in his belly marked where the top of his belt buckle had pressed while he slept. Though he couldn't see out of the cube and there was no shiver in the walls, no sign of shifting, he sensed it was moving.

The Dragonfly Girl stirred and bubbled up next to him. "Do you feel it? Do you feel it?"

He looked up dully and said, "Hey, KarooKachoo. Yeah, something's going on."

He unbent his stiff limbs, grunting like an old man as he stood up. Now, Danny Ray had never tasted coffee before, but something told him he'd welcome a hot cup of it just now. He yawned and said, "Who is this magician guy, anyway? Something's not right with him."

"He is awful! Just awful!" she replied. "He flies into a rage, his evil face showing, and performs his terrible magic on poor prisoners. Then he apologizes with his kinder face, and turns to his next victim."

"Sounds to me like he's two different people—guess that explains the two halves of his face, evil and good."

"Oh, yes!" she said, fluttering. "Unstable is he—and doesn't know the meaning of real regret, or even anger. I have a poem about such a person!"

"Why ain't I surprised?" The cowboy sighed.

The Dragonfly Girl shook herself into a pose, laying out a seven-fingered hand as if holding an invisible platter, her other hand over her heart, and began:

"True and holy sorrow
Does not cry
But tomorrow
Seeks to rectify.

A tear is but water
And is gone
And is of no matter
When deeds are not done!"

"What the heck does all that mean?

"It means that crying and saying you're sorry over and over again for the same thing doesn't matter—you have to stop hurting others."

Danny Ray gritted his teeth. "I've had just about enough of being cooped up in this here chicken crate." He braced himself against the wall and said to KarooKachoo, "You best step back."

He raised up his foot, swinging back the heel of his cowboy boot as hard as he could, slamming the spur against the window-thin stone. The wall shivered slightly but no cracks appeared. "That's the darnedest thing I ever saw!"

"Oh!" cried KarooKachoo. "He'll see you! He'll see you!"

"Do you have to say every danged thing twice?" The cowboy chose this crucial moment to pause at the task at hand. "It's like you have some kind of echo disease, or something."

"Sorry! Oh, sorry!" she said, and then bit her lip and giggled. "Oh, there I go again!"

"Confounded girls, wherever you go!" he muttered. Just like this stinky, weird girl KarooKachoo, he thought, or Cherry, or Caroline Robertson back home.

He kicked the wall again, and then again: nothing.

He doubted the rope of thrillium would do him much good in here—nothing to grab hold of. Yeah, but his shining red companion—well, that was a different story! He retrieved his slingshot from his back pocket and felt the grip. He fished in his pocket and took out a forgotten tarnished brass token with ENTERTAINMENT WORLD engraved on it.

"Wait!" warned KarooKachoo, but it was too late. The cowboy had already reared back with the slingshot and fired the token at the far wall.

BING! The token hit the wall and shot back at them. They dove out of the way. BING! It ricocheted off the near wall and the cowboy had to dance out of the way. BING! Here it came again, parting KarooKachoo's hair, *BING!*, grazing Danny Ray's hat. *BING—WHACK!*

"Ouch!" yelled KarooKachoo, as the token tinkled to the ground. She rubbed her rear end and shot Danny Ray a furious look. "I told you to wait!"

"Gosh!" said the cowboy. "That's the darnedest thing I ever—"

"Everything's the darnedest thing you ever saw, Danny Ray," said the Dragonfly Girl hotly.

The cowboy had a mind to be angry right back at her for making fun of him like that, but when he saw KarooKachoo's crazy eyes and the way her hair flashed more vibrantly when she was mad, he chuckled. "Yeah, I guess I say that a lot, don't I?"

But the Dragonfly Girl didn't answer back. "Oh!" she squealed through all fourteen of her fingers, her hair standing straight on end. "It's working! Danny Ray! It's working!"

What started as a small hairline crack branched like lightning across the whole length of the wall, crisscrossing wildly until, in a shower of brightly colored shards, the entire wall shattered and clattered to the floor like a curtain of thin shells!

"Let's get outta here!" urged the cowboy.

But louder by far than the crushing, rushing avalanche of glass was the wave of applause that engulfed the two escapees as they halted in their steps just outside the box. Danny Ray winked and KarooKachoo blinked with her wild eyes retreating back into her head.

They found themselves standing in the center ring in a vast stadium with a huge crowd and the magician in his tuxedo and tall stovetop hat, applauding them happily. He announced loudly,

"Let's hear a warm round of applause for Danny Ray, the Otherworld Rodeo Cowboy, and KarooKachoo, the Dragonfly Girl!"

He seemed not at all upset that one complete wall of the glass cube had been destroyed. Evidently, Danny Ray's escape had been a fortunate event of a bigger show.

The crowd reacted with rude, raucous noise, not the pleasant rustle of applause, for all of them were missing hands for clapping and slapping, or heads for cheering and jeering, or feet for romping and stomping.

"Scary! Scary!" said KarooKachoo, her eyes fastening on a tall apparatus towering ominously behind the magician: the magical guillotine. "That looks scary! Oh! That looks scary, Danny Ray!"

"You can say that again," the cowboy declared, apparently not noticing that the Dragonfly Girl had said it no less than four times!

"Let's hear it for the spunkies!" called out the magician.

A fresh wave of noise surrounded little winged blue fairies no bigger than your little finger who flittered here and there around the guillotine, some dancing along the hoisting rope, some polishing the tall wooden structure, some sharpening the cruel, silver blade at the top of that structure with tiny, delicate files. It was the diagonal, glinting blade that caught Danny Ray's eye, and it made his blood run cold.

"Please!" said the magician to KarooKachoo while gesturing to the guillotine. "Step this way!"

"No!" gasped the Dragonfly Girl.

"Why don't you just leave her alone?" The cowboy's boots

crunched in the gravel of the ring as he stepped in front of her and placed his hands on his hips.

"I'll tell you why," said the bad magician, smiling from the happy part of his face. "This is what comes from sneaking and thieving around my island!"

"The Queen of Dragonflies is sick," replied the cowboy. "KarooKachoo's looking—"

"I take it you still refuse to be my assistant?" he interjected, the evil side of his face contorting enough to spit out the words.

"If you can't get your magic right, then stop!" The cowboy pointed around to all the injured people in the stadium who had grown strangely quiet. "Looking out over this crowd of folks, I think you've had enough practice already."

"If you guess my secret, I'll stop!" he replied. He jabbed out with a long reach and grasped KarooKachoo cruelly by the hand.

"Let me go!" she shrieked, but her cry was drowned out by the confused, eerie noise issuing from the crowd. KarooKachoo's hair flamed out on the tips.

The magician wrestled her over to the guillotine and laid her on it roughly, his tall hat tumbling off onto the gravel in the process. The spunkies whirled in a maddening frenzy around the grim machine while the noise of the crowd rose and rose. And then—

"Ouch!" yelled the magician, standing bolt upright.

There stood Danny Ray, his spent slingshot at his side.

"What did you do that for?" blazed the magician, rubbing his arm where the cowboy had just shot him with a stone.

"I'm sorry," said Danny Ray in his most humble voice.

The magician slowly turned and began the business of securing the Dragonfly Girl's wrists and ankles with silver clasps.

"Ouch!" he cried again, and wheeled around on the cowboy. There stood Danny Ray, as before, with a smoking slingshot.

"I'm sorry," repeated Danny Ray. "I gotta learn to control this thing!"

"Sounds like a good idea to me!" snapped the magician.

Once again the cowboy pulled back his slingshot, and once more a stone rocketed toward the magician, but this time it slapped him painfully and squarely in the rear end.

"I've had it with you, Danny Ray!" he snapped and lunged at the cowboy, catching him around the neck with a viselike grip.

"Sorry about that," said the cowboy, as the magician, full of frenzy and fury, dragged him over to the guillotine, unclasped KarooKachoo and kicked her away in an untidy heap. "You shall take the Dragonfly Girl's place!"

He slammed Danny Ray facedown so hard on the wooden bed of the guillotine that he tasted blood. "I said I was sorry," he said groggily.

"Sorry doesn't begin to cover it," blazed the magician. "You can't keep doing the same bad thing over and over and just apologize for it."

"Isn't that what you're doing?" Danny Ray said, trying to catch his eye. "You just keep maiming people and—"

"It's not the same!" he replied in Danny Ray's ear. "If I can get just one trick right, if I can make my magic true, then I can perhaps get her back."

"Her who? Ouch!" He grunted as the magician kneeled in

the middle of his back. Danny Ray winced—ouch! cold hard clasps closed down around his wrists, but they were way too small.

"Sorry about that!" the magician said sarcastically. He reached down and retrieved his hat, waving to the disorderly crowd. He gripped the rope that would bring the heavy blade sizzling down on Danny Ray's neck. "Any last words, Otherworld Cowboy?"

"You know this magic trick ain't gonna work!" spat out the cowboy. "You're a big joke!"

"I don't see you laughing, Danny Ray!" he said, a drop of sweat rolling down the evil side of his face.

"You ought to be ashamed of yourself!"

"I've been ashamed of myself for some time, now," he said, with a murderous grin. "I've got an amazing secret."

"I know your secret," gasped Danny Ray as the spunkies buzzed around his head, laughing and giggling, and pulling off his cowboy hat and yanking playfully on his hair.

"It will die with you," said the tall magician.

He jerked on the rope as the blade came free. The cowboy exhaled a huff of air, waiting for the sharp, life-ending pain— and then oblivion. It shot into his mind that he would die without his cowboy hat on—what a crazy thought at a time like this! Here came a hissing sound, closer, closer.

Danny Ray grimaced as he felt a slap around his shoulders— he cried out!

THWACK! But instead of finding death, the cowboy was snatched away from the falling blade.

Danny Ray breathed deeply, and found himself nose to nose

with the magician, who asked: "What is my secret, Danny Ray?"

The cowboy tried to speak, but he was relishing the fact that he was still alive.

"I want to give you a sporting chance, Danny Ray. Guess my secret. If you're wrong, I'll put you back beneath the blade—and believe me, I won't save you this time!"

KarooKachoo picked herself up and looked at the pair.

The evil side of his mouth repeated the question: "What is my secret, little cowboy?"

Danny Ray looked wide-eyed at him.

Mr. Tabbashavar went to grab him again so Danny Ray said, "All right, I'll guess. But what's in it for me if I'm right?"

"You won't be right," said Mr. Tabbashavar with an evil chuckle. "No, no, no, you can't possibly know my secret!"

"But what if I do? Will you let me and KarooKachoo go?"

"And show us the way out of this dreadful cave?" added Ka-rooKachoo.

"I'll do better than that," Mr. Tabbashavar said confidently. "I'll supply you with all of the magic charms and weapons you want, and load you with more treasure than you can hold. But, as I said, you cannot possibly guess my secret."

Danny Ray scratched his head and thought for a moment. There had to be a clue somewhere, something that gave the magician away.

"Well? What's your answer!"

"Danny Ray!" said KarooKachoo, coming up beside him. "What is your answer?"

"Just hold on a second, doggone it!"

Danny Ray brought his hand up under his chin. Hmmm.

Something was going off in his head, like an alarm, like a clue. Wait! Mr. Tabbashavar had introduced him as the Otherworld Rodeo Cowboy—how did he know that? Danny Ray hadn't told him he was a rodeo cowboy. And something about his hat and clothes had bothered Danny Ray to no end. And a slight trace of a familiar accent. It was as if Mr. Tabbashavar were really . . .

Danny Ray cleared his throat. The whole stadium went quiet. The magician and KarooKachoo leaned in to hear his answer.

"I reckon . . ." said Danny Ray.

"Yes?" said Mr. Tabbashavar smoothly.

"Yes? Yes?" asked KarooKachoo nervously.

"I reckon you're not from this world at all. You're really from the Otherworld, just like me."

The bad magician looked narrowly at him.

The smiling side of his face finally spoke as he shook the cowboy's hand. "Unbelievable—but you've done it! I'm Mr. Tabbashavar from Huntington, West Virginia. Pleased to meet you, Danny Ray!"

✦ 16 ✦

The Treasure Vault

Folks from West Virginia keep their word, and Mr. Tabbashavar was no exception. He kept his promise, and began leading Danny Ray and KarooKachoo out of his glittery realm.

"So, Danny Ray, how did you ever guess I was from the Otherworld?" he asked as they wound their way through the mountain's heart.

"Well," responded the cowboy. "First, you're dressed in clothes like back home, if maybe a little out of style. Plus, you knew I was a cowboy without me telling you so, and every so often you sound like you're from the South."

"Ha!" said Mr. Tabbashavar, from the happy side of his face. "The more I listen to you, Danny Ray, the more words I remember—and the accent's coming back to me."

"How long you been away?" Danny Ray asked, while examining a small bite hole in his cowboy hat that the spunkies had made.

"Oh, just after the Civil War, I was a driver out west for Wells Fargo. Drove the route from Salt Lake to Virginia City and Deep Creek. Best driver around—I could cut a fly off the rump of the lead horse with my whip! Been on this island about a thousand years or so."

Danny Ray whistled and then said in a quieter tone, "What I can't figure, is why the Lord Advocate sent you here."

"Same as you. One day I walked through a magical doorway. I was supposed to deal with this fellow named Dru-Mordeloch—"

"I know him!" said Danny Ray with a start. "He's the scoundrel that's been causing all the trouble for King Krystal in Elidor!"

"Yeah, well, in a way that's all my fault. I got sidetracked along the way and did some things I shouldn't have."

Danny's face was all questions.

"I fell in love, you see, with a girl from this side of the doorway. Don't ever do that, Danny Ray. I can tell you, it'll only lead to heartache. Then, I tried to go after Dru-Mordeloch on his terms. I learned magic as best I could and tried it out on—" He stopped for a moment, his eyes becoming a little wet. "Under my power—my wretched, awful power—my own dear Eiliana disappeared, and I . . . I couldn't bring her back. I figured if I could get one of my tricks to work, just once, then I might possess the magic powerful enough to find her, wherever she is."

"So that's why all those people back there—"

"That's right. I shoulda stopped a long time ago, but I just kept trying and trying—but no luck."

"Sorry to hear that," said the cowboy, and he meant it.

The bad magician wiped his nose. "Yeah, well, in the end I nearly defeated Dru-Mordeloch. But he got away from me. I raided his castle and carried away some pretty potent stuff; jewels, weapons, charms, and such—some of it good, as it turns out, and some of it bad. But I had failed in my quest, really, so I sailed to this island. Back then it was covered with trees and wildlife—"

"What d'ye mean?" cried Danny Ray. "Sugarwood Island's like a big Christmas ornament!"

"About a thousand years' worth of powerful magic, trans-forming magic, have changed this island into something very beautiful," he said, looking around him at the crystal forma-tions closing them in. "And yet something terrible at the same time. The crystals have slowly taken over the island so there's hardly any dirt or trees left."

"You don't look a thousand years old!" exclaimed the cow-boy, closely appraising the magician as if he were a prize steer at the county fair.

"And neither would you after staying in this world a hundred years, or a thousand. Or a million." Mr. Tabbashavar shook his head. "Oh, Danny Ray, the everlastingness of immortality weighs me down. To exist between two worlds—to sit beneath the uni-verse of stars and realize that you are as immovable, as fixed, as one of them. Time passes, seasons in their cycles, and the luster and vigor of life fade out like the moon in her phases, only to start up again. But still your flame burns, burns and burns on into infinity." He looked steadily at the cowboy and said: "Beware: magic's a real seductive thing. Believe me, I can do things you wouldn't believe."

The cowboy was silent for a moment. It dawned on him that time in Elidor passed much faster than in the other world. Mr. Tabbashavar had been gone about one hundred and fifty years in the otherworld. But a thousand years had passed here. That also explained how King Krystal and Lord Red and Lord Green had forgotten him so soon.

The cowboy said seriously: "Let me ask you something, Mr. Tabbashavar, and you tell me the truth. You weren't gonna really cut off my head, were ya?"

"Nah," he replied. A sad look spread over both sides of his face. "When I laid eyes on you, Danny Ray, and heard your accent, I knew you were from back home, from the Otherworld. Maybe it's a sign that it's time for me to go home."

"How would we get off this island, anyway?" asked the cowboy. "I don't see a ship."

"You forget!" KarooKachoo said, flicking her fingers across her pearl necklaces. "I am the Dragonfly Girl!"

"Yeah, right." The cowboy looked back to the magician.

"I do have a way off this here island, Danny Ray," he said stiffly, "but it'll take you and me back to the Otherworld. Your quest to rescue Princess Amber would fail. And, to tell the truth, I'm not sure I want to go back yet."

They came to a tall, thin door made of translucent rock. As he produced a key, magically, a keyhole appeared.

Click! He turned the key and swung the door outward. They passed inside and Danny Ray pushed back his hat. What kind of room was this with its blank walls and high ceiling? A gasp of impatient air popped out of KarooKachoo's mouth; maybe she was thinking the same thing.

"This vault's where I store my treasure."

"But treasure rooms ought to have treasure," prompted the cowboy. "Like big piles of gold and silver coins—right?—and heaps of gems lying all over the place."

Mr. Tabbashavar stood facing a stark wall, and waved his hand. A drawer appeared and he pulled it outward.

"Wow! Oh, wow!" exclaimed KarooKachoo.

Danny Ray's face swelled with excitement. "Lookee there!"

"To help you both on your way—a king's ransom!" said Mr. Tabbashavar. He brought out a fistful of glittering diamonds and let them cascade back into the drawer. He took a leather pouch and filled it, handing it to the cowboy. Bracelets he presented to the cowboy, more gems, along with unrecognizable baubles and trinkets, tinkly things that hung off other glittery jingly things. Danny Ray began to sag with the weight of them all.

"Wait—I got something to hold your treasures!" the magician said. He reached in another drawer and pulled out a solid silver box the size and shape of a book, adorned with rubies and gold, labeled MAGICAL THINGS, and opened its clasps. "Put everything in here, Danny Ray!"

But the box quickly became so full that the cowboy couldn't come close to closing the clasps. So he placed the pouch of diamonds in his shirt pocket and Mr. Tabbashavar retrieved a green cloth sack where he put the silver book and a few more odds and ends from other drawers.

"Hey, Dragonfly Girl," he said, looking at KarooKachoo, who had begun to pout slightly. "I'm gonna give you this!"

He produced an orange book entitled *Magical Herbs: Their Properties and Powers.*

"Oh, thank you! Thank you!" she said, blubbering profusely.

"If you hadn't noticed, she repeats everything," said the cowboy in a low voice.

So they left the treasure room and walked along in silence

for a time until they came to an opening of a cave, sparkling in the brilliant morning sun.

"Wow!" shouted Danny Ray. His heart soared—oh! to see the sunlight again!

"At last! At last!" cried the excited Dragonfly Girl.

They were high up, looking out over the Checkered Sea from the northern cliffs of the island. Towering battlements of pink and blue crystal, reflecting the rays of the sun, hemmed in a harbor of black-and-white squares on three sides. Danny Ray grinned, pushing the rim of his hat down to shade his eyes from the sun's harsh reflection off the surface of the marble. He felt an unexpected warmth, deep down, just seeing the sea again— maybe he was becoming more sailor than cowboy.

The cowboy returned to the diffused light of the cave where the tall, lanky magician leaned against a vein of baby-blue crystals flecked with yellow that danced in the light like tulips in the sky.

"Aren't you gonna show us the way down to the sea?" asked the cowboy.

"I don't dare go out there—not in the sunlight. She . . . She is out there!"

"I don't see nobody," replied the cowboy with a frown, looking back.

"The path down to the bay is pretty easy," prompted Mr. Tabbashavar.

KarooKachoo darkened the doorway of the cave. "Voices! Voices! I hear voices!"

"That would be your friends," said Mr. Tabbashavar simply.

"They're down at the bottom of the path!" said the Dragonfly Girl, "Danny Ray! They—"

"I heard you, doggone it," he muttered, hoisting his treasure bag over his back. He knew he should be more excited than he was, but for some reason, he had become strangely attached to the magician. Sure, Mr. Tabbashavar was from back home, but maybe it was because they both shared the deep-down desire to rescue a woman they loved. Well, wait a minute, thought Danny Ray, he didn't really love Princess Amber, did he?

The cowboy went to shake Mr. Tabbashavar's hand, but the tall man waved him off. "No goodbyes, Danny Ray. Something tells me we will meet again real soon."

✦ 17 ✦

The Crystal Transformer

"We can't leave Danny Ray behind!" shouted Cherry. She pointed a wicked finger at Prince Blue while Tûk stood off watching the pair go at it.

"Well, we can't just stand out here doing nothing," said the prince, frowning. He tightened his belt around his purple robe and looked out over the Checkered Sea. He sighed the same sigh as the wind blowing through the towering mineral pinnacles and the few remaining trees that bordered the harbor.

"We need to go look for Danny Ray!" blazed the little girl, taking up the fight again.

"I don't much like saying it," said the prince sharply, "but Danny Ray will have to look after himself!"

"I'm staying on Sugarwood Island until we find him!"

"I am your prince and future king," pronounced Prince Blue. "You will do exactly as I say! There's no point in searching for Danny Ray. We'd only get lost—or worse! Then we'd be in a pretty predicament, wouldn't we?"

"But how we should leave?" said the hellwain, wagging his head. "Tûk has no wings, ha!"

Suddenly, the devil stood up straight, his pointed tail as rigid as an arrow, his red hooked nose twitching. Out came his sword. He shaded his eyes from the sunlight as he looked up the side of the mountain to a higher balcony.

"Hey, you guys!" called a voice from overhead.

Cherry's mouth opened in shock. "Danny Ray!" She jumped up and down, did a silly, giddy dance, and then hugged the prince. "It's Danny Ray! He's all right!"

The cowboy waved and then skipped down the stairs with KarooKachoo just behind him, his bag of trinkets and charms tinkling and tankling. Cherry hugged him while the Dragonfly Girl stood off and marveled at the tall, slim devil who regarded her with the same level of amazement.

"Shucks! I never thought I'd see you guys again!" The cowboy looked down at Cherry's smudged and torn dress, reminding him of their skiing experience in the middle of the night. Gosh—that seemed so long ago!

With a deep breath Cherry asked, "But what happened to you, Danny Ray?"

"It was a real circus," assured the cowboy, smiling inwardly at his private joke.

"What strange person, Danny Ray, all afire in hair and face, ha?" asked Tûk.

"This is KarooKachoo," he replied.

The Dragonfly Girl giggled and then bowed. Her hair pulsated with color. "Great day!" she cried out, stretching her arms up and wiggling her fourteen fingers about. "And good to meet you!"

"A bit over the top, Danny Ray?" said the prince quietly.

"You should see what she does with her eyes," he responded.

She glanced back over the top of the harbor to the crest of the flat mountain. "Up there I am! Up there!"

Danny Ray muttered under his breath, "She thinks she's a dragonfly."

Cherry giggled and Tûk shot Danny Ray a wide-eyed look.

Danny Ray caught the prince's eye. The air crackled with tension. "Sorry for blowing up at you before," said Danny Ray. "Maybe we should let bygones be bygones."

Prince Blue nodded and started to say something but fell silent. After an awkward moment, he rubbed his hands together and said: "Shall we think of what to do next, now that everyone's been introduced?"

"Everyone? What about me?"

That question came from a man who staggered out from behind a nearby tree. He wore a black captain's uniform and hat trimmed in gold. Behind him, in matching outfits of black and yellow, stood a company of grim gargoyles with cutlasses and boarding axes.

"Allow me to—allow me to make my acquaintance." The tall, gangly man staggered a little closer and swayed back and forth, a bottle of rum in one hand. "I am none other . . . other than Captain Giddyfickle. And yonder"—he pointed with the hand holding the bottle, nearly dropping it—"is my ship—now where did my ship go?"

"Over there, Cap'n," said one of the gargoyles.

"Ah! Yes, there is my ship, *Wasp!*" The captain looked back at them and wiped at his nose. In the distance sailed the tall and elegant bishop, the morning sun catching her delicate purple upper works as she slowly cruised her way diagonally into the harbor. No sign of *Serpentine* or the commodore.

The captain wobbled and turned to Danny Ray and his company of travelers. "And where in the infernal blue blazes have you been? Fall off *Serpentine*, did you?"

"Yeah," said Danny Ray sarcastically, "all of us, at once."

The cowboy thought of the little gossip that had flown out of Prince Blue's watch—it would have told Commodore Mumblefub every detail of their escape. They were being toyed with by this captain—why not toy back? The hellwain devil had already guessed as much and held his sword at the ready—good ol' Tûk!

A red glow emanated from around the captain's eyes. And even now, as the form of the captain and the gargoyles began to shimmer and change, the cowboy's worst fears came to pass.

"Ah!" cried KarooKachoo.

Cherry gripped the cowboy's shirt from behind. Her heart pounded loudly in her chest. "Fantasm!"

A fearfully familiar pillar of shadow rose before them that even the bright, glad sunlight of a summer day could not penetrate. Cruel orange eyes glowed beneath broad black brows like flickering firelight beneath the heavy eaves of a witch's abode, deep in a dark, haunted wood. And the voice, the villainous voice that issued forth in command to the whiners hulking to either side of it, caused Danny Ray's neck hairs to curl.

There was no escape back to the island. The magician had returned to his strange, mysterious realm. And there was no escape to sea with *Wasp* dominating the harbor.

They were trapped!

Danny Ray found he couldn't move his arms or his legs—it was as though they were cast in invisible cement. The others were held fast as well, Cherry crying pitifully, KarooKachoo trembling with fright, Prince Blue seething with rage, and Tûk growling and squirming to free himself from the unseen bonds that held him.

The fantasm and whiners were too preoccupied with their advantage to notice *Wasp*, out in the harbor, signaling with its lights and sounding a warning whistle. Each of the whiners pulled out long, red knives while the fantasm drew out a cruel thin blade, hissing like a snake as it cleared the scabbard. But as formidable as the fantasm was, and as sinister his followers, the cowboy's attention was drawn to what had panicked *Wasp* and had caused her to signal.

The tall crystal towers close at hand had begun to move, silently, methodically. Shorter towers joined the main mass to become arms, to become legs. Chiseled features, grim and hard, appeared in the very top of the spike-shaped head.

"Wow!" said Danny Ray, gazing up at the pink and purple giant. "It's a huge crystal transformer!"

Wasp flashed its panic lights and fired a warning cannon. The ground began to tremble, more and more violently, as the crystal giant walked toward them, lifting its massive feet and setting them down on the ground. The fantasm looked up in time to see the sun obliterated as the shadow of the transformed stone giant settled over them. Fingers appeared in the translucent block of stone at the end of its arm that came to hover over the fantasm and his whiners—it was an immense crystal fist!

Threateningly, the fantasm raised his black hand. A bolt of

blue lightning shot upward, dancing wickedly about the giant's body and head! The stone creature fell to one knee and froze.

"The poor giant is dead!" whimpered Cherry.

The fantasm swiveled its eyes back on them. "Take the prince and Otherworld cowboy alive. Kill the others!" he commanded the whiners.

Danny Ray tried to reach for his rope. Tûk snarled and said something harsh in his native tongue.

The leader of the whiners, a hulking brute with four clawed arms on each side of his body, signaled to his minions, and their wings began to hum. Just as they lifted off the ground—*KABOOM!*—the giant's monolithic fist came down! The shock waves knocked the cowboy down on top of his treasure bag and the others fell flat on their backs.

Danny Ray scrambled up and helped Cherry and KarooKachoo to their feet. At the exact place where the terrifying fantasm and his evil minions had stood, there simmered and fumed a black, soupy puddle with wisps of smoke rising from its surface.

KABOOM!

The giant brought its fist down again in the same spot, thundering against the ground so hard that the foundation of a nearby spire disintegrated. The tower of stone leaned askew with an awful grinding sound and fell over with a terrible crash.

The giant raised its fist. The puddle had vanished, driven so deep into the ground that all that remained was a fist-shaped hollow. The giant got to its feet with an ominous grating sound, piercing white lights shooting out from beneath its crystal brows as it gave them a quizzical look. It turned its head to peer out over the harbor and then strode away around the bank toward the dismayed bishop ship.

Wasp had signaled in vain to her captain. Now, she realized her own mortal danger as the giant's attention was turned toward her. A whining sound filled the air, the panicked bishop's engines reversing to flee the harbor. Danny Ray scratched his chin and wondered what sort of engines *Wasp* housed; tantarrabobs, clabbernappers, zanzoomies?

But the giant closed on *Wasp* quickly, and came to stand on the edge of the shore.

With an awful groan, the giant pushed at an immensely high column of stone. The tower rocked toward the harbor but then its momentum brought it back to the giant. It grunted as it took the weight of the tower against its shoulder. Danny Ray could only imagine the panic on the bishop, the chaos and mayhem on deck: that tower was tall enough to smash them if it fell over!

Wasp still had steerage way. Her engines were intact and humming, and in a few seconds, she would be free of the harbor and rocket away. With a flash of white fire shooting from its eyes, the giant let out a deep, hollow cry and leaned into the tower, heaving it forward. This time, the mass of stone snapped at its base and tottered, falling, falling—

"Oh!" cried Cherry, pointing out over the harbor.

The tower fell directly on top of *Wasp*. Her upper ball was driven into her main deck, which collapsed farther into her main column. The bishop disintegrated in an eruptive cloud of smoke.

Danny Ray cringed, and gritted his teeth as the thundering

of falling rock rushed across the harbor with a great—
HROOOOOOOM! The bishop had simply disappeared, crushed
to smithereens beneath tons of falling rock. The shiny marble
around her was covered in a film of fine purple dust, the powder of what was once a mighty and beautiful ship.

The smoke cleared.

The giant looked back their way.

"Run for it!" yelled Danny Ray.

But there was no place to run. And in a few long, thunderous
strides the giant stood over them. It worked its mouth back and
forth, but only a deep rumbling came out, like the sound of an
avalanche.

"He's trying to talk to us!" said Danny Ray, relieved that the
giant might not smash them under its weighty fist.

"He may know a way off this island," said Cherry hopefully.

"Maybe he has ship, ha?" put in Tûk with his devil grin.

"I think he just destroyed the only ship around for miles,"
said the prince dourly.

"I wonder why he didn't smush us in the ground, too," said
Danny Ray.

"Because of me!"

"Mr. Tabbashavar!" gasped the cowboy. There stood the magician, and Danny Ray noticed a brilliant yellow stone dangling
from the magician's neck. He looked around. "What—how did
you?—when?"

"I thought you might need some help."

"You mean, that's *your* giant?"

"I told you I could do unbelievable things."

"Yeah, but—" Then he laughed. "Well, I know you said we'd

see each other again soon, but I never figured it would be this soon!"

Danny Ray introduced the magician to his friends. Prince Blue looked haughtily down his nose at him while Tûk growled suspiciously. Then, much to the hellwain's surprise and delight, the magician produced a most interesting gift for the devil, fashioned from the hardest pink crystal.

"Pitchfork!" exclaimed Tûk, holding the weapon like a cherished baby.

"No self-respectin' devil should be without one!" said the magician.

Tûk's knobby red fingers gripped the long pole, his black fingernails fingering the razor-sharp prongs on the end. He offered the magician a quick nod of approval.

"I reckon I still wield some powers," Mr. Tabbashavar said proudly, touching the yellow stone on his necklace.

"Thanks for taking care of Captain Giddyfick—I mean that fantasm—for us! And thanks again for this here sack of treasure!"

"You'll need more than what's in that sack to battle the likes of fantasms." He fished a necklace out of his pocket, much like the one he was wearing except glittering with a white light. "This here magical stone is named Arcile. Take it. Keep it around your neck for protection."

It felt light in the cowboy's hand. But the white flicker of fire within the gem, just like the blue rope on his belt, gave him a calm feeling of assurance.

It was Cherry who spoke up politely and said, "Mr. Tabbashavar, sir, do you want to come with us?"

He shook his head sadly. And as the clouds parted momentarily and the sun shone through, he pulled out a white handkerchief and wiped away a tear.

"What's wrong, sir?" asked the cowboy.

"She . . . She is here!" replied Mr. Tabbashavar.

"Who is?" Danny Ray looked around.

But then he glanced at the ground, and a shiver went up his spine. Mr. Tabbashavar's shadow was a delicate profile of a woman in a long, full dress!

"It is Eiliana, beloved!" he whispered into his handkerchief. He was virtually paralyzed, afraid even to look down.

Cherry's eyes widened as Danny Ray nodded. "So that's your old sweetheart, sir, the one who disappeared?"

"Yes! Yes! Did I not tell you she dogs my steps in the full sunlight?" His voice was now a sad, tormented whisper. Both sides of his face shared in the agony. "I must go, Danny Ray. I cannot bear it any longer!"

Mr. Tabbashavar's hand closed around the small gem glittering on his chest. He said one last time: "Farewell, Otherworld friend! Do not take the wrong paths I took, or make the bad choices I made. Goodbye, and good luck, Danny Ray!"

The cowboy felt a lump in his throat. He watched him disappear up the path to the mountainside, the shadow of the woman keeping pace with him.

"Now where did KarooKachoo get to?" Danny Ray asked, coming out of his thoughts.

"Oh!" she called excitedly.

Everyone gathered around. The Dragonfly Girl knelt where a bright yellow flower bloomed among thorny leaves. Delicately she pulled the small plant from the ground and held it in her trembling hand. Her cheek bands pulsated with color and her eyes circled around maddeningly in their sockets.

"Look, see, Danny Ray! Look, see! I ventured into the magician's lair seeking what lay outside—the magical herb aurora!"

Slapping his leg and laughing out loud, the cowboy cried out, "Aurora? Shoot! That ain't nothin' but a dandelion!"

"A what?"

"A dandelion! A dag-nummed weed!" replied the cowboy. He laughed even harder when he remembered her description of the flower, with petals that float up to heaven—the dandelion in its fluffypuff stage. "Lordy! Dandelions grow all over the place back in Oklahoma!"

"Really, Danny Ray, really! I cannot believe you might say such a thing!" said KarooKachoo, clearly insulted.

"She's right!" said Cherry with a deep frown. "Aurora is no weed!"

Danny wiped his smile away as the Dragonfly Girl reverently wrapped the dandelion in a handkerchief and placed it in her pocket, patting it solemnly with her hand to make sure it was truly there. Tûk laid back his head and cackled at the cowboy, whose ears were still tinged faintly red with embarrassment.

"We still have no plan for how to get off this island," announced Prince Blue.

The giant was standing there, silent, commanding. The Dragonfly Girl raised her voice and called out to him, "Would you please lift us up there?" She pointed to a particular cliff edge.

The giant grumbled an assent. With the sound of rock grating against rock, he lowered his hand to the ground, palm open.

"He wants us to climb on!" squealed Cherry.

"What are we going to do up there?" fumed Prince Blue.

"We don't need a clumsy, clunky old ship; bishop, rook, or queen," announced the Dragonfly Girl confidently, striking a pose and unfurling a dramatic hand. "I will fly us away from here!"

Danny Ray snorted. "Yeah, sure you will."

The giant's hand was so massive that they had to climb up into the palm. Danny Ray and the others felt nervous as they were being lifted by that huge rock hand high over the ground, along with the rumbling and grumbling of rock. Cherry held on to the cowboy's belt with frantic hands, and even Tûk decided to kneel once he saw how high up the mountainside they were being raised.

As they were lifted higher and higher in the air, Danny Ray scanned the Checkered Sea. No *Serpentine* in sight, thank goodness. No fantasm, either, with its haunting maliciousness and cruel eyes glowing with the torch of bitter envy and strife. Below, the wreckage of *Wasp* still smoldered in the harbor: one fantasm down, two more to go.

"Over there!" directed KarooKachoo, looking up kindly into that grim crystal face. The giant silently obliged.

As they stepped off his hand onto a wide shelf of rock, Danny Ray's mouth opened even wider than his eyes.

"Lookee there!" he shouted. The cowboy set his treasure bag down on the ground with a clinkety-clank.

He wouldn't . . . he just couldn't believe what he saw!

❖ 18 ❖

The Rainbow Empress

 The travelers stood beneath a black dragonfly, as large as an airplane, sitting lifeless, unmoving, on that hidden rocky shelf bordered with tall, wheat-colored grass. It was devoid of any color and seemed dead, except for an occasional flicker of its four long wings, two to a side, as the wind gusted through the long grass. The honeycombed eyes seemed hollow, the legs frozen in a crouching posture.

"I don't understand why we're up here on the side of the mountain with a big, dead dragonfly!" said Prince Blue, hands on hips.

"We better get running, or flying, or whatever," said Danny Ray to the others. "*Serpentine* might show up anytime!"

"Oh, awful boys!" chortled KarooKachoo, walking under the massive wings of the dragonfly. "First, you call the illustrious magical herb aurora a weed . . . a weed! Next, you call my outer skin . . . dead! Oh, vile, senseless boys!"

The cowboy surveyed the gigantic flying creature: it looked dead to him, too, but he wasn't about to chime in with the prince. "Wait a minute, Karoo!" Danny Ray exclaimed. "You saying you got a license to fly this thing?"

"Better than that!" she responded, clicking her nails over her mound of pearls. She climbed up one of the dragonfly's legs and, in a flash, came out on top of the dragonfly's head. "It is a rainbow empress!"

She sat down and crossed her legs, closed her eyes, and began breathing deeply. Her hair looked like it might catch fire, and her pearls began rattling. Slowly, she began to sink into the very armor of the flying creature.

Danny Ray looked back and made a wild face to the prince. But Prince Blue wasn't even looking at the cowboy as an amazed look passed over his royal features.

A strong wind hit Danny Ray from behind so that he had to clamp his hand down on his hat to keep it from blowing out over the harbor. He turned to find that the huge dragonfly's humming wings were tipped with red and yellow, and that her long tail section and body glowed bright green and blue, with bright white lights dotting the ends of the hairs atop the magnificent creature's head.

KarooKachoo was nowhere to be seen— Wait! It dawned on the cowboy that the colors of the rainbow empress were the exact colors on the Dragonfly Girl's cheek, and the twinkling lights on its head were her pearls!

When he was a little boy, Danny Ray's Scottish grandmother told him tales about the seal maidens, or selkies, and how they would come ashore to shed their skins and dance on the beach as beautiful women, only to don their seal skins again at twilight and swim away in the dark waters of the North Sea. It dawned on Danny Ray that KarooKachoo had not been crazy when she had said they didn't need a ship to get off the island. She had put on her natural shell, uniting her inner soul with her outer shell, just like the selkies.

Gosh! thought Danny Ray. KarooKachoo *was* actually a dragonfly!

The cowboy bit his lower lip as he looked up into those powerful jagged jaws—dragonflies were known for having voracious appetites. Would KarooKachoo remember him in her new state, that they had been prisoners together, that he had saved her from the blade of the guillotine? Or would she just eat all of them right on the spot?

The rainbow empress looked down and a glint of recognition flashed across those honeycombed eyes. She lifted a spidery leg and motioned to him.

"All right!" cried Danny Ray, and heaved up his bag of treasure. "Let's go, you guys!" he called over his shoulder to his astonished friends. "We got a dragonfly to catch!"

The rainbow empress lifted off from the small landing area with a certain rodeo cowboy, a pugnacious little girl, a stuffy prince, and a red hellwain devil riding on her back—along with a sack of trinkets!

"We fly!" said Tûk, laying back his horned head and laughing heartily.

"Scooch up!" called Cherry, over the loud droning of the empress's wings. Danny Ray squirmed to the front as far as he could, wedging his bag of treasure just behind the dragonfly's massive head. Tûk rode at the rear. The cowboy secured his chinstrap and had the manners to point his toes forward—no way KarooKachoo would enjoy being poked by his spurs!

The vibrating of the dragonfly's wings increased. Cherry squealed in astonishment as they rose and hovered above the sparkling ridges of Sugarwood Island. The wind hit Danny Ray full in the face as they slowly gathered speed, skimming across the angular stone mountains and valleys.

KarooKachoo's tail lifted slightly, Tûk's small black horns were outlined against the end of her blue tail, and her speed increased dramatically. Danny Ray thought he saw the magician standing in the shade of a cave. But then he dwindled away until he looked like a child, then a dot, then the island swallowed him up, and then the island was hidden by clouds.

"Good morning to you!" came a low, melodic voice. Spunkies! Danny Ray couldn't believe his eyes as the neck of his treasure bag opened wider and an important-looking spunky stuck out his head, doffing his hat. "Appreciate the lift!"

Oh, great! When Mr. Tabbashavar returned to his realm and found them missing, he'd think Danny Ray was a thief. But the cowboy couldn't keep frowning for long, as a crowd of other spunky faces appeared, pealing out their congratulations, felicitations, and complimentations in a merry chorus. They looked like tiny blue elves with pointed ears, and an unmistakable twinkle of mischief lit up their eyes.

"Gosh! You guys aren't very heavy," added Danny Ray. "I didn't even feel you when I lifted the bag!"

The cowboy's light moment was short-lived.

"Look!" bellowed Prince Blue, pointing below as the clouds

cleared away. There, tall, majestic, and alone on the Checkered Sea, sailed *Serpentine*. Pinpricks of light sparkled from her helm—telescopes trained up into the sky. The bishop ship accelerated on the diagonal.

"She's seen us!" cried Danny Ray. Cherry scooted up and wrapped her arms tight around the cowboy. "You best get back in the bag where it's safe," added the cowboy to the spunkies. "We're in for a peck of trouble!"

⇜ 19 ⇝

Dogfight over Big Lizard

 "We have visitors!" yelled Danny Ray.

Up from *Serpentine* issued a dark brown swarm that turned to burgundy and then to red as it drew closer.

"Whiners!" said Prince Blue.

Danny Ray unhooked his magic blue rope and shouted behind him, "Grab something to fight with!"

"Beesa Blue!" said Tûk, handing the prince his sword and the very dagger that the cowboy had pressed against his neck. The devil heaved up his fearsome pitchfork.

"Hey!" yelled the cowboy. He felt something yanked out of his back pocket: his slingshot.

"I need rocks! Stones!" called Cherry above the increased hum of the wings.

Gosh! thought the cowboy. I don't have any—wait! Danny Ray felt his shirt pocket—yes! He opened the small pouch and pulled out a handful of sparkling diamonds and handed them back to Cherry. "Careful with those!" he called. "Don't waste 'em!"

A large rocky blob appeared below, its major outcropping of

rock looking like a chameleon or iguana lying on its stomach with its mouth open: the island of Big Lizard.

"Here they come!" called the prince.

"Inbound bogeys!" screamed the cowboy.

Something flew close by the cowboy with a high-pitched shriek—no wonder they called them whiners!

"Bogey straight ahead!" yelled the cowboy. He went to lift his rope when he heard something *whizzzzzzz!* past his ear from behind. Suddenly the whiner doubled over and fell from the sky, its wings limp, a diamond buried in its throat. "Nice shot, Cherry!" yelled the cowboy over his shoulder. The little girl grinned, her blond hair blowing straight back.

"Whoooaaaa!" yelled the cowboy. The big dragonfly leaned over on her left wing, making a mass of whiners miss with their dive. Their humming grew faint and then louder again as they circled for another attack.

"There's too many of them!" said Cherry.

The cowboy fumbled with the necklace on his chest. How'd this dang Arcile stone work, anyway? It was supposed to protect them!

All of a sudden, the sky in front of them grew dark. A mountain appeared right in their path where there had been clear sky. A gaping mouth appeared in that huge land mass, covered with swaying trees and grass.

"We're flying through!" cried Danny Ray as they passed into deep shade and out the other side. With a horrible *WHOOOOMPF,* the mouth closed down on the multitude of pursuing whiners.

"That island came to life!" shouted a shocked Prince Blue,

pointing down as the colossal head lowered to its original posture and once again became as still as stone.

Danny Ray nodded to himself—Mr. Tabbashavar's powers truly did extend to all the islands!

"More whiners!" Cherry gestured into the sky with the slingshot.

Here came a group of the bloodsuckers banking on the wind. Danny Ray snared a whiner by the wing with his rope as it flew across in front of him—*SNAP!* Off came its left wing, crumpling like balsa wood, and it plunged below in a tight spin, like water circling down the bathtub drain.

CRUNCH! The rainbow empress snagged a whiner and bit its head off. Then *CRUNCH!*, down went the rest of her meal, as she feasted in midair while the smaller, nimbler whiners swarmed menacingly all around them.

Twang! went the slingshot. Another whiner dropped from the skies. *Twang!* Another whiner shrieked while hovering in midair close to Cherry, a diamond lodged in its head. Another whiner appeared out of nowhere; Prince Blue grabbed it by its clawed foreleg and plunged his dagger deep into its chest.

Tûk showed amazing balance and agility by standing upright on the dragonfly's tail, swinging his pitchfork as only a hellwain devil can do. *Whoosh! Whoosh!* Back and forth went the lethal weapon. He caught one whiner with the sharp crystal edges of the pitchfork's prongs, slicing the thing clean in two.

CRUNCH! Madam Empress had caught two more of the flying menaces and devoured them whole.

Twang! Twang! Cherry was busy with her slingshot. "More diamonds, Danny Ray!" she called.

Ain't that just like a girl! chuckled the cowboy to himself. The cowboy cleaned out his front pocket and handed back all the gems he had left.

Just then, the cowboy heard something over his shoulder—*whizzz!*

"Behind us!" yelled Cherry.

Danny Ray ducked to one side and felt a hot, searing pain as the long, needlelike nose of a whiner glanced along the side of his neck. He grabbed it with both hands—it felt hard, sharp, strong, like a broom handle. He pulled the whiner over his shoulder, and then jerked up savagely, breaking it off the whiner's face just above the mouth, blood spraying back at him in the screaming wind.

"Oh, my white dress!" screamed Cherry indignantly.

"Here they come again!" screamed Danny Ray. "Bogey at three o'clock!" He reached back just in time and pulled Cherry down as a brown shape shot over them.

Tûk was covered with streaks of purple blood. His pitchfork flashed, caught a whiner flying by, and sheared off its wing, and the thing tumbled over. With his return stroke the devil hacked off its other wing and it dropped like a lead pellet. The prince hacked at a whiner flying by and nearly lost his balance.

Danny Ray looked below. Big Lizard was well behind them now. They were out over the open sea, the small black-and-white checks stretching out to the horizon.

Twang! Twang! The magical slingshot sang in Cherry's hand. *Twang!* Danny Ray was glad now that the little blond girl had practiced with it back at their campsite on Sugarwood Island. Gosh—she was good with that thing!

All of a sudden something gripped Danny Ray's arms from overhead and settled down in front of him—the largest whiner he had yet seen, with two sets of wings instead of one, and golden hairs framing its red eyes.

"Cherry!" yelled Danny Ray back to the little girl. She fumbled with a diamond, her hand shaking so much that she dropped it over the side. She watched it fall, twinkling out of sight.

"Shoot it, Cherry!" screamed Danny Ray hysterically. His arms were pinned.

"I'm trying!" She fished in her lap—dropped another diamond over the side.

"What are you doing!" cried the cowboy.

The whiner's eyes flamed red, its thin mouth grinning greedily.

"Cherry! Shoot it!" he shrieked. "Shoot it! Shoot it!"

"Just hold on, Mr. Impatient!" called Cherry.

The whiner drew back its razor-sharp proboscis, to stab deeply into the cowboy's innards, to drink richly. It grinned all the more to see Danny Ray's eyes light up with helplessness. But then its grin faded. Over the cowboy's shoulder peeked a determined blond cherub holding a strange but formidable weapon at point-blank range.

THWAAAAK!

A sharp diamond blazed, drilling a small, black hole in the

whiner's forehead. It let go of the cowboy and tumbled life-lessly down the side of the dragonfly.

"Could you be a little quicker on the draw next time?" Danny Ray's heart was still in his throat. *"Whooooooooooaaaah!"*

Without warning, the dragonfly pointed up and flew straight into the sky.

"Grab hold!" cried Danny Ray, feeling his weight falling back.

"What's KarooKachoo doing?" screamed Cherry.

Tûk fell down to his hands and knees and hugged the empress's tail. Higher they flew, and now Danny Ray saw what KarooKachoo was doing. A floating cloud bank as dense as a pillow hovered overhead, inviting them in—a great hiding place from the whiners! They passed into the misty, secretive grayness and leveled off.

The cowboy shivered. He could hardly see the back of the empress's head, so thick was the cloud! She had dimmed her pearl-white lights and even her wings hummed more softly so as not to attract attention.

Serpentine had been left for behind and there was no sign of their attackers. But Danny Ray thought he could hear a distant whine now and then as their pursuers crisscrossed through the gray soup, trying to locate them. Prince Blue placed the dagger in his belt. Tûk sat down but remained wary, skimming off pieces of paperlike wing from his pitchfork with his thumb and forefinger. But the rainbow empress flew steadily on, following some inner compass.

After a while, the cowboy could hear nothing but the steady drone of her wings. He closed his eyes and his chin fell to his chest.

———

Danny Ray never remembered coming out of the cloud bank, never recalled the sudden appearance of the sun again and the sparkling Checkered Sea far below them. He had long ago nodded off to sleep to the steady droning of KarooKachoo's wings and the secure feeling of flying on the huge dragonfly.

"Land!" yelled Cherry. The excited pitch of her voice jolted the cowboy awake.

He yawned and stretched, remembering suddenly he was hundreds of feet in the air. His hand shot to his rope as a group of flying attendants issued out from the distant coast. But the rainbow empress showed no signs of fleeing or of taking evasive action.

"More dragonflies!" said Prince Blue, craning his neck to see the approaching armada of bright damselflies and dragonflies.

"Fly with us will they!" snapped Tûk in his rough, guttural show of approval. "Ha, ha!"

Like a heavy bomber being escorted by fighter planes, the rainbow empress entered Dragonfly Bay surrounded by marvelous consorts: blue darners, amber wings, and violet dancers; ruby-spotted damselflies and orange skimmers with translucent wings; brown hawkers and crystalline dancers; each displaying his own signature of vibrant, metallic colors and glowing hues of orange, green, blue, and splashes of electrifying purple.

"The White Kings!" cried Prince Blue, pointing off to the right.

Against the northern cliff sat four immense statues of kings with forbidding stares, carved out of the cliffside. Their hollow eyes frowned in the long shadows of the failing westerly sun, their grim countenances shifting and stirring through the dragonfly's shimmering, iridescent wings.

The rainbow empress banked to begin her final approach into Dragonfly Bay as the late lights began to twinkle on, one by one, as did the stars overhead.

The cowboy had grown very quiet.

"Why are you so glum, Danny Ray?" asked Cherry, leaning her chin on his shoulder.

"Aw, it's nothing . . ."

"But we're safe now! Aren't you proud how we killed all those whiners?"

"Sure," said the cowboy, and then he felt his empty pocket where the diamonds used to be. "Except it cost me a million bucks to do it!"

❧ 20 ❧

Mirrathaní

Dark walls of Belagamma teak streaked with gold; shimmering yellow curtains hanging from far overhead, waving like waterfalls of coins; two huge puffy beds, piled with red and black pillows; a soft floor carpeted in rich damask; this was Danny Ray's exquisite room that he shared with Tûk in the royal palace of Her Majesty, Queen of Dragonflies. Cherry was in her own private chamber fast asleep.

"Snore, Beesa Ray?" asked Tûk gruffly, his arms crossed, watching the cowboy empty his bag of fabulous treasure onto his bedcover.

"What do you mean?" asked Danny Ray.

"Tûk asks if you snore? Do you snore?" said the blue spunkies, laughing. They were everywhere: hanging in the curtains, sitting on the head of the bed, lying lazily on the dresser, dangling from a hummingbird light.

"Do I snore?" The cowboy snickered. "Shoot—I don't know! I ain't never been awake to listen—ha, ha!"

The spunkies giggled mischievously while Tûk only mumbled

moodily. He didn't like being away from Beesa Blue. But the prince, because of his royal status, had been given his own room.

"Tûk, you don't have to call me Beesa Ray," said the cowboy. "Just relax and take it easy. We've all been through a lot today."

Danny Ray unclasped his rope and hung it on a peg.

"Mm." The hellwain devil glanced about the room. He raised a black eyebrow when he spotted the puffy mounds of covers and pillows. Tûk sleeping in a bed—ha! Tûk would do no such thing. He would be more comfortable balancing on his two legs and tail!

"Hey, I forgot about this!" said the cowboy. He opened the silver box labeled MAGICAL THINGS and pulled out a full pouch of diamonds. "I gotta hide these from Cherry."

Sad music wafted into their room, accompanied by a fresh wave of mournful weeping from the direction of the room where the Queen of Dragonflies lay dying. When they had first arrived in Dragonfly Bay, it was revealed that KarooKachoo was actually the Princess of Dragonflies. The cowboy had peeked into her mother's royal chamber where she lay on her vast bed, surrounded by so many colorful dignitaries, each red-eyed from weeping, sniffling with handkerchiefs. But their sadness had turned to joy when Princess KarooKachoo had unwrapped the precious, magical healing herb, aurora. Danny Ray had fought down the urge to laugh at the limp, spiny-leafed dandelion with its drooping yellow flower. But that had been an hour or so ago—the queen should have recovered by now.

"Beesa—Danny Ray!" gasped Tûk.

Danny Ray snapped out of his daydream to find the devil staring down, transfixed. A silver face had pushed up through the bottom of the empty box. It looked like a mannequin's face dipped in chrome, expressionless, neither male nor female.

"Magical things that begin with the letter *O*," it said with no inflection, in a level voice that was neither high nor low.

"What the heck—" whispered Danny Ray to himself, his face screwing up in astonishment.

"Magical things that begin with the letter *O*," it repeated. The voice wasn't really machinelike. It was too smooth with feeling for that.

"Mirrathaní!" exclaimed Tûk, pointing. "Danny Ray—Mirrathaní! More worth than heaps of diamonds!"

"Mirrathaní! Mirrathaní!" cackled the spunkies in chorus, some of them dancing and snapping their fingers. "Mirrathaní!"

"Aw, hush up!" said the cowboy dully, without taking his eyes off the face that had filled up the cavity of the box. He waved his hand over its silver features. Nothing. Why hadn't the face appeared before?

"How do you know this is a mirra . . . a whatever you call it?" asked Danny Ray.

"Pirates know everything!" said Tûk, smirking with those awful teeth. "Pirates sail all the world!"

"Tûk, what . . . does it do?"

The devil pointed to the different-colored gems that lined the inner edge of the box. "You touch, Danny Ray!"

So that was it! When he had retrieved the pouch of diamonds, his hand had accidentally brushed against one of the gems, gems that were really buttons. Slowly, deliberately, the cowboy lowered his finger to touch another gem.

"Magical things that begin with the letter *W*," it recited.

"Wow!" he said, looking down into the face.

" 'Wow' is not a magical thing," it responded, neither amused nor upset.

The face had heard him! The cowboy scratched his chin. Hey! Wait a minute! He touched a few other buttons at random until he found the one he was looking for.

"Magical things that start with the letter *F*."

Danny Ray looked up at Tûk, who shrugged.

"Fantasms," said the cowboy.

There was a pause: it was thinking.

"Fantasms," said the face. "Five powerful spirits in the Age of Stars; destroyed in the War of Judgment by the All-Father, the Golden God of Showering Lights. Only Ikkus-Sark, the King of the Fantasms, survived. He was imprisoned, yet every thousand years he is turned loose upon the world for one week to attempt to restore the number of his kings to five."

"And if this Ikkus-Sark feller does that," surmised Danny Ray, remembering Lord Green's testimony, "then comes the final age of this here world, with no sun, no moon, only stars."

"Correct," replied the mirrathaní evenly. "But first, the fantasms must number five."

"I heard you, darn it," said Danny Ray half to himself, remembering the three dark shapes surrounding Princess Amber. "Captain Giddyfickle was smashed into a pool of goop. So that leaves only two fantasms."

"Incorrect," said the shiny face. "Ikkus-Sark, the King of Fantasms, holds their lives. They are immortal. Only the All-Father himself may completely destroy them."

"So how are we ever gonna whup these fantasm guys?"

"What is meant—'whup'?" The silver face went blank.

"You know," said Danny Ray. "Beat 'em. Whup up on 'em. Kick their tails!"

"Defeat, ha?" said Tûk helpfully, baring his fangs in a grin.

"Fantasms. Defeat the King of Fantasms and you defeat them all. If Ikkus-Sark is returned to his dark vault, the others must follow for the next age of one thousand years."

"I wonder who these fantasms are." Danny Ray looked over at Tûk and frowned, trying to piece it together. As the cowboy thought, his fingers gently touched the scrape on his neck. That had been a close call with the whiner.

"E' bootoosh ha, Fashina?" asked Tûk, looking at the face in the box.

"Fashina," replied the face, speaking in Chilldown, the devil's native language. "Innuasch anna reathinath sûk."

"It say, fantasms be kings of earth to choose evil," Tûk informed him.

"Kings of men," corrected the mirrathaní, "that Ikkus-Sark deceives to embrace evil."

"So, over the ages this Ikkus-Sark fellow will try to get four other kings to choose evil—"

"To *embrace* evil," the mirrathaní corrected Danny Ray. "Once the fantasm number of five is attained, they congregate upon the Seat of Power and stand at the five points of the pentagram, calling down the sun and moon from the sky. The Age of Stars is reborn, lasting for eternity."

"Too mixed up in the mind!" exclaimed Tûk, shaking his head.

"Yep, pretty confusing," said Danny Ray. He pushed his hat back and rubbed his forehead, eyes closed.

"Okay. Wait a minute: let me see if I understand this." Danny Ray stretched his hands out in front of him to steady his thoughts. "This is kinda like chess, right? If we destroy this King of the Fantasms fella, game over: he gets sent back to jail with his two creepy buddies for another thousand years. But as long as the King of Fantasms is loose, he'll be trying to lure two more kings into choosing—into embracing evil, to bring his number to five."

"Correct," replied the mirrathaní.

Prince Blue had slipped into their room at some point and was sitting near the door in an overstuffed, elaborate chair, his purple robe clashing with the bright red cushions. His face bore lines indicating that he had slept fitfully. He gave out a wide, gaping yawn and said: "So, the fantasm that was destroyed back at Sugar-wood Island, this Captain Giddyfickle fellow, he's like a captured chess piece sitting off on the side of the board. He can't play any-more. But if Ikkus-Sark gets two more kings, he gets new life and counts toward the total number of five kings."

"Correct," repeated the mirrathaní.

"How do we destroy Ikkus-Sark, the King of Fantasms?" asked the prince.

"Unknown," put in the silvery voice in the chrome face. "Re-quest unanswerable."

The three of them fell into deep thought. After a time of in-activity, the face receded, leaving an empty silver box.

Prince Blue shot to his feet as the door banged open. In strode KarooKachoo wearing her orange, red, and green royal robe, followed by an entourage of important officials. They crowded around his chair. Her hands gestured frantically as she cried out, "Danny Ray! I have lost the orange book—the orange book of herbs!"

"What?"

KarooKachoo picked up Danny Ray's treasure bag and peered inside.

Empty.

"Danny Ray! I've searched everywhere—even places the book couldn't possibly be, couldn't possibly be!"

The cowboy searched through the trinkets on his bedcover.

No orange book. And without the directions to prepare aurora, the wondrous herb was useless; powerless.

"Oh! Somewhere along the way—along the way, I must have dropped it." KarooKachoo wrung her hands. "Misplaced it! Oh, dear! The queen is slipping away quickly! Quickly! She won't last the night!"

The High King of Spunkies bowed elaborately and spoke up: "I think I speak for each member of my company when I say we know nothing about the magical herb aurora—I'm sorry! We cannot aid you in your distress!"

"Who asked you?" growled Danny Ray.

The room was filled with weeping and moaning, crying and groaning.

"Well, we can't go back for the book," Danny Ray thought out loud. "We've logged way too many miles. I wouldn't even know where to start looking."

KarooKachoo's face fell. It dawned on them all that the Queen of Dragonflies was doomed. "I cannot prepare aurora!" she murmured. "All is lost!"

She turned her back to the cowboy, she and all her subjects, and they began filing quietly out of the room.

"Wait a minute!" cried Danny Ray.

They gathered around the bed. He leaned over the silver box labeled MAGICAL THINGS. He slowly lowered his forefinger and pressed his best-guess button.

Up came the chrome face, plain, unsmiling. KarooKachoo's eyes widened in astonishment and she covered her mouth.

"Magical things that start with the letter *A*," it intoned.

"Aurora," said the cowboy. The face paused, thinking. "A small magical herb with thorny green leaves and a pleasant-smelling yellow flower. Its many healing properties are released using the following method . . ."

Danny Ray looked up from the box and grinned.

❧ 21 ❧

Queen of the Dragonflies

Danny Ray's head popped out of a mound of confetti at exactly the same time as Cherry's, their two noses inches apart. They laughed hysterically in each other's faces, the cowboy raising two handfuls of the yellow, blue, red, green, and white flakes and throwing them up into the air. Cherry did the same and giggled. A big red foot with sharp black toenails stuck out from a pile of glimmering shavings as Tûk's face shook free from a mask of confetti, pointed his nose into the air, and howled an animal-like call. Even the prince, lying nearby, joined in the laughter.

They were being carried in a huge, immense sack by four huge dragonflies that hovered overhead with translucent wings, each grasping a corner of the rich tapestrylike rug. Vast quantities of confetti had collected around the three travelers, floating down from cheering multitudes who waved from overlying balconies that spiraled up to a peak. It was like looking up from the inside of a hollow ice-cream cone.

"We're going down!" called out Danny Ray as their floating bag lurched around and began to slowly descend, the walls of the Dragonfly Queen's banqueting hall moving away on all sides, the air shimmering with all the colors of the rainbow as more and more crowds came into view, tossing their own showers of celebration. The cowboy felt his backside come to rest against something solid. The bag had landed. Danny Ray and his companions scrambled to their feet as best they could in the piles of confetti, dusting off their clothes. The dragonflies dropped the corners of the elaborate sack, the wind from their wings whipping up the piles of confetti into a whirlwind.

The colorful storm cleared. There stood the Queen of Dragonflies.

Danny Ray, holding Cherry's trembling hand, along with Prince Blue and the hellwain devil, bowed before her. The queen's sparkling green dress flowed out to cover nearly half the dais, her pale cheeks pulsating with stripes of red and yellow, and her hair pinned up in a great mound of flaming red and sprinkled with pearls. Danny Ray tried to guess what species of dragonfly she might be, what colors her wings might exhibit.

The queen's cold, hard eyes took in Tûk but then softened as she observed the rodeo cowboy who wore the strange clothes.

"Rise!" she said. Her voice was higher than Danny Ray expected, almost indistinguishable from that of KarooKachoo, the Princess of Dragonflies, who came to stand next to her mother.

"Danny Ray!" said KarooKachoo. Her face beamed brightly in rainbow colors, her eyes spinning around dizzily in excitement.

"Yes," said the queen delightedly, "the child of the Otherworld with the mirrathaní—the mirrathaní that saved my life by revealing to us how to prepare the wonderful, magical herb aurora!"

"All the squeezing!" said the court physician.

"All the mashing!" said the royal pharmacist.

"All the boiling!" said the official alchemist.

"Please give an ear to my song!" announced a court jester with blue and red streaks on his cheeks and wearing a ridiculously huge green and blue striped hat. "I wrote it, with some help from the hero Danny Ray, for this special occasion of Her Majesty's splendid recovery!"

He spread his hands and beamed a smile as the hall grew quiet.

"Dandelion, Dandelion, Dandelion wine!
Squeeze it out, serve it up,
Saved her just in time!

We're just glad, you see
We dodged a travesty
We saved Her Majesty
Saved her just in time!

So, maybe let me think some
Maybe let me drink some
Dandelion, Dandelion, Dandelion wine!"

Raucous applause broke out even though neither the court officials nor the queen, nor any of her subjects for that matter, had even the faintest idea what a dandelion was.

"Excuse me, ma'am," continued Danny Ray. "I'm not wanting to take any credit. Your daughter, KarooKachoo, had a lot to do with us escaping the Islands of Magic and getting back here to save you."

"Yes!" said the queen, pinching KarooKachoo's cheek. "Oh! Is she not worth more to me than seven sons? And Danny Ray, may I say that you and your companions are most welcome, most welcome in the Kingdom of the Dragonflies! We will show you a great deal of gratitude, Danny Ray, and help you as we may on your quest to rescue Princess Amber. For she is a friend, oh, yes! A friend of all dragonflies, for her royal dress is adorned with our likeness!"

"And damselflies," said a squeaky court clerk.

"And damselflies!" agreed Her Majesty. "Again I say, welcome!"

"We accept your greetings," Prince Blue interjected in a stuffy voice, bowing, doing his best to match the importance of the event. Danny Ray smirked.

"I now begin returning my thanks, most humbly," replied the queen with a nod and upraised arms that flashed with gold and silver bracelets. "Now! Yes, now! Let the celebration begin!"

Danny Ray and his companions were whisked off their feet and carried over the heads of a delighted crowd, ending up in a heap of cushions and velvet pillows.

"Beesa Blue!" The hellwain pointed. Prince Blue and Cherry rose up off their elbows and craned their necks.

Clip-clop! Clip-clop! Twelve white horses with yellow, green, red, and blue spots on their rumps pulled a colossal copper vat on wheels. Two red imps balanced on the vat's rim, stirring the green exotic drink with long copper spoons the size of brooms. The driver gripped the reins in one hand and held up a golden trumpet with the other. As he passed by, he blew a loud blast on the horn while the imps waved with their spoons. The horses pranced proudly, snorted and arched their necks, and then galloped away with fruity green suds sloshing merrily against the sides of the vat. What especially caught the cowboy's eye was that each horse had three legs in front and in back: he wondered how wildly they might buck back home in the rodeo arena!

Servants knelt beside them, offering platefuls of all manner of piping hot foods, like piles of toasted pinwheels of bread with cheese, with sausage, with herbs and spices; slightly steaming foods, like breaded and fried cheese and burger bites; sweet foods, like knuckleberry pastries striped with purple frosting, and white, sugar-crusted cookies with candi-yum jelly; cold foods, like white-dusted crumpets and delicious stuffed sugar cones of chocolate pudding sprinkled with candy tidbits. Danny Ray's stomach cried out in hunger—how long had it been since he had eaten? He sat up from the cushions and delved into the delectable feast, heavenly meats and incomparable sauces caressing his tongue, and then he stopped short as he realized he was smacking loudly. But one look around him assured him that the others were smacking, too, and Danny Ray chuckled to himself.

"These cakes are like sponges!" Cherry frowned, turning up her nose.

"I like to eat sponges!" retorted Tûk, with brown frosting around his mouth, and Danny Ray put his head back and laughed.

The cowboy had nearly cleared one of his plates when up buzzed a spunky laden with an armful of hot rolls and pastries and laid them respectfully in the cowboy's plate.

"Much obliged," stated Danny Ray. He went to tip his cowboy hat but, like all well-mannered young men, he had removed it for mealtime.

"Beesa Ray!" said another one of the spunkies, buzzing around his neck, adjusting the napkin stuffed in his collar.

"Beesa Ray! Beesa Ray!" the others chimed in, sitting around the cowboy on pillows.

"Knock it off, you guys!" said Danny Ray, but the spunkies only chuckled mischievously, while another wiped a gravy smudge away from the corner of his mouth.

"You see how easy it becomes?" pointed out Prince Blue. "I mean, to let others serve you?"

"I don't like it none," Danny Ray said, frowning.

"Maybe not, but how do you refuse them, delighted as they are to wait on your every need, your every whim, simply because you rescued them from Mr. Tabbashavar's lair?" Prince Blue smiled. "You see, you and I are not that unalike."

"One-bubble, sir?" came the question as a goblet nudged his elbow. There stood a servant with a glass pitcher holding the green drink drawn from the vat.

"One-bubble?" asked the cowboy. "What—"

The servant poured the drink slowly, carefully, the green beverage as cold as crystal and flickering like green lightning. A bubble formed on the drink's surface. "Do you see? Do you see?" asked the servant.

Danny Ray smiled to himself. He had that same annoying repeating habit as KarooKachoo. "Yeah, I see the bubble," he said.

"The instant the bubble disappears," said the servant, still eyeing the trickle of fluid, "I must stop pouring—oh! stop pouring! For then the drink turns bitter and poisonous!"

The bubble popped and the servant jerked the mouth of the pitcher back and smiled, very pleased with himself. The cowboy sniffed at the fruity drink and then took a healthy, unguarded swig from his goblet.

"Yessir!" he said, nodding to the servant. "That's sure good stuff!"

Danny Ray ate some more, and drank some more, and then ate some more on top of that, and, well, the cowboy began feeling pretty contented. He yawned and stretched like a lion that has just eaten half a zebra on a Sunday afternoon.

"Well, hello, Mr. Spunky!" said Danny Ray as one of the pale blue fairies flew by and refilled his empty goblet with one-bubble, pouring it exactly right. The spunky's tiny brown eyes observed the cowboy from beneath a prominent forehead, and its clear wings vibrated as fast as a hummingbird's. It chuckled at the cowboy, flying around his head, and then playfully flapped its big, pointed ears like wings to hover in front of Danny Ray's nose. In a sparkle and a flash, it zoomed away.

The prince, on the other hand, was too busy and too pleased being waited on to acknowledge anyone, so Danny Ray got up with a grunt and made his way alone through the colorful crowd, costumes cascading before him, each set of clothes signifying which species of dragonfly or damselfly the person was.

A loud tambourine with bells announced an amazing sight. Here came a huge, portly man, laughing and calling out. He wore biscuit pants and a roast beef overcoat with olives for buttons and cranberries for cuff links. His tall white hat was made of cream cheese dotted with walnuts. Everyone giggled good-naturedly and tore off little bits of his apparel as he passed by, and Danny Ray found himself tearing off a piece of the man's coat sleeve and dipping it in the cream cheese. The cowboy champed down and licked his lips—gosh, that was good!

Raucous cheering broke out, the people wild with singing:

"Knick-knack, patty-whack
Make me up a snick-snack!
Ram it down my food crack
Then carry me home!

Rack-ma-tack, thunder crack!
Pants made out of flapjacks!
Bake me up a muffin hat
That I can wear home!

Crick-crack, lip-smack
Cookies in a knapsack
Bring me crumpets piggyback
Then leave me alone!

Whoooooah! Whoooooah!
Eat all I can then leave me alone!

Knick-knack, patty-whack
Make me up a snick-snack!
Ram it down my food crack
Then carry me home!

Rack-ma-tack, thunder crack!
Pants made out of flapjacks!
Bake me up a muffin hat
That I can wear home!

Crick-crack, lip-smack
Cookies in a knapsack
Bring me crumpets piggyback
Then leave me alone!"

Danny Ray, still munching on the beef and a dab of the cream cheese, made his way to a wide circle of cheering people. In the middle stood Tûk. The tall, red devil's eyes were closed as he moved in a slow, wraithlike dance, swinging his pitchfork around his body. He took a few steps and lunged with the gleaming weapon, just missing the amazed spectators who shrieked in good humor. He twirled the weapon like a baton, jabbing out again at an imaginary enemy.

Nearby, another circle erupted in cheering. When Danny Ray saw what all the noise was about, his eyes narrowed. There was Cherry, her white dress glittering and shimmering like new, aiming the slingshot and—*whap!*—hitting a target dead-on with a chestnut. She hit the mark every time, and every time the crowd shouted and clapped. The cowboy had a mind to be angry, but then a spunky circled overhead and flew down to him with another goblet full of one-bubble.

Danny Ray took a swig; he had to admit, Cherry was getting pretty good with that slingshot, but he'd be double-danged if he'd tell her so.

"Danny Ray!" It was KarooKachoo. She grabbed his hand. "How are you enjoying the party?"

"We are enjoying it thoroughly!" spoke up Prince Blue, appearing at Danny Ray's elbow and crossing his arms in a self-important way. "And, might I add, the food being served is up to the standard of any king!" he said with the utmost gravity, taking a deliberately slow bite out of a flaky crumpet.

"Or any queen!" said a new voice. The crowd parted, bowing, as the Queen of Dragonflies strode forward followed by her officials. She bowed her head slightly, although not toward her daughter or Prince Blue, but to the cowboy. "I am glad to see you rested and fed—this party is in your honor, Danny Ray!"

"And in honor of Your Majesty's recovery," interjected Prince Blue politely. "May I say how welcome it is to see you in good health!"

"I liked the man with the yummy-yummy clothes," said Danny Ray. He licked some remaining cream cheese off the corner of his mouth. "And the food song made me laugh!"

"It is a wonderful kingdom over which I rule, is it not?" responded the queen. "We have whole days set apart for the glory of food, to revel in feasting! Surely, the Otherworld has such days, such songs?"

"Shoot—yeah!" said Danny Ray. "On Thanksgiving Day we remember how the Pilgrims and Indians and Vikings and Columbus had a feast to celebrate making it through a bad winter. So, we roast up a turkey—"

"Turkey?" asked KarooKachoo.

"Yeah, with cranberry sauce and ham and deviled eggs and smashed potatoes and stuffing—but I don't much care for stuffing—and corn and green beans and rolls and butter. And sweet potatoes—the orange kind. Don't much like those either, though. Heck, I even made up my own food song about a Thanksgiving turkey."

Danny Ray took off his hat and cleared his throat.

"Well, it's Thanksgivin' Day
And my head's a-wobblin' wobblin'!
I'm a-runnin' through the pumpkins
And my legs are hobblin', hobblin'!
I'm screamin' for my life
So my beak's a-gobblin', gobblin'!

My mama's long gone
So I've got no lovin'
Plop me in a pan
Stuffin' and a-shovin'
Look at me—my head's off
And Lord, I'm in the oven!"

Applause broke out, and Danny Ray beamed. He bowed profusely and repeatedly, plopped his hat back on and then crossed his arms, his smile outshining the glittery lights.

"We are elated that you shared that . . . that song with us, Danny Ray!" said the queen. "Yes, we are! We are!"

"Me, too!" exclaimed the cowboy. "It's neat to actually meet real dragonflies!" Danny Ray pointed to the different people standing near the queen, taking in their cheek colors and their glowing clothes. And they bowed as he named them off:

"Civil bluet, green darner, silver skimmer, rainbow oriental, ten-spotted dragonfly, broad-winged damselfly, and you, you're a yellow dancer!"

"Danny Ray!" exclaimed KarooKachoo. "We're so impressed!"

"Indeed, we are!" said the queen jubilantly. She spread her arms and motioned to the whole hall. "Hear this gem among the folk of men, so knowledgeable about us that he knows our species by sight!"

"Shucks!" said Danny Ray. "It ain't nothing. Me and Jesse, my youngest brother—we got a whole dragonfly collection at home!"

"Collection?" asked the queen's clerk, holding an inkwell and pen in one hand, his reading glasses in the other, and a roll of parchment tucked under his arm. "Collection?"

"A collection of dragonflies!" said Danny Ray. "In a box, I mean. Heck, over the years Jesse and me, we've caught a whole bunch of dragonflies and put 'em in a box with pins stuck through them. Oh, they're real pretty!"

Tûk caught his breath.

"You stick pins in dragonflies?" said the flabbergasted clerk.

The hall went silent. It suddenly dawned on the stunned cowboy what he had said.

"Whoa!"

A swirling windstorm blinded the cowboy. He just caught a brief glimpse of the queen's angry countenance, of her red hair blowing out in all directions, of the queen's court whipping up into a sudden frenzy of iridescent madness, and lastly, Karoo-Kachoo's hurt face.

Danny Ray fell forward and groped on all fours. In the

howling wind, he heard faint calls from Cherry, from Tûk, roaring out in confusion. He tried to shield his eyes, to see what had happened to his friends, but the dust and wind knocked him back down.

Danny Ray didn't know how long the storm lasted, but finally, finally, it subsided. He peeked up from his arms. He lay upon a rough bed of leaves and twigs and all around him the splendors of the dragonfly court had disappeared, leaving only the rough brown walls of a plain cave.

Prince Blue sat nearby, caked in dust and holding a goblet, with Tûk kneeling next to him, his glowing pitchfork supplying the only light in the cave. Cherry, her dress a filthy mess again, stared down at the cowboy with furious eyes.

"Well done, Danny Ray," said Prince Blue almost too smoothly. He tipped the goblet, allowing the dirt to spill out, and then the goblet turned to sand and fell through his fingers.

Danny Ray sat up and looked overhead. Gone were the balconies, gone were the chandeliers, gone, too, the crowds, the horse-drawn vat of one-bubble, the man with the roast beef coat; everything and everyone . . . gone.

"What happened?" asked the cowboy.

"The Queen of the Dragonflies and her people are the High Folk of the Varaldir," said Prince Blue simply. "When offended, and believe me, Danny Ray, what you said offended them, they disappear in a flash."

"Wow," he muttered.

"Wow, yourself, Danny Ray!" chided Cherry. "What a dumb thing to say!"

Even Tûk nodded in agreement and said: "Your boot does taste good, Danny Ray?"

"He means," put in Cherry venomously, "that you stuck your foot in your mouth!"

The cowboy got up and walked over to the cave's opening where his bag of treasure lay. Well, at least that hadn't disappeared. He looked out over Dragonfly Bay, bathed in star-shine. The rhythmic sound of crickets echoed through the empty cave. "Sorry, you guys," he said, looking back at his companions.

"Sorry doesn't begin to cover it," said Prince Blue.

"Well, heck, Prince Blue, or Purple, or whatever color you are now: at least I apologized!"

Prince Blue took in a deep breath, simmering, and then said: "You were right when you said you aren't the same old Danny Ray. You've completely botched this whole rescue. And, Mr. Otherworld Cowboy, I'd like to know what you plan to do now?"

"Head up yonder." Danny Ray nodded toward the east where a cliff of rock, barely discernible in the darkness, jutted out into the Checkered Sea. "It's high ground and we'll be able to see pert near the whole harbor."

"There's a graveyard up there," whimpered Cherry. "I saw it when we flew into the bay."

Tûk opened his pouch and took out a handful of small, black objects that turned out to be pieces of blackened bones. They clicked as the hellwain rubbed them between his palms and then let them fall on the dirt floor. He leaned forward and studied them in the dim light of his pitchfork, his yellow eyes squinting and his hooked nose twitching. He looked up and pointed the other way toward the harbor. "Bones say that way!"

"You see?" said Prince Blue, getting to his feet and coming to face the cowboy. "A handful of old bones are smarter than you, Danny Ray!"

"Well, I'm not going off half-cocked into the night because a bunch of old, burned bones told me to," said Danny Ray.

"We can't split up!" said Cherry with a quivering lower lip. "We did that once already!"

"You must follow me, Danny Ray!" said Prince Blue sternly.

"I'd rather take a beating," said the cowboy simply, slinging his bag over his shoulder, and setting his sights on the steep cliff on the bay's eastern shore. There, like a brooding crown atop the statues of the four kings, cold, stark, and forlorn, lay the grave-yard of kings.

He looked over at the little girl, who was on the verge of crying. She offered him something, a glimmer of red emanated from her trembling hand.

The slingshot.

"No, Cherry," he said thoughtfully. "Keep it for yourself. Believe me, you may need it."

❖ 22 ❖

An Old Enemy

In one motion Danny Ray hunkered down behind a tree and laid down his bag of treasure. He peeked out over Dragonfly Bay. Behind him loomed the four massive kings, jutting out of the cliffside, staring southwestward over the bay. Monstrous they seemed in the nighttime, their upraised hands like black towers against the starry sky.

Distant thunder announced the coming of a storm, but this was not what caught Danny Ray's attention. Below, in the middle of the bay, helm lights twinkling in the night, cruised *Serpentine*. The bishop had sniffed them out over hundreds of miles and now sailed steadily through Dragonfly Bay. On second thought, it must have been easy for Commodore Mumblefub to locate their destination, for *Serpentine* had last observed them flying straight north on the back of a dragonfly.

The cowboy backed away stealthily from the tree like a cat and began nimbly picking his way up the cliff's edge. He stopped higher up and chewed at his lip as he took another look at the bishop ship. He thought of drawing attention to himself to help Cherry, Tûk, and the prince on their way, but he had no idea where they were—probably on the far end of the harbor by now. He hoped they were all right.

Danny Ray couldn't figure out why the ground began to rumble and shake, for *Serpentine* was motionless. Strangely, too, she had run out her guns. Danny Ray covered his ears as the distant thunder increased to a feverish pitch.

And then he saw an amazing sight.

Into the bay sailed a massive white rook, nearly twenty stories high. Her stern was decorated with marble jesters, holding aloft crystal lanterns. Her signal lights, located up near the back rim, glowed yellow and blue. Her port lids opened and large black cannons poked out menacingly.

Danny Ray craned his neck to see a smaller white rook following her, with green stern cabin windows glowing in the night. In the distance Danny Ray spied a third ship, a white bishop, sealing off the bay from the other side. She was easily *Serpentine*'s equal in size and guns.

Serpentine was trapped!

Booooooom!—a gun spewed out orange fire from *Serpentine*'s upper deck toward the leading rook. *Booooooom!* went another. *BOOOOOM!* went the *Serpentine*'s well-timed broadside. Danny Ray could see the rook's name lit up in the cannon fire—*Diamond*—and behind, the smaller rook, *Emerald Castle*.

Serpentine continued to concentrate her fire on the heavy rook but parts of her own deck and rockwork were flying high in the air as *Pearl*, the elegant white bishop, fired repeatedly, steadily, from an extreme distance across the bay. Whoever commanded

Pearl had drilled her gun crews into a high level of accuracy and efficiency.

Danny Ray stared at the battle scene, transfixed. *Diamond* sailed determinedly toward *Serpentine* without yet firing a shot. Holes appeared in her white marble from *Serpentine*'s big guns firing from the lower ports. Danny Ray remembered hanging just above those ports with Cherry on his back. He wondered where on *Serpentine* Tipsy was now, if he was singing along in the midst of the battle, or if he was wounded or dead. Then he wondered about the commodore, hoping that, by chance, a stray shot had destroyed the fantasm.

The bishop *Pearl* ceased firing, afraid of hitting *Diamond* as the rook drew close to *Serpentine*. *Diamond*'s decks were silent, the calm before the storm, the last instant of order before the hounds of chaos were unleashed. The rook's heavy guns grinned horribly at *Serpentine*. Danny Ray saw the yellow and blue lights dip once, then again, as some sort of signal.

Suddenly, violently, *Diamond*'s guns disappeared in a cloud as the rook's well-aimed broadside tore into *Serpentine*. Danny Ray covered his ears to the tremendous roar of the cannons. The immense rook turned on her axis, slowly, ponderously, even as *Emerald Castle*, obeying the earlier signal, took her station past *Diamond* and discharged her own devastating broadside into the green bishop ship.

Serpentine was doomed. She had sustained unrelenting fire from three different ships. And now, *Diamond* and *Emerald Castle* had begun exercising their great guns, running them in and out like clockwork.

"Holy cow!" muttered Danny Ray. With an agonizing groan, the upper ball of the green bishop trembled as if taken by a sudden chill, and then collapsed straight down, devoured by a dense cloud of debris and cannon smoke.

Danny Ray sniffed at the smell of burned gunpowder that had just begun to reach him on the night breeze. *Serpentine* was destroyed, but a sneaking, ugly feeling told him that Mumblefub was still alive, that it would take more than just a cannonball to destroy a fantasm.

Here came *Pearl*, lovely and white, sailing through the smoke, running diagonally toward him and away from the destruction, her search lights running along the shore.

Wait a minute! Danny Ray ran that ship's name over in his memory—*Diamond!* A cold shock went over the cowboy. He remembered that *Diamond* had been sailed by the Sarksa pirates! So, the pirates had grown tired of waiting for Commodore Mumblefub to show up with him and the prince, and they had gone looking for the *Serpentine*. And now they had found the bishop and utterly destroyed her. The thought hit Danny Ray that once the pirates found that he wasn't on *Serpentine*, they would start searching the harbor for him.

Quick—before it was too late! Danny Ray grabbed his bag and scrambled up the rocky incline. He threw himself into the deep shadows of a ravine just as the thick white searchlight from *Pearl* swept over him. Ooooh, that was close!

He sprang up like a flash and again began picking his way along the rocky gorge.

After a while, the cannon fire died away, the cowboy's boots on the hard rock sounding as a loud, harsh accompaniment against the softly sighing wind. Onward he climbed, he trudged, he labored. Looking above, he could just see the rim of the cliff where small pinpricks of stars twinkled.

The gorge opened up steadily. Danny Ray paused again to take a breather, wiping his heated forehead with his arm. His heel hurt him mightily, the beginnings of a blister. These boots were for busting bulls and broncos, not for climbing cliffs! The feeling, heart part of him wished he knew where his companions were, but the other part of him, the toiling, climbing, sweating part of him, was glad he didn't have Cherry tied to his back right now.

Far, far below, the surface of Dragonfly Bay glowed black and white—boy! he had climbed quite a ways already! Only once had he seen the gleaming white walls of a passing ship. Hey! Maybe they had given up the search.

The cowboy shot a glance over at the profile of one of the kings. He was now even with its eyebrow.

A few more grunts, a few more heaves, and Danny Ray emerged out on top of the cliff, on the very tip of the eastern arm of the bay. He could see out over Dragonfly Bay and the limitless Checkered Sea.

There was a graveyard here, all right, the kind Danny Ray had seen in history books. Statues stood in rows, some of them kings with crowns, along with ancient, weathered monuments the size of cabins.

Overhead the stars twinkled, accompanied by the barest sliver of a moon. Soon would come the night of the new moon, when the moon would refuse to shine at all. He was running out of time: Princess Amber was running out of time.

Danny Ray caught the movement of something in the darkness, low, slinking, like a large dog. Then it was gone. Wait! There it was again, a low shadow flitting noiselessly between the gravestones.

He ducked behind a large monument and reached down for his rope. The coil shimmered blue, and touching it reassured the cowboy.

He peeked out.

Something was up here with him, something knew he was here. Danny Ray conjured up in his mind all sorts of frightful creatures that might haunt lonely graveyards at night. For all he could tell, there was just one of them. Gosh! He sure wished he hadn't loaned his slingshot to Cherry!

But then, like the surfacing in your subconscious of an old forgotten nightmare, a sense of dread came over him. His breathing became all shaky as he slowly turned his head, around, around, to a presence he felt behind him.

There it was, just a little ways off, a shadow standing on all fours, its eyes gleaming with sinister interest, staring at him.

The wolf.

Danny Ray had a terrible hunch: this was the same wolf he had seen in Buckholly Harbor on his previous trip to Elidor. But how had it found him here? Danny Ray could hear its rough panting, feel the hate of the thing directed at him. It appeared to have not eaten for ages, its ribs and haunches outlined through its patched fur. But it was the eyes, those gleaming white orbs, that showed no sign of wavering whatsoever. Just cold, unmitigated hate.

Quick as lightning, Danny Ray lunged down and grabbed a stone without so much as a pause, and flung it at the wolf. He was sure his aim was true, but the stone seemed to pass through the thing. It never flinched, never seemed concerned, bending its awful stare, its awful will toward the cowboy.

Why didn't the wolf attack?

Another wisp of white mist floated by, and the wolf floated away.

The cowboy breathed a sigh of relief. But what did the wolf want with him?

"Aha." Out from the statues stepped a looming figure wearing a commodore's uniform. Danny's blood ran cold. It was none other than Mumblefub. "Didn't figure to see me again—hm?"

A flicker of silver flashed in the commodore's fingers. He was trimming his nails with a sharp instrument and hadn't even bothered to look up at the cowboy.

"*Wasp* destroyed, and Captain Giddyfickle. All because of you, a troublesome, pugnacious little cowboy from the Otherworld." Now Mumblefub did glance up, his eyes glowing with the hue of a setting sun. Then he went about his nails again. "And now, my own beloved *Serpentine*, pulverized into dust."

Danny Ray looked to his left, then right. How was he going to get out of this fix?

Mumblefub took a step toward him. Danny Ray could see a line of yellow teeth as he grinned ear to ear. "You're a very ill-mannered young man—leaving the hospitality of my ship without so much as a goodbye, or even a tip of your hat? Noooo, not very polite of you."

The cowboy gasped.

"How we worried about you, Danny Ray!" The commodore had stopped filing his nails. "How frantically we searched for you!" Another moment of silence. "Of course, you must know by now that I'm a fantasm? Mm?"

"Figure that out all by yourself?" blurted the cowboy, the first words he had managed to speak from a throat tight with fear.

"Sarcastic and derisive to the end, eh?" commented the commodore. "Still not addressing me as 'sir'?"

For the first time Danny Ray noticed a gossip with singed wings sitting on Mumblefub's shoulder, presumably the same one that had been lodged secretly in Prince Blue's watch; the same gossip that had escaped Tûk's frantic efforts to capture it; the same little tattletale that had flown miles from Sugarwood Island to inform Mumblefub of their whereabouts.

"My little gossip, here, is unlike any other in the world," commented Mumblefub. "Do you know what it likes to eat? I take it by your rare silence that you do not. Well, for your information, it enjoys eating eyeballs. That's right, eyeballs just like yours. It likes pecking at them—don't you, little fellow? It likes drawing each eye out with its little sharp beak—ripping each one from its socket. Of course, haven't you heard? It gulps them down without chewing. But I've heard, and it's quite hard for me to believe, that the screams of its victim don't at all put the voracious little beast off its appetite, hm?"

The commodore hesitated as he caught sight of Arcile glittering white on the cowboy's chest. "I see you have a special companion. True, it may have some staying influence upon me, but *not* upon my companion!"

The wretched gossip grinned, licking its sharp mouth with a barbed tongue.

"Aha, hm. I think I'll keep my present form as commodore. Oh! How I love my medals so! And I want to hear you scream and yell for mercy, you contentious, irascible little gnat that has caused me such distress, such discomfort. What strange dream made you believe you might stand up against the fantasms? And now, you must pay for your arrogance, your misplaced pride."

The cowboy felt a drop of sweat roll down his back as the gossip rasped wickedly, its eyes flaring in anticipation of the coming gory feast. It braced itself to jump, stretching its burned leathery wings, and to grasp the cowboy's tender young face with its razor-sharp talons.

Danny Ray winced. An excruciatingly bright light surrounded them. A gurgling filled Mumblefub's throat.

"*KAAAAAAARRRKKK!*" screamed the gossip, and then its wings burst into flame, its body vanishing in a puff, leaving behind only a tendril of smoke.

The commodore trembled, shuddered in the blazing light. His image gave way to the awful form of the fantasm. But that fearful ogre had only a moment to cast a vengeful eye upon the cowboy before he was engulfed in fire, flames sweeping around his dark robes and out through his mouth, his eyes, out through the very top of his head. His sleeves billowed in the wind although there was no wind, and Danny Ray felt the heat of his destruction.

In a final roar of flame, the fantasm was gone.

Danny Ray felt his breathing catch, felt his heart labor. As

anxious as the cowboy had been about setting off without his
friends, as horrified as he had become of the bloodthirsty gossip, as utterly petrified as he was of the fantasms, far more terrifying was the astonishingly pure, exceedingly powerful light
that had now frightened all his other fears away.

❖ 23 ❖

The White Lady

In the blazing, enchanting light, Danny Ray forgot exactly where he was. When he could open his eyes, he detected the movement of ghostly forms on horseback riding slowly against a brilliantly white background.

"Olan s'hlerian adem yada!"

Danny Ray heard the voice: rich, velvety, like a river of buttercream frosting. The tall figure of a woman in white, haloed by an intense pulsating aura, beckoned him to step forward. But the cowboy was overcome with awe. He could only remove his hat and kneel with shaky legs.

"Stand, Child of Heaven!" she said.

The intense light slowly began to fade. The stars reappeared in the dark sky, the gravestones and monuments, the hoary, bent trees, the dark earth beneath his feet.

"Lady in white!" gasped the cowboy.

"You have uncommonly fierce enemies, Danny Ray!" She said, drawing near to him. The eyes that regarded the cowboy were clear, discerning, and yet her voice seemed distant. The

White Lady's great mound of snowy hair was infused with streaks of feathery frost surrounding forlorn faces of ice, and fastened with pins and combs of iron-ice. Her dress was whiter than a thousand weddings, gathered with patterned sashes of brilliant snowflakes and with pearls and clasps of ivory. She glowed with an iridescent, inner light as did those passing in solemn procession behind her, the spirits of lords and ladies on horseback being led by footmen and peasants.

Danny Ray was quietly terrified. He could hardly bring himself to look up into her face. "Who . . . who are those people?"

"Those with no longer any regard for this world. Those who are passing into the shadow of the Vale of the Moon."

"G-gosh, ma'am! You destroyed that fantasm like he was nothin'. But there's a wolf skulking around here, too—"

"Ah, the wolf," she responded dreamily and closed her eyes, playing with a strand of frosty lace dangling down from her headpiece. "The wolf must yield to me at this present age, for his strength has not yet come to full."

"Who are you?" breathed the cowboy.

"I am the lesser light," she responded. "Once, long ago, my home was upon the earth, before the giants arose, before the sun shone. But my former home is dark; now is my lamp extinguished. Dark and abused, my habitation is now the seat of dark powers. Once lovely, it is now forlorn and dim, used for sorcery and darkest magic."

Danny Ray didn't know how, but in one graceful gesture of her hand, she revealed her knowledge of his quest. There, behind her, on a dappled gray stallion, rode a pale woman wearing a pale crown. She looked neither to the left nor right, nor straight ahead seemingly, but far away over to distant hills where the long, slow caravan wound out of sight. Her countenance was one of hopelessness, of one sure of her dark destination and doom. But Danny Ray recognized that delicate, upturned nose, that perfect mouth and chin, that slender royal figure.

"Princess Amber!" cried Danny Ray. He wrung his hat in his trembling fists.

The face turned his way, but no light of recognition shone there, only sorrowful eyes looking through him, past him, as if a great chasm of time and of place separated them. He knew in his heart that he could not take the princess back with him, not here, not now. Tears cascaded from Danny Ray's eyes. He felt powerless to do anything except put his hat back on to hide his wet cheeks.

The magnificent beast that carried her seemed to float away, and then she was gone, lost in the following procession of knights and warriors, kings and underlings.

"The princess with the golden hair," whispered the White Lady. "She shall be well tended to in her restful place."

The cowboy shook his head and wiped his nose. "I gotta save her, ma'am. You don't understand. I've come a long way to see that she's returned safe and sound to her dad."

"I do understand, Child of Heaven," said the White Lady, "but sometimes, are there not tasks too great for us? Are there not deeds far beyond our meager abilities, beyond even a hero's reach?"

"But this task just can't be impossible!" said the cowboy, trembling. "I can't leave Princess Amber behind. And I won't, darn it!"

The White Lady opened her mouth, a bluish, frosty tongue flitting over her teeth. She tapped her cheek with fingernails as sharp as icicles.

"You would confront Ikkus-Sark, King of Fantasms?" she mused.

"Reckon I will, ma'am, if that's what it takes. I gotta stop him before he lassos two good, righteous kings and brings his number to five."

"There are very few good kings," she responded. "And fewer still that are righteous. But what confidence do you have, Otherworld Cowboy, in facing Ikkus-Sark, in confronting one so ancient, so resolute in awful power?"

The treasure bag wiggled and giggled and jiggled and then popped wide open as the blue, beaming faces of the spunkies appeared. "Danny Ray rescued us, didn't he?" they said in chorus as they flooded out in a blue torrent and whirled around her upturned face in a dizzying circle, crying, "Danny Ray is our hero!"

"Ah!" cried the White Lady, her face lit up, showing its first sign of any feeling or emotion. "Can this be? Ah! My crystal crown fairies!"

She looked fondly at the cowboy. "Long ago, in the Great Chastisement, was my fairy crown taken from me. Never again did I expect to see their fair forms. I had given them up for lost. But now, here they are, my precious, my glorious crown!" Just a faint glimmer of fondness flashed through her frozen features. "In return for this blessing, Danny Ray, ask of me what you will and I will supply you richly out of my treasure room."

"I don't want nothin' for myself, ma'am, just to get the princess back."

The White Lady lowered her frightful head and considered him. "Because you have not asked for power, or riches, or even longer life, I shall give you the most precious gift of all: wisdom. And for insight into the fantasms do I impart unto you this riddle, to enlighten you as to your real and substantial danger."

The cowboy looked deeply into her wondrous eyes that reflected stars upon stars, and rotating galaxies in deep space. Her breath was numbingly cold:

"Wild are the winds
Of the Checkered Sea
Circling the world
In tranquility

Seasons come
Seasons go
Marching in time
In a timeless flow

Strong and sure
The hinges of day
Weak in their turn
Of black, blue, and gray

Ponder the center
Of any chessboard
The battle pieces
The unsceptered hoard

This riddle flows
Like hourglass sand
Grain by grain
Let the hearer understand."

Danny Ray shook himself from his cold stupor. He asked quietly, "So, I'm going to have to face this Ikkus-Sark fellow, sooner or later, ain't I?"

"The future is dim, clouded. Surely, we may know only the past and present, but only to the present does my riddle speak. For time, like hourglass sand, flows, does it not, moment by moment, day by day?"

"But where is the King of Fantasms?"

"Why seek him? Perhaps he shall find you."

"Well, then, how do I defeat him? Seems to me he's gotta be a lot tougher to kill than the first two fantasms. And where is Princess Amber? How do I get her back?"

"Oh, Danny Ray of the Otherworld," replied the White Lady. "When you ask yourself the most important question—the most obvious question—only then shall the mystery unravel; only then shall the riddle reveal its secrets and all other things fall into place."

"Shoot! Can't you just tell me?" asked the cowboy impatiently. "Time's running out!"

"Yes, like hourglass sand!" Her words were framed in a wisp of frost. "Child of Heaven, have I not given you deep wisdom in the riddle?" Her eyes fell to the stone twinkling on his chest. "And have you not been given one of the great Stones of Audrehelm?"

"It's called Arcile," he responded meekly.

"Call it what you will, the stone is deadly to the fantasms. Keep it close for your protection."

"But what if I never ask the right question? And what if I can't figure out the riddle?" said Danny Ray, looking at her anxiously. "What if you're just a dream and I wake up and none of this is real?"

"My image shall stay with you. And I shall insure that you remember the Riddle of the Fantasms."

The White Lady reached out with cold fingers. Ever so delicately, almost affectionately, she touched the cowboy on his forehead, chilling him to the bone, deep down to his soul. The hauntingly cold, lonely lady began to fade from his sight. He heard her say, "Beware, Otherworld Cowboy, what friends you make. Fair may be foul, and foul, fair. Time to sleep. Farewell for now, Danny Ray."

❧ 24 ❧

The Beautiful Captain

 In pitch-blackness, one large drop as white as milk, as round as the moon, gave way to gravity and fell silently into a pool. The ripples spread out in perfect, creamy circles, and the center offered up an answering orb of its own, a nearly perfect white drop. That solitary drop seemed to hang there, shimmering and lovely, suspended in time and memory, as if it had occupied that exact place for eternity.

Danny Ray jerked fully awake. The drop in his dreams became Arcile, the magic gemstone lying on his chest, rising and falling to his measured breathing, and winking back at him.

A single silver lamp dangled from a heavy rafter close overhead. Sunlight streamed through a wall of glass, and Danny Ray pushed back a mound of covers and raised up on his elbows that sank into a marvelously soft mattress. His cowboy hat hung within arm's reach on the bedpost.

Pattering feet sounded across the ceiling. The cowboy was aboard a ship—the *Serpentine*? No, she had been destroyed—or had she? He rubbed his head and tried to shake out the cobwebs. He remembered climbing a cliff, or was that on Sugar-wood Island? A picture of Commodore Mumblefub flashed through his muddled memories, but he had been destroyed like the *Serpentine*, right?

A door opened, and a smiling face appeared. Danny Ray's mind cleared.

"Hey! I know you!" called out the cowboy, and as two more faces fitted in the doorway he added, "And you, and you!"

"Hello, Danny Ray!" said the sailor with a gray pigtail, lumbering across to his bed followed by a short, stubby captain with an orange face and green whiskers and a huge lieutenant with black, downturned horns going *thump! thump! thump!* on his wooden leg.

"Hey, Piper!" said the cowboy, positively beaming with delight. "Hey, Hoodie! Hey, Captain Quigglewigg! Wow, it's great to see you guys again!"

"We sailed into Elidor the day after you departed," said Captain Quigglewigg, shaking Danny Ray's hand.

"Ah!" came the low booming voice belonging to Hoodie Crow, standing dark and huge behind the captain. "King Krystal, he was all put out because the real *Serpentine* and *Wasp* had just sailed into Birdwhistle Bay—"

"So we knowed that the fantasms got you!" added Piper.

"We sailed straight north as fast as we could," finished Quigglewigg, "just in time to catch *Serpentine*—"

"The fake *Serpentine*," corrected Danny Ray.

"Well, yes. But I'm befuddled and besmirched that we never saw one of the fantasms!"

Fantasms. That set something off in the cowboy's head—

something about Mumblefub. What *had* happened with him? But the previous night was a blank.

"Danny Ray—what do you think of my new ship?" said Captain Quigglewigg, breaking in on the cowboy's thoughts.

"Ain't we aboard *Hog*?"

"No, sir, we are not!" Quigglewigg said, shaking his head. "Old *Hog*, bless her soul, is a transport now—all fetch-and-go, fetch-and-go. You are a guest on *Diamond*."

Diamond! Danny Ray's head was beginning to clear, as if a gust of clean air had blown in one ear and out the other. *Diamond*—the massive eighty-four-gun rook that last night had shattered *Serpentine* almost single-handedly.

"When I saw you sail into Dragonfly Bay last night, I thought *Diamond* was a Sarksa ship," the cowboy said, frowning.

"Remember, before you left us last time, how you asked King Krystal to give me a new ship? Well, *Diamond* is it! She is one of the rooks that we took from the Sarksa. And I have you to thank, Danny Ray. We repaired her and cleaned her up of all that terrible Sarksa pirate smell!"

"And just so you know, Danny Ray, we brung the clabbernappers as engines over from *Hog*," said Hoodie Crow, his white eyes shining excitedly. "*Diamond* sails so sweet and solid—not a shimmer, not a shake!"

"And them great big guns we got fer *Hog* back in Port Palnacky, remember?" cackled Piper, the master gunner. "We brung 'em all over to *Diamond*!"

The cowboy nodded grimly. He remembered, in this world so full of exotic colors and violent savagery, the destruction

Hog's cannon had wreaked on the pirate bishops *Vulture* and *Wick*, and its totally destroying *Clackmannon*, a heavy rook. With the clabbernappers as engines, *Diamond* must be the most formidable rook on the Checkered Sea.

"But first things first," said Captain Quigglewigg seriously. "How are you feeling, Danny Ray? You was as pale as pipe clay when we found you a-lying in the graveyard last night."

The cowboy's face was all questions.

"You're not remembered of last night, eh?" asked the captain worriedly.

Piper scurried around the bed. He held up an open hand wide: "How many fingers?"

"Four," responded Danny Ray, and Piper's freckled face screwed up with concern. "And one thumb!" finished the cowboy with a smirk. "Come to think on it, Piper, I ain't got no fingers at all. 'Cause my dad says I'm all thumbs!"

"Oh, ha, ha, ha!" cried Captain Quigglewigg, slapping Piper on the back. Even Hoodie Crow, normally a very serious first lieutenant, roared out a laugh. "A point for Danny Ray!"

"Wait!" cried out Danny Ray, the clouds in his memory clearing. "I need to find Prince Blue! And Cherry and Tûk!"

"Not to worry," replied Captain Quigglewigg, still grinning like a big orange. As if on cue, the cabin door opened. "Ah! Here comes my precious niece!"

"Danny Ray!" squealed Cherry, running across the cabin in her flashing white dress and nudging past the captain to hug the cowboy. "I was afraid we'd never see you again!"

"Your niece?" asked Danny Ray.

"Captain Quigglewigg's my uncle!" She beamed as she stood back and the captain patted her blond hair affectionately.

"Quiggs is her last name, ain't it now?" asked Captain Quigglewigg, putting up his hand. "Short for Quigglewigg, like me."

Cherry shrugged before the cowboy could ask the obvious. "I don't look anything like my uncle, for sure, but—"

"But I must prohibit you from running around with these risky rescuers!" interrupted her uncle with a mixture of fondness and warning in his voice.

"Tûk!" cried Danny Ray, catching sight of the devil's red face peering in through the door.

The hellwain devil had to hunch down to keep from smacking his head against the deck beams as he sauntered across the cabin and stood at the foot of the bed. He smiled warmly at the cowboy while Hoodie Crow eyed the hellwain devil suspiciously, recalling that Tûk had been a leader of the kidnappers of *Winter Queen*.

"Danny Ray! Worried of you I was!"

Prince Blue stood beside the devil. He nodded stiffly to the cowboy. Captain Quigglewigg felt the sudden tension between them and quickly asked, "Now tell us, Danny Ray, what happened to you."

"I'm trying to remember," replied the cowboy with a frown. "I done saw *Serpentine* get blown to bits and then, I think, I started climbing somewhere. Then I woke up here. But hey, Cherry! Your dress looks like new!"

Cherry's face changed and she pointed at his head. "Don't you try to make up with me, Danny Ray! I remember, now, I was mad at you for leaving us—"

There came a twilling of pipes and the beating of drums. A little midshipman with a pixie face stuck his head through the door and said with a squeaky voice, "Cap'n Peach is here, sir!"

"Now, Mr. Kelpy," admonished Captain Quigglewigg, rising to his tiptoes. "Stand at attention and make your report properly!"

The midshipman entered, stood up straight, took off his hat, and cleared his throat. "Mr. Jenkins sends his compliments, sir, and Cap'n Ritchie Peach of *Emerald Castle* is come aboard."

"Very good, Mr. Kelpy. You may show him below."

Danny Ray had just managed to struggle to a sitting position, leaning back against a bank of huge, white pillows, when a mountain of a man walked through the door and, like Tûk, ducked beneath the ceiling beams. Most notable about Ritchie Peach, once he had tucked his captain's hat under his arm, was his bright blond hair, his yellow skin, and red cheeks dusted with white fuzz—just like a peach! He displayed a wide smile, and two tiny brown horns jutted from his forehead. His bright blue coat was adorned at the shoulders with two gold epaulettes, marking him as a very experienced captain.

"Captain Peach, commander of *Emerald Castle*, a seventy-four-gun ship," remarked Quigglewigg, making the introductions. "Ritchie, this is my principal friend, Danny Ray, champion rodeo cowboy from Oklahoma . . . from the Otherworld."

Quigglewigg noticed that Danny Ray winced at the title.

"Pleased a'meeting of you," Captain Ritchie Peach said, regarding the cowboy curiously. He caught sight of Danny Ray's blue rope dangling from the bedpost and took a slight step backward. "So, you must be a wizard?"

"It don't take a wizard to see how your ship pounded the *Serpentine* something fierce!" said Danny Ray respectfully.

"Coo! Why, thank you, young sir! I'm passing grateful to you for a-noticing of it!"

"And I notice, too, what a neat name you have, Captain Peach!" replied the cowboy. "Shoot—you look just like a peach!"

"You should meet my sister," he replied, his fuzzy features splitting into an ever wider grin, and a twinkle lighting up his eyes. "She is quite melancholy: she has a head like a melon and a face like a collie!"

"Har, har, har!" chortled Piper.

"Oh, ha, ha, ha!" cried the captain over a chorus of good-natured laughter that made the stern windows rattle. But then, Ritchie Peach's smile faded as he spotted the hellwain devil, Tûk, and his blue eyes grew cold as ice. Tûk growled under his breath, for Ritchie Peach was a demon, and it is well understood that devils and demons are not friends.

Midshipman Kelpy reappeared at the door and announced: "Mr. Jenkins's compliments, sir, and come aboard, too, is the cap'n of *Pearl*, sir."

Pearl had been the elegant white bishop with the amazingly accurate guns that had pummeled *Serpentine* from clear across the harbor. In his previous adventure, Danny Ray had helped to fire Arlette, a cannon named a "long nine," and had blown off the top knob of a bishop ship. He knew how difficult it was to fire a cannon and hit a mark a ways off, and for that reason alone he could hardly wait to meet *Pearl*'s captain.

Everyone began filing silently out of the cabin, Tûk and Ritchie Peach keeping their distance from each other. Captain

Quigglewigg, the last one out the door, turned and bowed slightly. "To your very good health, Danny Ray!"

"Why is everybody leaving?" called the cowboy from his mound of pillows.

When the captain of *Pearl* entered the room, he understood why.

Danny Ray saw dark brown eyes blinking at him from across the room, eyes as large as the whole huge doggone universe, and the glittering captain's uniform she wore paled in comparison to the exquisite loveliness of those eyes. Her short, lithe form seemed to float across the floor, and Danny Ray noticed a familiar pin fastened on her chest bearing the likeness of a prancing tiger. Her teeth dazzled white from a complexion of cinnamon-colored skin as she smiled and said, "Hello, Danny Ray."

The cowboy had been shocked to meet up again with Piper, and Hoodie Crow and Captain Quigglewigg. But he had never, ever expected to see the Sultana Sumferi Sar.

"What are you doing here?" exclaimed Danny Ray.

"Nice to see you again, too," stated the Sultana demurely.

"No! Shucks, I mean, I expected you to be back at your highfalutin palace in Port Palnacky! But it's real nice to see you! Real nice!" The rest of his words choked up in his throat, and he blushed as she tilted her lovely face to study his.

Danny Ray all of a sudden felt very grungy, dirty, and awkward in her dazzling presence. He reached up and grabbed his hat and placed it over his messy hair.

"So, here you are recovering in bed again," she said with a smirk.

"Ain't that just the cut of it?" said the cowboy. He grinned to think that the first time they had met, he had been flat on his back in bed, recuperating in her ornate palace in Port Palnacky.

"Oh! After sailing the Checkered Sea with you pursuing *Winter Queen,* flying on the back of that huge red bat, and being attacked and captured by Sarksa pirates—"

"Don't forget almost getting eaten by that Sarksa queen!"

"Yes! Well, I became spoiled, Danny Ray," said the sultana. "I wanted to be at sea again so I purchased *Pearl* and armed her with cannon and a good and trusted crew. Gimmion Gott—you remember him, the big purple giant treasurer person?—he watches over Port Palnacky now. Anyway, I've spent most of my time sailing the coastline, and I happened to spot *Serpentine* as she headed north to Dragonfly Bay. I secretly followed her. I knew something was up when I caught sight of *Diamond* and *Emerald Castle* approaching."

"Boy, you're a good shot," the cowboy said in a quiet voice. "I seen what your guns did to *Serpentine.*"

"And *Pearl* will certainly give a good accounting of herself when we catch up to the King of the Fantasms!" she said proudly.

"Maybe he'll find us."

The sultana shot him a questioning look. She studied him for a moment. "What's wrong, Danny Ray?"

He felt light-headed and he laid his head back against the pillow. He closed his eyes as a whirling scene took him back to Oklahoma:

HRAAAAANG! A pair of horns appeared out of the mist of his dreams and banged and twisted the metal gate he sat on.

Danny Ray looped his legs over the top bar and eased himself down on top of the broad bundle of tussle and muscle. He could feel the heat of the beast, smell the sweat, the sheer bloodlust and violence of the brute, impatient and angry beneath him.

"From Tahlequah, the reigning Junior Bull-riding Champion!" came a far-off echo through the rodeo arena, garbled like, as if the announcer were speaking into a large can. "Let's give a warm Oklahoma welcome to Danny Ray!"

Danny Ray sat bolt upright on the huge bull.

"And today he'll be riding none other than Tomahawk!" The name rose like a sinister force above the rush of applause.

Tomahawk.

Danny Ray caught his breath just hearing the name. Tomahawk: the meanest bull around, with large, wine-red eyes the color of spilled blood, and a heart blacker than Satan. Tomahawk: the ride of your life, or your death; like strapping your legs around a two-ton keg of rompin', stompin' dynamite.

Danny Ray's tongue was dry against the sides of his mouth. His knuckles grated hard against his rawhide glove as he gripped the rigging strap with his left hand and pounded it tight with his other. The bull strained to turn its grisly head around as far as it would go, pressing its horns against the cowboy's leg.

Danny Ray lowered his head. He closed his eyes. He breathed deeply.

"Check your grip, son," came a familiar voice. Danny Ray's father reached over from the top of the gate and patted his son on the back. The young cowboy's gloved hand loosened and tightened on the rigging. "Keep your spurs forward—good. When it comes time to let loose of the rope and you catch air, roll and run when you hit the ground 'cause Tomahawk'll come lookin' for you, boy. Roll and run! Roll and run! D'ye hear me, Danny Ray?"

He barely choked out the words: "Yes, sir."

"Tomahawk's a money bull—you can win on him, Danny Ray! A money bull! Ride 'im rough. Make me proud!"

"Yes, sir." He had whispered his last response so softly that it had almost been only a thought. He blew a blast of air through a small O in his mouth.

He checked his grip again.

He was the defending bull-riding champion. This ride was for all the marbles.

The time had come.

He nodded his head.

WHANG! The gate flew open!

Danny Ray jerked back, the lights in the ceiling whirling around in a cloud of sawdust as he blasted into the open arena riding a bone-crushing roller coaster. His right hand flew into the air for balance as Tomahawk's hind end bucked up, spun around and around, and bucked again, spinning, spinning, again and again. Danny Ray stayed with him and leaned into the spin, looking down into the well.

Tomahawk switched back in a flash! His hand was jerked violently from its grip! The arena tilted on end. He flew into the air, chaps flapping, the colors of the crowd dancing drunkenly around. *WHAM!* A jolting shock as he hit the ground—dust flying all around him. He rolled over—run, Danny Ray, run! His dad's urgent voice echoed in his head—*run*! The ground shook with thundering hoofs. Something huge and snorting was bearing down on him with black horns, wild eyes—

Danny Ray rose up from the pillow with a gasp. His upper lip was all sweaty and he felt the cool hand of the sultana flow down the side of his cheek.

He sniffed, looking down, and said, "I ain't the same Danny Ray no more."

"And I am not the same Sultana Sumferi Sar!" she tittered happily. "How do I look as a captain? Oh! My epaulette keeps slipping! Is it straight?"

"That's not what I mean," he said in his best tough-guy voice. He adjusted his hat and hung his head so that she couldn't see his face. "I ain't a rodeo champion no more," he said dejectedly. "Tomahawk threw me."

"Tomahawk?" Confusion replaced concern on the sultana's face.

"Yeah, Tomahawk: the meanest, quickest, evilest bull that ever was—my dad says he's a white-livered son of Satan," explained Danny Ray, "and boy, I believe him!"

The sultana watched him quietly.

"And so, I ain't a champion no more!" said Danny Ray. "Things have changed for me here, too. Last time around, looking for *Winter Queen*, I felt like I was getting somewhere. But now, everything's wrong, sort of sideways. I feel like I'm on some wild-goose chase—like a blind man in a dark room lookin' for a black cat that ain't there. I'm all confused about the fantasms— who we have to fight, and if they're destroyed whether they're even going to stay dead. And time's running out for Princess Amber—the new moon's coming tonight, or tomorrow night, or the night after next, I don't know which. I don't even know what happened to me last night."

The sultana thought for a moment. "Well, Danny Ray. You saved all of Elidor when you were here last—have you forgotten? I don't care about this nasty bull, Tomahawk. You're still a champion in this world!"

The cowboy shook his head and muttered, "Girls! They don't understand nothing!"

"And I'm a captain!" She posed with her sparkling uniform.

He brightened up and reached out good-naturedly and yanked on her hair. "You're still just a stinky old girl to me!"

"Oh, Danny Ray!" She felt a strand of raven-colored hair loosen and tried to pin it up. "I should pop you one in the nose! I can't be seen like this!" She looked about the room and snapped, "Oh! Where is a mirror in this whole ship?"

She finally succeeded in securing her wayward lock of hair. She held her arms out and pirouetted around and around to show off her lavender uniform and the gold epaulette on her left shoulder. In a flash, she leaned over the cowboy and kissed him lightly on the cheek.

Danny Ray quickly wiped his cheek. "Now why'd you go and do that? Gosh darn it! What am I, anyway—a kissing target?" He shot a look at the door to make sure no one had seen him being kissed by a girl.

"Well! Aren't we Mr. Slouchy and Grouchy this morning!"

"I don't like it none, being kissed on my face like that. A gal can suck a feller's face clean off!"

Danny Ray wiped his cheek again, but then his eyes met hers and all of his temper and shyness melted away in an instant.

She smiled, half whispering, "I've missed you, Danny Ray, championship rodeo cowboy."

A rush of hope and security flowed over him as his hand closed around something small, something round, something tangible: Arcile, the sparkling gem of his necklace. He opened his fist. There, in the vast depth of that single, solitary gem he was amazed to see the other worlds, the slow turning of frozen stars, and gassy nebulas with sparkling clouds of celestial majesty.

In a rush, all the events from the night before flooded into his mind in vivid detail: the graveyard; the obliteration of Commodore Mumblefub; the ghost of Princess Amber on horseback; but first and foremost in his mind was the image of the White Lady.

"What is it, Danny Ray?"

"The Riddle of the Fantasms," he said. "'Wild are the winds of the Checkered Sea . . .'" He recited the riddle out loud, word for word, stanza for stanza. He rested his head back against the pillows.

"Why, Danny Ray! How did you memorize that whole poem?" she said in an amazed voice.

"Yeah, ain't that something? I know it word for word." He thought for a moment. "I fainted dead away when the White Lady touched me, right here on my noggin. Maybe it was her way of making sure I remembered the riddle and every doggone thing she said—in detail, like."

"The White Lady?" The Sultana Sumferi Sar scrunched up her face. "Are you not feeling well, Danny Ray?"

"You'll never guess what else," he said, as the sultana leaned in close to him. He felt her cool hand on his forehead. "It was there. I saw it again. The same one that was in Buckholly Harbor."

Now it was the sultana who turned impatient and said: "Will you do me the service of coming to the point? I'm not fond of guessing games."

"The wolf."

She abruptly withdrew her hand, as if Danny Ray had uttered something unholy. She looked at him out of the corner of her eye. "How do you know it was the same wolf? Danny Ray, are you all right?"

She followed his stare to a picture of a chessboard hanging on the wall near the door, just above the washbasin.

"A chessboard doesn't really have a center," she said, guessing that he was remembering that particular stanza of the riddle. "So the riddle really doesn't make sense."

"You're thinking I made this whole thing up—about the White Lady and all?" Danny Ray's face wrinkled up. "And I'll bet you think I'm just crying wolf!"

"Not exactly," responded the sultana with a shrug. "I'll try to help you, Danny Ray, you know that."

"Then tell me, what the heck are the battle pieces on the chessboard? What's the unsceptered hoard?"

"Let me think." The sultana crossed her arms and rested her chin against her forefinger. "Well, only the king holds a scepter, so I guess it would be those pieces other than the king—the rook, and the knight, the bishop and queen—the ones that do the fighting. But I don't see how that tells us anything about the fantasms. Or where they have taken Princess Amber."

"That ain't the right question," replied the cowboy matter-of-factly, remembering something else the White Lady had said.

"Whatever do you mean?"

"Right now I don't know what the right question is, but as soon as I find out, everything else will fall into place." He licked his lips as the sultana shot him a baffled look. "You'll see. Everything will fall into place."

❖ 25 ❖
Six Rooks

 From the tremendous height of *Diamond*'s upper deck, the expanse of the Checkered Sea stretched away in all directions as far as the eye could see, black-and-white squares so polished that the fleeting flock of low-skimming birds was mirrored exactly on its surface. Far overhead the lookout perched on the top of a long pole, a black speck against the cloudless sky, where a long blue pendant fluttered in the wind.

"Wait! Where's Dragonfly Bay?" asked the cowboy.

"We are hundreds of mile south of there," replied the sultana. "After we destroyed *Serpentine*, Captain Quigglewigg thought there might be other enemy ships lurking about." As she pointed to the east, her gem-laden bracelets glinted and sparkled in the noonday sun. "Just over that horizon is Dumzil-Daz, and Scorpion Bay."

Danny Ray stared in the direction of *Pearl*, the bishop's graceful curves and white stonework and bulwarks soaring above the mighty rook, her perfect golden top knob glinting in the cloudless sky. The Sultana Sumferi Sar had wondered what the cowboy's reaction would be to her wonderful ship, but his face was difficult to read. He pushed his hat back and a gust of wind played with his hair.

"What is it?" she asked.

"The wind—the Riddle of the Fantasms mentions the wind."

"Oh," she said.

Danny Ray looked up and saw a glittering comet blaze through the bright sky. He hadn't really even seen her elegant ship of war, and he didn't seem to notice the disappointment in her voice. "'Wild are the winds of the Checkered Sea, circling the world in tranquility,'" he recited, half to himself. "Hmmm."

"How can something be wild and tranquil at the same time?" asked the sultana, her diamond hoop-shaped earrings dancing as she shook her head.

"Maybe it's a clue that the fantasms ain't predictable," replied the cowboy.

"Yes, but doesn't the riddle say something about seasons?" she countered. "The seasons are very predictable."

"Shoot! Why'd you have to go and say that?" Danny Ray scratched the back of his neck, knocking his hat too far forward on his forehead.

Eight bells tingled out sharply, accompanied by the padded sound of sailors' feet running across the deck as the watch changed; one group of sailors from below, newly rested, replaced the tired group on duty.

"Deck there!" came a faraway call.

Danny Ray spun around and looked up the rook's single mast, the dark dot of the lookout pointing westward, black against the blue sky.

"Where away?" boomed Hoodie Crow, limping up on his wooden leg, telescope in hand.

"Off the stern, sir, behind us!" he shouted down.

Captain Quigglewigg appeared out of nowhere, walking quickly to the rear of the ship, and trained his glass out to the horizon, trying to focus on the strange ship.

"The White Lady said he'd find us," said Danny Ray, half to himself.

The sultana shot him an alarmed look. "Who would find us?"

"Ikkus-Sark," replied the cowboy, nodding in the direction of the ships. He touched Arcile, twinkling on his chest. "King of the Fantasms."

"Please, Danny Ray!" Quigglewigg said, taking his eye away from the glass and looking back at him. "None of your wild speculations, sir—you will spook my crew. Chances are she's a merchantman, surely."

"Bring out the Heart of Ildirim!" said the sultana excitedly. "It will tell us if that ship is a friend or an enemy."

The cowboy shrugged. "I left the Trouble Stone at home," he said with a nervous chuckle. "That's what I call it, my Trouble Stone. 'Heart of Ildirim' is too hard to say—my tongue gets all twisted up!"

The Heart of Ildirim, a magical crystal that flickered red when an enemy was near, had been instrumental in warning them of danger when they had tried to avoid the Sarksa pirates as they hunted down *Winter Queen*.

The sultana folded her arms and scowled, looking the cowboy up and down. "The Trouble Stone, as you so crudely call it, is very, very valuable, Danny Ray! Gimmion Gott will never forgive you for losing it!"

Gimmion Gott, the sultana's giant treasure hunter and guard, had been completely discombobulated when she had removed the Heart of Ildirim from the treasure vault in Port Palnacky. Oh—how Gimmion's purple body must have quivered and shivered when he learned she had given it away to Danny Ray before he had returned to the Otherworld!

"I didn't lose it!" exclaimed the cowboy. "It's back home on my dresser . . . I think. Or in my old toy box."

"Toy box!" she cried.

Danny Ray shot back: "Listen here, I ain't in the habit of riding the rodeo or going to school with a magical stone the size of an egg in my pocket! For crying out loud—it ain't like I can wear it around my neck! Folks would think I'm plum crazy!"

"I already think you're crazy!" she snapped, wagging her finger at him in a most unsultanalike way.

"I'll remember to bring my Trouble Stone if I visit here again. But for now—get off my back!"

"Don't you take that tone with me, Danny Ray!" the sultana countered, hands on hips. "It's not my fault you forgot it. And it's not my fault you're no longer Mr. Championship Cowboy! When you got thrown off that bull something in your head came loose!"

"Hey!" said Danny Ray in a low voice, glancing around the deck. "That's supposed to be a secret!"

Quigglewigg and Hoodie made bad efforts at pretending not to hear.

The lookout called again: "Deck there! It's two ships, sir. No—three ships! Rooks o' war, sir!"

"No harm in assuming them to be hostile," stated the captain, ignoring the fuming cowboy and sultana. "Mr. Kelpy, signal *Emerald Castle:* three enemy rooks sailing in column to stern. Though I fancy Captain Ritchie Peach already knows it."

The words had hardly passed the captain's lips when a puff of smoke and a loud retort issued from the side of *Emerald Castle*— a signal cannon warning of the same suspicious squadron, and flags flew up her signal halyard to the top of the mast.

"Hoodie," said Quigglewigg, looking away from his glass. "I'll thank you to beat to quarters."

Rat-a-tat tat—rat-a tat! Rat-a-tat tat—rat-a tat! went the drummer boy's signal. The ship burst into a disturbed nest of bees as all sailors above and below decks ran here and there through the ship, across the decks, lieutenants yelling out orders, gun captains hollering for their crews to report. Rat-a-tat tat—rat-a tat! Sand was scattered across the deck to keep feet from slipping, cannonballs were piled into cradles next to the superb cannon whose lashings were cast off. Rat-a-tat tat—rat-a tat! Powder boys with extra cartridges of gunpowder scurried from below deck just as the plugs in the muzzles of the cannons were pulled out and sailors with long-handled sponges swabbed out the deep mouths of the guns.

Wait—where had the sultana gone? The cowboy whipped around—too late. She had gotten back aboard her ship quickly, and even now the gangway leading to *Pearl* had been gathered in. The bishop let out a soft whine as her engines revved up. Danny Ray looked overhead at the bishop's upper works, towering over the massive, bulky rook. He thought he caught a glimpse of the sultana's slim, sparkling form, pointing calmly here, waving there, preparing her ship for battle. To his surprise he saw the forms of Tûk and Cherry looking down from the bishop's rim. Between them stood Prince Blue. Caught unaware while visiting the beautiful ship, they were unable to make it back. Amid the pandemonium on *Diamond*'s deck, Danny Ray raised a hand goodbye. Surprisingly, it was Prince Blue who waved back.

Danny Ray's stomach felt tight. This was three times that he had been separated from his friends.

"Make it four enemy rooks, sir," said Hoodie Crow dully. "Three of them are seventy-four-gun ships, sir, and they're closing with us fast."

"We'll run away for now," said the captain simply, snapping shut his telescope. "Mr. Kelpy, signal *Emerald Castle* to take station ahead of us and lead the way south—all ahead full. And signal *Pearl* to keep safely away."

"Aye, aye, sir," squeaked the midshipman, and ran off toward the massive steering wheel near the tall lookout mast.

"Can't the sultana help us, sir?" asked the cowboy.

A thick crease appeared on Quigglewigg's orange forehead. "Bishops are not line-of-battle ships, Danny Ray—those heavy rooks would make mincemeat of *Pearl*."

Colorful signal flags broke out and flapped in the breeze as *Diamond* surged ahead. She was a fast rook, even for her considerable size and heavy armament, and had no trouble keeping station directly behind the smaller *Emerald Castle*. *Pearl*, being a bishop, slanted sharply southeast and was nearly out of sight.

"Mr. Piper!" announced the captain as the master gunner

appeared from below. "I trust all cannon on the lower decks are primed and ready."

"Aye, aye, sir!" Piper's freckled face split into a grin. "We'll shoot two broadsides for their one, sir!" The prospect of battle excited him. Never mind that in a few moments he might be dead or maimed from cannon fire. His sole delight was in handing out more hot iron than he got.

"We'll give 'em a belly load of shot, sir!" boasted one gunner, leaning against a long pole with a sponge on the end.

"We'll thump it home, sir!" agreed another, patting a huge, squat cannon with a blackened hand. "Yessir! Thump it home!"

"Silence there!" growled Piper. "Attend to your duties!"

Danny Ray grabbed a telescope and peered northward. "Here they come, sir!" he yelled. The dark smudge on the horizon sharpened into sinister detail as he focused the eyepiece: four black rooks sailing in single file, their ports open and black, stubby cannon run out.

Captain Quigglewigg looked through his telescope, eyeing their black flags, the same color as their stonework, and bearing the five-pointed star—ancient symbol of the fantasms.

"Gods preserve us!" muttered Hoodie Crow, just focusing on them.

Captain Quigglewigg made his way over near *Diamond*'s massive steerage wheel where a coal troll, dressed in grimy overalls, saluted him. He looked like Hoodie Crow's twin except shorter.

"Yakky, chief of the Engine Room, zur. Sent for me?"

The captain pointed back behind them to the four rooks. "Now see here, Yakky," he said. "When I give the word, bring down *Diamond* to a quarter speed, but not so sudden that we roll into the scuppers, understand? I need them to catch up to us sudden like. Then stop the ship completely."

"Yezzur." Yakky's massive downturned horns nodded.

"That'll catch 'em by surprise, hopefully." The captain wiped his mouth. "Now Yakky, there's a thirty-square space between each of those rooks. As the first rook's momentum carries her past us, I want to jump between her and the second rook. Do you understand?"

Yakky growled and nodded his head. "Yezzur. I'll do it, zur, me and me lads. Them clabbernappers is good-tuned to orders; ship's gears is solid and greased up good. Jest give us the word, zur."

"Very good," said the captain, and the engineer shuffled away. "Now, Mr. Kelpy, be so good to signal the *Emerald Castle* as to our intentions: Captain Peach will know what to do."

The six rooks sailed swiftly south under a blue, cloudless sky beneath the slow moving sun. *Emerald Castle* led the way with *Diamond* behind her while to starboard and some distance back, the four enemy rooks cruised menacingly.

Danny Ray glanced to larboard, to the left of the ship, but saw nothing of the frail bishop, *Pearl.* He was glad Quigglewigg had ordered her to sail safely away—at least little Cherry, Tûk, Prince Blue, and the sultana would be safe. The cowboy had stark memories of heavily armed rooks dueling it out with their big guns and thick walls: the smoke, chaos, and destruction.

Danny Ray jumped as Captain Quigglewigg appeared at his side. "Now listen carefully, young cowboy, sir. I will be busy watching the movements of the enemy, Hoodie will be with the helm, and Piper with his guns. I need you to be ready at the speaking tube to relay my orders, eh? When I give the signal, you give the order for *Diamond* to slow down to a quarter speed."

"Yessir—aye, aye, sir," said the cowboy.

"Helmsman, keep our speed right where she is."

"Aye, aye, sir," came the answer.

Boom! A distant retort caused them to run to the rear of the ship. A trail of smoke blew away from the front-most enemy rook. She had tried a shot at long range. Something hummed close overhead and disappeared south. A cannonball.

"Good practice," commented Captain Quigglewigg. Danny Ray didn't have to be told that it was high time he took his place at the speaking tube rising out of the deck. But it felt oddly warm . . .

As the four enemy rooks drew steadily closer, the third rook in their line, a magnificent eighty-gun rook, broke out a long black and purple admiral's pendant in an extreme chest-thumping display of bravado. Captain Quigglewigg's fingers tapped on his magnificent ceremonial sword that had been presented to him at Port Palnacky for destroying the pirate bishop *Vulture*. And then his fingers stopped.

It was time.

"Danny Ray!" he shouted. "Now!"

"Back to a quarter speed!" shouted the cowboy down the tube.

"Danny Ray! That's the smokestack for the galley stove!" boomed Hoodie Crow.

The cowboy's heart leaped into his throat! No wonder it had seemed warm! He scampered over to the shiny brass speaking tube and yelled: "Slow down to a quarter speed!"

Just in time.

The effect on *Diamond* was astounding. Danny Ray braced himself as the rook wound down, the wind on the deck dying to a small breeze. And then the powerful rook stopped.

"Helm—steer to starboard!" shouted Quigglewigg. Hoodie Crow and the stout helmsman spun the huge double wheel to the right and *Diamond* pivoted until she faced straight west.

There came a deep rumble as the enemy squadron was abruptly upon them. Danny Ray heard the whining of engines as the front-most rook passed them, trying in vain to stop. *Diamond* lurched into the gap behind the first two enemy rooks. Danny Ray read the name over the first rook's stern: *Viper*.

"Stand by!" Captain Quigglewigg drew his sword and raised it high, the superb blade flashing blue and yellow in the sun. "Starboard guns—stand to the ready!"

Diamond would spend her first, well-aimed broadside on the second rook, which rapidly loomed up on their right side. The cowboy could see the panic on the enemy rook's upper deck as *Diamond*'s primed and ready guns appeared directly in front of them. They scurried from their larboard cannon to man the front guns. But they were too late.

"Fire!" yelled Quigglewigg.

BOOOOM! Diamond's heavy guns leaped back, belching out fire, her massive broadside catching the black rook full on, causing her to stagger and turn, a fatal mistake that presented her vulnerable stern to *Diamond*.

"*Python*," said Danny Ray to himself, reading the second rook's name.

"Helm-a-lee!" cried the captain, and the helmsman, a grim smile smeared across his face, spun the wheel. The cowboy heard a distant broadside. *Emerald Castle* had doubled back and was engaging the leading rook, *Viper*, fighting her furiously.

"Mr. Piper, sir!" shouted someone close by. A massive cannonball from *Python* had plowed through the left side of the rim near a forty-two-pounder, killing two of the gun's crew. But the master gunner didn't hear them, striding the deck, gesturing in the smoke and noise, blowing his whistle and shouting orders.

"I'll help!" said the cowboy, running up and stepping over the dead bodies. But his face was all questions.

"Grab this here crowbar, lacky!" said a smudge-faced gunner. Danny Ray followed his directions, hunkering down behind the breech of the massive artillery piece.

"Easy there!" came a low voice.

"Who said that?" cried the cowboy.

"Pugg's who said it!" The cowboy looked down to see a puffy iron face fashioned out of the rear of the cannon.

"My name's Danny Ray—"

"Didn't ask your name!" Pugg puffed. "I knows a new matey when I feels one!"

"Hey!" said the cowboy, grunting as he helped lever Pugg around until he pointed once again at the enemy rook. "I talked to a cannon before, but her name was Arlette—a nine-pounder."

"Nine-pounder—Hah!" scoffed Pugg.

"Hey! She was real elegant!"

"Elegant—smellegant! We forty-two-pounders does the lion's work! Now, mind you, I don't weigh forty-two pounds: I shoot a cannonball that weighs forty-two pounds!"

"I know that already." Danny Ray frowned.

"Well, then, if you knows that, you know we load and fire, load and fire! Hot work at close range—that's why they nicknamed me Pugg the Masher Smasher. You'll see what I can do!"

"Swab out!" bellowed the gun captain as one of the powder boys ran up with a gunpowder cartridge.

Danny Ray had seen that done enough times. He took the long-handled wet sponge—"Easy, there!" grumbled Pugg—and swabbed out the deep mouth of the gun, the hot metal hissing as he pulled it out again.

"Load!"

The powder was poured in and tamped. A massive cannon-ball, bigger than a bowling ball, was rolled into Pugg as *Diamond* came around slowly, inexorably, her larboard side guns grinning mercilessly at the stunned *Python*.

"Fire!" shouted Quigglewigg.

"BOOM!" went Pugg and the rest of *Diamond's* larboard side, the side of the rook disappearing in smoke as her massive guns discharged yet another broadside of metal into the enemy rook. The starboard gun crews swabbed out their iron monsters and reloaded them with grapeshot. The acrid smell of gunpowder, of battle, wafted across the deck, and the cowboy found it surprisingly pleasant.

Diamond's next thunderous broadside knocked the fight out of *Python*. Her officers and crew lay dead, her steerage wheel blown to bits, her cannon upended.

Through the smoke, Pugg, the forty-two-pounder cannon, winked up at the cowboy, who still held the long-handled sponge in his hand. "Not bad shootin', eh, matey?" he growled with a wink.

"Strike your colors!" bellowed Hoodie Crow through a speaking trumpet. The huge first lieutenant was demanding *Python* haul down her flag, signaling surrender. Farther to the south, *Emerald Castle* was pounding *Viper* into submission.

That left two undefeated rooks, two heavy rooks that, even now, crept up into the theater of battle. The blue of the sky gave way to a fuzzy brown cloud rising from them.

Danny Ray pointed into the sky and yelled, "Whiners!"

Captain Quigglewigg blew his whistle and yelled, "All hands! Prepare to repel boarders!"

✦ 26 ✦

The Battle of Scorpion Bay

 Danny Ray's hand closed down around the handle of a thick, curved sword lying on the cutlass rack. Lines of firm determination formed on his face. He unfastened his magical blue rope.

A familiar dreadful whining filled the air, growing deeper and deeper in tone as the whiners dove down toward the crew of *Diamond*.

"Here they come!" cried the cowboy as huge red mosquito-like bandits swooped over the deck.

Whirrrr! Whirrrr! Whirrrr! went the rope of thrillium over his head as he let out the loop in a bigger and bigger circle, snagging a passing whiner by the leg and—*THUNK!*—bringing it down hard, smashing its head against a brass cannon.

Danny Ray swung his cutlass wildly at the flying monsters. One whiner ventured too close and, with a lightninglike swing, the cowboy sheared off its legs. It buzzed out of control and disappeared over the rim of the rook. The cowboy slapped at another whiner with the flat of his blade, knocking it to the deck where Piper finished it off, yelling, "That's done fer ya!" and driving a pike into its thorax.

Another whiner, its eyes glittering like red murder, came to hover over the cowboy, its long sharp proboscis waving from side to side beneath the hum of its wings. An image of the poor pipsqueak flashed through Danny Ray's mind, the battle over Big Lizard and the searing pain on his neck where a whiner had just missed killing him with its long, sword-shaped beak.

ZZZZzzzZZZZ! went its wings. It jabbed down with its sharp nose. Danny Ray leaped to the side. The whiner jabbed again, its nose sticking like a needle in the wooden planking of the deck. The cowboy felt a jarring impact up his arm as he drove his cutlass into the creature's abdomen.

Danny Ray looked up and his heart fell. Here came a fresh wave of whiners, a hundred or more, screaming down toward *Diamond.*

"Captain!" he shrieked. Quigglewigg and a company of sailors were huddled near the steerage wheel, hacking upward with pikes and swords. Hoodie Crow, all alone, wielded a boarding axe back and forth, trying to ward off the flying bloodsuckers.

BOOOM! The unexpected blast of cannon came out of no-where. The squadron of whiners disintegrated in midair as the massive white ball of a bishop loomed over *Diamond*'s deck.

"It's *Pearl!*" yelled the cowboy gladly. The bishop slanted in and fired another full broadside of small nuts and bolts, pellets of lead and grapeshot. Like a machine gun, it had mowed down countless whiners out of the sky!

Danny Ray's heart flip-flopped into his throat as a whiner grasped little Mr. Kelpy with its cruel, barbed claws and lifted him into the air. "Kelpy!" cried Danny Ray helplessly as the whiner hurled the boy over the side of the rook to fall hundreds of feet to his death.

Danny Ray gritted his teeth. He lunged for his rope—*ZZZZzzzZZZZ!*—something flew close by and knocked him clean off his feet and into the scuppers. *Bong!*—he hit his head against one of Mr. Piper's magnificent cannon and his world twirled around like he was in the spin cycle of a washing machine. He tried desperately to shake out the cobwebs when a danger signal went off in his head as he felt a presence standing over him. He reached for his cutlass but a long, barbed claw knocked it away.

Danny Ray looked up.

There stood the largest whiner he had ever seen, nearly twice the size of the others, with red and yellow streaks lining its abdomen. The thing grinned, an evil, hideous grin. It had no weapons: no sword to draw; no spear to jab. For, in its gleaming proboscis, it possessed both sword and spear.

Overhead, the sky darkened all the more with swarming insects. No way out this time, the cowboy thought grimly—there were too many of them! Poor Princess Amber. Danny Ray trembled, wondering how a needle that big would feel stabbing into his chest, how fierily the whiner's eyes would light up as it drank deeply to its devilish delight.

The cowboy began panting as it raised its metallic mouth, quivering feverishly with anticipation.

WOOOOOOOSH! Something large flew by with a deep-throated hum, reaching down with long claws and snatching the whiner away! Danny Ray dove to his left across the deck as another whiner stabbed at him from behind. In a flash, that whiner, too, was whisked away by another huge flying insect!

Danny Ray scrambled to his feet and looked up. He couldn't believe his eyes—dragonflies! The sky was filled with them!

The cowboy grabbed his cutlass and wheeled around. He saw a group of whiners trying to fend off the mad rush of incoming dragonflies, but they were lifted off the deck and eaten piecemeal. Blue darners flashed here, brown hawkers slashed there, zooming across and back, zipping and flipping over in midair to grab a handful of whiners and swallow them whole. Violet dancers buzzed violently as they dove from the heavens, holding their claws like baskets and gathering up a harvest of crunchy, munchy whiners. Even those whiners that lay twitching on the deck were whisked away.

Danny Ray looked overhead. Something hovered close, huge and ominous: a dragonfly descended slowly. The humming from its wings was deafening. Its honeycombed eyes considered Danny Ray as he held his hat from blowing off with one hand and his weapon threateningly in the other while his rope lay on the deck at his feet. Maybe the dragonfly was considering whether or not he was a whiner, whether or not to eat him. But then Danny Ray noticed its crown of pearls, the streaks of color in its wings—a rainbow empress!

"KarooKachoo!" cried Danny Ray.

The dragonfly nodded her head.

"We sure appreciate your help! We'd have been in a real peck o' trouble without you!"

Danny Ray reached up and affectionately touched her claw. He smiled to remember her bizarre hair and cheek-stripes, her layers of necklaces and quirky motions. She tilted her wings back and forth, a gesture of goodbye.

Like lightning she flitted away. Gosh! he thought. How could something that big move so quickly? The sun reappeared and the sky became brilliant blue again as the swarm of dragonflies flew away with their gory booty, heading northward, heading home.

"Well, Danny Ray—just like old times, is it not?" cried Quigglewigg, slapping him on the back with a big, orange hand. "Remember how we barely fought off the Sarksa pirates at Port Palnacky? Ha, ha, ha! And see the prizes we've won—four rooks! Look'ee there! *Viper* has struck its flag to *Emerald Castle!*"

The cowboy saw that *Viper* now flew a new purple flag with a white crown—the flag of Elidor. He began gathering up his rope and fastened it to his belt.

"I just wonder how the dragonflies knew we needed help?" asked Captain Quigglewigg.

"They probably saw what was left of *Serpentine* in Dragonfly Bay, sir, and flew south looking for us—and I'm glad they did!"

Pearl threw her gangway across to *Diamond*, and here came Cherry, squealing with delight, followed by Tûk brandishing his pitchfork and Prince Blue his sword, their weapons grimy with whiner blood and insect parts. Behind them walked the beautiful sultana.

"Danny Ray!" cried Cherry, bounding up to him and hugging him around the waist. "You should have seen me! I killed three hundred whiners with my slingshot! I mean, *your* slingshot!"

"Three hundred!" muttered Tûk and rolled his eyes.

"Howdy, Prince," said the cowboy stiffly, touching the rim of his hat.

"Danny Ray," Prince Blue said back.

"Thanks for saving our necks, Captain Sultana," said the cowboy. "You really knocked those whiners outta the sky!"

The sultana just nodded at him, glancing down at the little blond girl who still hadn't let go of the cowboy.

Captain Quigglewigg, shadowed by Hoodie Crow, said, "Well, shall we go and take possession of our captured ships?"

And so they laid a plank across to the decimated deck of *Python*. Piper rubbed his hands deliciously together to see the many salvageable cannon while Hoodie Crow estimated the effort it would take to put the rook to rights again.

Danny Ray walked to the far edge of the rim and looked across at the alien deck of *Dragon*, the third rook in line, and a nervous apprehension came over him. He felt a presence at his elbow. It was Prince Blue, who said, "Let's you and me go over to *Dragon* alone."

The cowboy swallowed hard. He considered Prince Blue's cold eyes, and the cold tone in the first words that had passed between them for a considerable time.

Danny Ray nodded and hitched up his cutlass and rope. His feeling of uneasiness intensified into one of danger as he and Prince Blue jumped the small gap to *Dragon*. Her lookout pole tilted sharply to one side, having taken a random cannonball from *Diamond*, where a metal grommet dangled from her dejected admiral's pendant, bumping softly against a massive iron cannon, sounding off like a bell: *doom . . . doom . . . doom.*

Beyond *Dragon* lay the fourth rook, *Vampire*, just as empty, just as forsaken . . . *doom . . . doom . . . doom.*

Dragon's cannon were all intact (Piper would be glad of that) and the binnacle lantern was unbroken, along with the ship's bell and compass. Danny Ray quickly determined that *Dragon*'s entire crew had been whiners, for her deck was completely deserted. Her great double wheel creaked slightly as the soft wind nudged it back and forth, keeping time with the cannon's hollow *doom . . . doom . . . doom!*

"Downright creepy," said the cowboy, just above a whisper. Arcile flashed wildly on his chest. "Don't like this none."

The tempo of the cannon's hollow warning picked up with the wind—*doom! doom! doom!*

Even in the bright sunlight it was as if they stood in reverence at some unseen crypt, attending to the dead. White sea birds from far away Scorpion Bay circled in the air, strangely mute, hovering long enough to catch the hint, the faint scent of something unholy, and then wheeling madly away on the strengthening wind's edge and beating hectic wings eastward toward home.

Doom! Doom! Doom!

"Yes," said the prince loudly as he worked the handle of his sword, his blue cloak billowing in the wind. "Something's very wrong."

Danny Ray remembered feeling this way before. He searched back through his mind. Of course! During the battle at Port Palnacky when the Sarksa had attacked unexpectedly—from behind!

DOOM!

☙ 27 ☙

The Third Fantasm

Danny Ray and Prince Blue spun around at the same instant. Over the edge of the rim a dreadful figure arose. In the shadows of its black hood flickered orange eyes like solemn candles about a burial pyre, and Danny Ray heard a hiss issuing forth from its red mouth. The awful specter grew in stature, the wind picking up and swirling.

"Ahhh!" little Cherry cried out from over on *Python*'s deck, and fainted dead away. Tûk caught her in his arms.

The fantasm raised a hand and there came a deep rumbling as he used his sheer will to move *Dragon* away from the other ships.

"We're on our own, Danny Ray," said Prince Blue, loud enough to be heard above the wind.

"Two fantasms down," the cowboy said firmly. "One to go!"

The cowboy from Oklahoma and the prince from Elidor stood firm: Prince Blue holding out his sword in front of him, Danny Ray gripping his magical rope with one hand and his cutlass with the other.

"Danny Ray!" cried the sultana from *Python*'s deck as the fantasm stepped down from the wall, his robe strangely unaffected by the wind, and pulled back his hood. Danny Ray saw a hellish crown upon the fantasm's head, of gleaming brimstone set with gems flaming with the fires of the Underworld, from the infernal vaults deep below the earth.

"Finally, we meet, Danny Ray rodeo cowboy!" said the thin, merciless voice, like the razor-sharpness of a knife.

"Real pleasure."

"You know who I am."

"Yeah, you're Ikkus-Sark, but you don't scare me none—king or no king!" said the cowboy, shaking in his boots but still holding his ground.

"Come to me, Danny Ray!" the crowned fantasm laughed. The sound of its sharp tone caused a sweat to break out on the cowboy's forehead. "I shall give up your body to the Fiends to savage and to rip and to devour; your tongue to the wolf of the weald to tear out at the roots and eat; your eyes to the savage black vultures of Dumzil-Daz to be pecked out and feasted upon!"

"You fantasms sure talk a lot about eatin' eyeballs!" said the cowboy. He cleared his throat and said. "Now, listen up. Hand over Princess Amber or I'll stick you good with this here cutlass—I ain't kidding!"

"Who are you to demand anything of me?" So cold was the questioning voice that the cowboy felt unable to move, his cutlass frozen in place. "Prepare yourself, Danny Ray, for I shall now reveal the full extent of my power!"

With a sickening oozing sound, the fantasm's skin split open down the back, the form of a serpent emerging, fantastically large. Fearful horns tore their way out of the fantasm's forehead and its face ripped open to reveal something frightful, a nightmare of scales and sharp teeth. Its body and legs wiggled free of its shell, armored in golden scales with a regiment of plates, angular and sharp, marching down its back. It trampled the black robe beneath its huge bulk. The monster stood serpentlike, towering over them and peering down with bloodred eyes, and the mouth sagged open to reveal a long, slippery tongue.

"He was ugly enough as it was," said Danny Ray, stepping back. "At least he didn't stink like a big lizard!"

"Watch out!" cried the prince.

The monster raised a heavy clawed foot, slamming it down on the steerage wheel, which exploded in a shower of splinters.

"Get back to *Diamond* with the others!" yelled the cowboy, Arcile sparkling hot on his chest with an enemy so near. "I can hold him back!"

"I'm staying," said Prince Blue, coming to stand by the cowboy.

"Look out!" cried Danny Ray.

The serpent swung its spiked tail and lifted a cannon from the deck, sending it screaming at the pair of boys! They fell backward—the mass of gray iron moaned over them to within an inch of their noses! It crashed through the far rim, sending stones and dust into the air, falling hundreds of feet below to the rock-hard surface of the sea.

The dragon's black forked tongue flickered in and out over its thin lips. It stalked toward the prone pair.

"Look!" blurted Prince Blue.

Danny Ray's blood ran cold. The beast lowered its head and opened its vast jaws, and with its mouth gaping wide, there appeared a fair face from down in its throat—it was Princess Amber!

"I see her!" said Danny Ray. His blood, so cold a second before, now boiled.

Whirrr! Whirrr! Whirrr! sang the cowboy's sparkling rope of thrillium as he twirled it over his head. "Time to rope me a dinosaur!"

The dragon lunged at Prince Blue with its knife-sharp teeth. Instantly, Danny Ray let go his rope, looping it around the monster's neck.

"*ARRRRRRRRRRRRG!*" moaned the dragon, whipping its frightful, horned head up toward the clouds.

"Yeeeeeeeeeeeeeeeehah!" yelled the cowboy as he was catapulted off his feet and swung up high in the air! In a flash, Danny Ray could see the entire deck and the other rooks lined up in a row. He caught a faraway glimpse of Tûk pointing up at him from *Python*'s deck, of Captain Quigglewigg who stood next to the sultana, whose mouth was opened in an anguished scream. Down he swung, his boots skimming the deck, then into the air again, twirling and twisting as the rope wrapped again and again around the evil fantasm's neck.

"Loopty-loop! Yeeeeeeeehah!" screamed the cowboy, swinging around again as the rope tightened. "I've ridden some pretty mean steers, Mr. Ikkus-Sark, but none as ugly as you, and none that stank this bad, neither!"

The dragon lolled its head, its eyes bulging out from its sockets—buggy and bloodshot.

"Ummmphf!" grunted Danny Ray as he came down hard on the beast and let go of the rope. He slid down and clung to a sharp armored plate, his boots dancing high above the deck. The great lizard roared ferociously, raking at its neck with a clawed foot as the rope of gleaming thrillium continued to tighten.

A small section of the dragon's plate armor began to crackle and burn where Danny Ray lay against it. The dragon pointed its sharp snout to the heavens and roared in pain. It became clear to Danny Ray—Arcile! The White Lady had said the magic stone around his neck was death to the fantasms, and now, pressed against the dragon, it had burned away an armor plate from its throat.

WHAM! The cowboy plummeted onto the deck as the dragon shook him off, making a gurgling sound.

Whiiiiiiing! Something flew by Danny Ray's head, a twirling rotating sword! Its aim was deadly, its aim was true, and it struck deep in the vulnerable bare patch on the fantasm's throat.

"Look out!" screamed the sultana from a distance.

The dragon-creature staggered, let out one more pitiful moan, and crashed to the deck, the impact throwing Danny Ray and Prince Blue back against the wall of the rim. The cowboy lost no time. He grabbed his cutlass and ran at the beast, raising the heavy blade over his head and slashing down on its scaly neck in a swift, sure stroke, severing it halfway.

The rise and fall of the creature's faint breathing ceased.

"Lookee there!" crowed Danny Ray, poking the red inside of its neck with his sword. "USDA prime cut fillet!"

"We did it again, Danny Ray!" beamed the prince, shaking the cowboy's hand. It was the first time in a long time Danny Ray had seen the prince smile. "Like when we rescued *Winter Queen* and killed the Sarksa commodore, remember?"

"Just like old times!" agreed Danny Ray, leaning back against a brass cannon and tipping back the brim of his hat.

"Wait!" gasped Prince Blue. He quickly knelt down between the dragon's gaping teeth and began tugging, tugging, tugging at something. A pair of wet hands appeared out of that open mouth and frantically grasped his! The prince gave one last pull and someone oozed out. With her hair all wet and slimy, her beautiful robe all coated in gook and goo, there lay Princess Amber, gasping for air!

"No! Stay away!" she said, clinging to the prince while glaring up with frightened eyes at the cowboy.

"Princess Amber!" said the cowboy, hurt. "It's me, Danny Ray!"

"Stay away from me!"

Dragon vibrated as *Python* nudged up against her. Captain Quigglewigg came running up, followed by the sultana, Tûk, Cherry, Hoodie Crow, and the rest of *Diamond*'s crew. The hellwain devil shot immediately to Prince Blue's side and then growled at the lifeless form of the serpent.

"Congratulations, Danny Ray!" cried the captain, shaking the cowboy's hand. He noticed the cowboy's discouraged face. "But of course the poor princess is shocked at the sight of you—all agore with dragon blood!"

"Get away from her—everyone!" Cherry said, pushing

through the crowd. She knelt down beside Princess Amber and held her trembling hand, saying softly, "Your Majesty—it's me, Cherry, your Traveling Maiden!"

"Cherry?" Princess Amber said weakly, and shielded her eyes from the harsh sunlight.

"Leave her alone! All of you!" ordered Cherry, waving them away with a frantic arm.

As Danny Ray turned away, he felt a hand laid on his shoulder. "You did it, Danny Ray!" exclaimed the sultana. "The princess is safe!"

He looked back to watch Cherry fussing with her mistress, and frowned slightly.

"What is it?" she asked.

"It just now hit me—how much Princess Amber looks like Caroline Robertson."

"Caroline?" she asked, raising an eyebrow.

"My girlfriend back home," he said, and then instantly regretted it.

"Oh," said the sultana.

"Wait . . . not really. I mean, she's not really—"

"Never mind," said the sultana, brightening up.

But Danny Ray noticed that her brown eyes weren't shining anymore. They had a dead look. "It's time for me to return to my ship. Goodbye, Danny Ray."

The cowboy sighed. Sure, Caroline Robertson was the prettiest girl in school, and sometimes he sorta liked her, but it wasn't like he really, really, really liked her.

He wondered what name they had in this world for a low-down sap-suckin' jerk who hurt his girl's feelings. And then it dawned on him: the sultana wasn't his girl—he'd never even told her he liked her.

He watched her glittering figure walk away, head down. He wanted to run after her, to tell her he liked her a whole bunch, that she was the main reason he had come back to Elidor. But shoot! She'd only laugh at him. Just his luck—the first girl he ever really, really liked, didn't like him back. Plus, she was from another doggone world!

Danny Ray stomped his foot with temper. Yeah, just his luck. Just his dirty, rotten, stinkin', low-down, no-good, rock-bottom luck!

⋇ 28 ⋇

A Gold Ring

The late evening stars marched up from the east, chasing away the blue sky as the sun dipped below the western horizon. Danny Ray stood in the darkness of *Diamond*'s lower gun deck at the back of the ship, watching the black-and-white squares of the Checkered Sea disappear into the gloom where followed the other rooks: *Viper*, commanded by Hoodie Crow; *Python*, by Piper; *Dragon*, by *Diamond*'s second lieutenant, Jenkins; and *Vampire* by Tûk. Quigglewigg had been reluctant to give command of a ship to a hellwain devil and former pirate, and Tûk had been equally reluctant to leave Prince Blue's side. But clearly, the devil had proved his loyalty and knew the business of sailing a rook. *Emerald Castle*, being the lightest and fastest of the rooks, had sailed off to Elidor ahead of the squadron to alert King Krystal to the good news of his daughter's rescue.

Pearl, commanded by the Sultana Sumferi Sar, had departed. Danny Ray's heart sank. He would miss the sultana, and he would miss the graceful bishop's diagonal zigzaging among the grim, stubby, unimaginative rooks as they plied vertically straight south toward Elidor.

The cowboy shivered, and pulled the fluffy collar of his sleeping robe closer about his neck.

"Danny Ray?" Princess Amber emerged out of the shadows. Cherry followed behind the princess and placed a furry cloak around her shoulders to ward off the cold.

The cowboy became tongue-tied as she joined him, for even without her royal jewels, her necklace and earrings of diamonds and emeralds, she possessed a soft, mesmerizing beauty.

"I didn't recognize you without your rodeo clothes," she said, smiling.

Danny Ray hung his head. "Well, I gotta wear this ol' robe until my clothes get washed up clean. Sorry I scared you before—I must have been a sight, all covered with dragon guts and stuff."

She looked up into the night sky. "There is no moon this night. Once again you have saved my life just in time, Danny Ray—I have not forgotten you rescued me from marrying King Dru-Mordeloch of Trowland!"

"I wasn't alone in fighting Ikkus-Sark, Your Highness," pointed out the cowboy. "Prince Blue sure helped."

"Oh, him," she said. A line appeared across her forehead. She hesitated and then said: "He seems to have changed, Danny Ray. Have you noticed?"

The cowboy took a deep breath. "Well, I reckon he's under a lot of pressure from being the future King of Elidor and all. I wouldn't think too much of it if I was you."

"That's not what you said about the prince before, Danny Ray!" piped up Cherry.

"Be still there, Cherry!" cautioned Princess Amber. She looked back at the cowboy, a whimsical smile playing about her lips, and then up into the night sky. "Oh! Look into the heavens! It is the night of the new moon!"

Sure enough, not even the barest sliver of a moon accompanied the stars. And with that, Princess Amber kissed him on the cheek and he shivered all over again. As she placed her hands in his, the cowboy's eyes widened.

"Gosh, your hands are cold, Your Highness!"

Princess Amber's smile became sad. "I feel as though I am still in the grip of death, Danny Ray, that the door is so thin between me and the grave! Please, oh, please, don't let go of my hands! It's the only warmth I've felt in such a long time!"

"Do you remember the White Lady?" asked Danny Ray. Princess Amber looked at him with blank eyes. "She was cold as ice, too!"

"I remember the chains of fire that I wore," she said, grimacing.

"Well, I saw you with a bunch of other folks riding horses real slow."

"Why, yes . . . I think I do remember riding a steed, yes," she said uncertainly.

"Did the fantasms hurt you, Princess?"

"I don't want to talk about it."

The cowboy understood. He made up his mind then and there not to let anything happen to her the rest of the way back to Elidor.

"What's bothering you, Danny Ray?" she asked somberly.

He scratched the back of his neck. "The White Lady, she told me a riddle—and doggone it all if I could ever figure it out! But now, with you back safe with us and ol' Ikkus-Sark killed, that riddle don't seem to matter anymore! Still, it bugs the life outta me why she'd bother to give me a puzzle I didn't even need."

Danny Ray fell under the spell of Amber's dreamy eyes as she studied him. Her light laughter distracted him from his thoughts. "Oh! I am so impossible!" she chided. "Where are my manners, la? I simply must reward my hero from Oklahoma! Give me your hand!"

The princess brought out a gold ring and placed it on the cowboy's finger. Danny Ray felt light-headed and giddy.

"Well, shoot! I'm starting to collect some pretty fancy things!" laughed the cowboy at last, looking at the new ring glimmering on his finger. "Downstairs in my cabin I have a necklace—Mr. Tabbashavar gave it to me. It's real pretty! I'm not saying this ring ain't real nice, mind you, Your Highness. But Arcile—that's the name of the gem on my necklace—well, it's magic. It burned a hole right through that ol' serpent's chest, scales and all! But, you know, since I have this here ring from you, I may give Arcile as a gift to King Krystal."

"Arcile was given as a gift to you, Danny Ray!" said Princess Amber with a smile a good deal warmer than her hands, he noted. "You must learn to treasure your treasures, to keep them for yourself!"

"That got me in trouble, already," said Danny Ray grimly. "I left the Heart of Ildirim sitting on my dresser back home—the sultana got on to me for it."

"Danny Ray, a gift is something that the giver should never require to be returned." The princess tenderly squeezed his hands and smiled. "If the sultana can give you a magical stone, then I can give you a present, la? This ring forms a strong bond between us, Danny Ray."

She looked up into his eyes with such warm emotion that the roof of his mouth tingled. He blushed and breathed nervously, looking down at the ring. It was like going steady or something—like getting engaged to a princess!

Danny Ray felt very tired, downright bone-weary. The exhausting events of the day were catching up to him fast.

She seemed to sense it, and said: "Good night, Danny Ray."

Danny Ray tipped his hat and trudged toward bed.

Ah! Fresh, chilly wind!

It was morning and Danny Ray, standing on deck, pushed back his hat and let his hair wave in the wind. He took grateful gulps of the biting cold air. The ship's scrub-a-dub man had done a good job: the cowboy's blue and white checked shirt was clean and crisp and his jeans were as good as new. *Diamond*'s crew had done the same kind of cleanup for the ship, preparing her marvelously for King Krystal's review in Elidor. Those few cannon that were brass had been polished till they gleamed, along with the ship's bell and all the silver knobs and handles. The sailors had newly plaited pigtails and fresh frocks and trousers. Ropes lay in neat coils and the deck was gleaming white, having been sanded and flogged dry as the sun cleared the glittering horizon.

Danny Ray's heart was glad and yet a weariness lay over him. Arcile lay sparkling on his chest, and his ring glowed strangely warm and dull. He looked behind *Diamond* to see the four captured rooks, now flying the purple and white flag of Elidor, flapping, clapping, and slapping in the stiff breeze.

Two bells sounded out.

"Land ho!"

Feet pattered across the deck as more sailors appeared out of every nook and cranny of the ship, heeding the call from the lookout as they scurried to their proper stations. Danny Ray's heart skipped a beat as the blue line of the Elidorian mountains peeked up from the south.

Captain Quigglewigg appeared on deck and smiled across to the cowboy as he leveled his glass toward the land mass that grew larger by the minute.

"Danny Ray." Prince Blue nodded, his neatly laundered blue robe showing no signs of combat. His demeanor was somewhat stiff again as he looked over the cowboy's stain-free clothes and the magical rope of thrillium hitched to his belt.

"Morning to you!" said the cowboy and pointed. "Yonder's Elidor. Shucks! We'll be there in no time! We'll sleep in a bed tonight that doesn't shake!"

"Where'd you get the gold ring, Danny Ray?" asked Prince Blue.

"Oh! That's nothin'." The cowboy shrugged. "Princess Amber sorta gave it to me—don't know why, really."

Prince Blue walked away in silence.

The wonderful towers and harbor of Elidor with their colorful banners sparkled in the strong sunlight! *Diamond*, leading the four captured rooks, sailed between the twin guardians of Birdwhistle Bay, the Tower of Fire and Tower of the Rose, and into the harbor. A huge wave of celebration, of jubilation, engulfed them. Brightly colored streamers twirled down onto the deck from excited spectators watching from the walls of the bay, watching from the towers, watching from the palace's high ground, or watching from the heights of Mount Featherfrost.

Captain Peach's *Emerald Castle* was docked nearby, and as *Diamond* drew closer, Danny Ray could make out on her deck the tall, golden-robed figure of King Krystal, his glass crown glinting in the sun. He could hardly wait to see King Krystal's face when he laid his tired, yearning eyes on his daughter!

Captain Quigglewigg, with Prince Blue behind him, came to stand at the bow of the ship as a purple-carpeted plank, complete with brass hand railings, was placed between the two rooks.

Here came King Krystal walking along the gangway, his face beaming, his cheeks rosier than Danny Ray had ever seen them. Behind him walked Captain Ritchie Peach, Lord Red, along with the rest of Elidor's distinguished royal court. Only Lord Green stayed back on *Emerald Castle*.

"Your Majesty!" said Quigglewigg solemnly, taking off his half-moon hat and bowing with one leg extended forward.

Prince Blue bowed.

Danny Ray folded his arms. There was nothing to do but smile. They were back home in Elidor!

An Unlikely Hero

"Captain Quigglewigg!" announced King Krystal to the orange-faced commander. "Once again, a quest under your auspicious leadership has ended in timely success! And now, where is my princess? Where is my lovely Amber?"

"Still below in her cabin, Your Majesty," replied the captain. "Still freshening up for this grandest of all reunions!"

An old, gray-haired sailor nudged Danny Ray. "What a change, eh, in one passin' of the hinges?"

"How's that?" asked the cowboy.

"Well, I mean, yisdidy mornin' we'ms fightin' fer our lives what we ain't even yet laid eyes on the princesses. And here we is, next morn, and we'm in Birdwhistle Bay, what wid the king all happy an' his datter all safe n' sound like."

"Wait a darn minute." Something like a warning bell went off in the cowboy's head. "You said something about hinges?"

"Oh." The sailor waved. "Hinges of the day. That's an old accountin' for the passing o' one day to the next: they's noontide, dusk, midnight, early dawn—four or 'em." He nudged

Danny Ray and displayed a smile with no upper teeth. "No-body but us old-timers uses that phrase no more."

A cold shock went through the cowboy. The stanzas of the White Lady's riddle flitted through his brain. Of course! He had made the riddle way too complicated.

"The answer is four!" Danny Ray said out loud.

"What that, then?" asked the old sailor, cupping his ear to hear over the ruckus and renewed cheering as King Krystal's foot touched *Diamond*'s deck and Captain Quigglewigg walked forward to shake his royal, ring-covered hand.

There were four hinges of the day; there were four seasons—fall, winter, spring, summer; four winds—east, south, north, west; four chess pieces besides the king—queen, bishop, knight, rook; four squares in the middle of the chessboard!

The riddle's answer was simple—it was the number four! That was what the White Lady had meant to tell him all along: there were not just three fantasms—there were four! Doggone it! The fantasms needed only one more king, not two, to plunge the world into everlasting darkness!

Danny Ray's breathing became short, panicky. Now what was it the mirrathaní, the silver face, had said to him? The fantasms would attempt to bring their number to five by getting a good, righteous king to embrace evil: to *EMBRACE* evil!

The cowboy shot a look over to the king and then to the back of the ship. The princess was still below. Good—at least she was safe . . . for now. Danny Ray's eyes riveted onto Prince Blue, saw him step forward, saw him smile at the aged, defenseless king, who naturally brought up his arms to embrace his prince.

This was the terrible moment—he had to move fast!

Clop! Clop! Clop! went his cowboy boots as he raced across the deck, the wind whistling in his ears as he picked up speed. He lowered his shoulder like an Oklahoma Sooner linebacker and collided with the unsuspecting prince, and his cowboy hat flew up in the air.

Ummmf! The sound popped out of Prince Blue as excruciating pain mixed with surprise as he was knocked clean off his feet and across the deck into the scuppers. The multitude of Elidorians let their hands drop as they gasped in horror.

King Krystal was too shocked to speak, and before he could even move, the cowboy straightened up, took off his necklace, and placed Arcile about the king's neck.

"There!" said the cowboy, patting the amazed monarch on the chest. "This will protect you, sir!"

"What . . . what is the meaning of this, Danny Ray!" the old king blazed.

Lord Red had recovered his wits enough to pull the cowboy's arms behind his back and propel him over hard against the rim. Danny Ray chuckled like a crazy man and looked out over the expanse of Birdwhistle Bay hundreds of feet below him. "I'm placing you under arrest," Lord Red said, "you infuriating, insulting little—"

"What's wrong with you, Danny Ray!" gasped Captain Quigglewigg.

Lord Red pronounced, "It's Dumbledown Dungeon for you after all, Otherworld Cowboy Hero!"

If the crowd's cheering had been loud in their chorus of rapt joy, an even louder wave of indignant outrage flowed over *Diamond* like a tidal wave. Tûk shouted and stomped up and down in frenzied rage from the rim of *Vampire*, waving his pitchfork, furious with the cowboy from Oklahoma for what he had done to his master, and furious with himself for having left Prince Blue's side.

The cowboy felt a face come very near to his, the mouth inches from his ear. It was the prince, who had gathered himself up from the deck, his voice almost hissing with controlled rage. "So, Danny Ray, you have finally done it. Here in front of everyone—finally gone completely mad!"

The cowboy grinned but then groaned—"uh!"—as Lord Red pinned his arms tighter behind his back. Danny Ray looked sideways at Prince Blue. "I was right about you the first time, Prince. Yep. You're a fantasm, all right!"

Lord Red stood him up and turned him around, keeping an iron grip on his elbow, his black mustachio twitching with temper.

The king came to face the cowboy. "Danny Ray, I cannot begin to voice my disappointment and displeasure at your conduct!" The king thumped the deck with his silver cane. "Here, at our grandest, happiest hour you display the vilest, meanest behavior!"

"He's not the same cowboy that rescued *Winter Queen*, Your Majesty," said Prince Blue.

"You'd like to make them think I'm off my rocker, wouldn't you, Prince?" shot back Danny Ray. "But I got you figured out, boy! And you're going to find it mighty hard to embrace the king with that there gem around his neck!"

"Embrace me?" asked the king, shocked.

"The fantasms are after you, Your Majesty!" said Danny Ray, sniffing. "I just now figured out the riddle the White Lady told me: the fantasms only need one more king, not two, to complete their number—to make it to five! And then this world, your world, sir, will be returned to darkness, like the day of doom when there's no sun or moon—the Age of Stars!"

"What's this about a White Lady?" The king looked down at the gem sparkling on his chest. His crown sparkled as he shook his head, trying to make sense of what the cowboy was saying.

"I never saw a White Lady," offered Prince Blue smoothly. "Neither did anyone else—except Danny Ray."

"Explain where I got Arcile if there ain't no White Lady!" said the cowboy crossly.

The prince winced with pain as he leaned back against the rook's rim. "Maybe from your treasure bag?"

"One thought has troubled me from the outset," said the king offhandedly. "Why did the fantasms even bother to kidnap Princess Amber?"

Danny Ray's mind reeled. "Wait, sir!" he said. "That's it!"

"What's it?" asked both the king and prince at the same time.

Danny Ray was quiet. Thinking.

"He's gone mad, is what's it!" said Lord Red, nodding vehemently.

"Father!"

There, across the deck, stood the beautiful Princess Amber with Cherry holding the train of her dress, a cream-colored gown that accentuated the beautiful lightness of her eyes. She beckoned with her arms outstretched and repeated, "Father!"

"My dear daughter! My dearest Amber!" King Krystal stood, as if in a trance, and a single tear of singular joy found its way down his cheek. "And Cherry!"

Cherry lost all restraint and ran across the full length of the deck, hugging King Krystal and burying her face in the folds of his robe. He patted her on top of the head and chuckled, "Oh, my little Cherry has come home to me!"

"Father!" repeated Princess Amber.

King Krystal took a step forward and then caught himself. He looked back and said to Lord Red: "Keep your hold on Danny Ray—he must not bring harm to my daughter! We will sift through this later when he is safely in the Dumbledown Dungeon!"

"Wait a minute—please, Your Majesty!" said Danny Ray. A frightening memory hit him. "The White Lady: she told me that asking the right question would clear everything up." He slapped himself on the thigh. "It was right in front of my dog-gone face the whole doggone time! You just asked the million-dollar question, sir. Why did the fantasms bother to kidnap the princess in the first place?"

King Krystal opened his mouth and then plopped it shut again.

"You tell us, rodeo cowboy," said Lord Red.

Danny Ray looked straight at the king. "The fantasms know, Your Majesty, that when Amber returned, the first thing you would do is give her a big hug!"

"Oh, the embrace thing again!" snorted Prince Blue.

"So now you are accusing my own daughter of treachery!" blazed the king.

"Impossible!" said Cherry with a grimace.

"Inexcusable!" declared Lord Red.

"First, you entirely neglect to bow before me, to show me respect as ruler of Elidor!" said King Krystal, pointing at the cowboy with his cane. "Then, you wrongly assault and injure the prince right before my eyes!"

Danny Ray hung his head. "You're right, sir, I was wrong about the prince."

Prince Blue clapped his hands lightly together. "Bravo, Danny Ray."

But the king was not done with him. "And then, when you realize your mistake, Danny Ray, you accuse my own precious Amber!" He thumped his silver cane again angrily.

King Krystal turned to go to his daughter. Danny Ray realized he would have to act quick.

"Wait, sir! Didn't you tell me, sir, that the birds in Birdwhistle Bay would fly around happy like and start chirping again, and that the trees would stop droopin' their branches—once the princess returned?"

Prince Blue stood bolt upright. He and the king shot a look over *Diamond*'s rim, down to the gardens and roadway bordering the bay.

"Father!" cried the princess again, pleading. She had come halfway across the deck.

"Hmmm," said the king, twirling a wisp of his white beard around his forefinger. "The birds are not singing. And the great Tree of Wisdom is as despondent as ever, leaning over wretchedly, like an old man. How can this be?"

"It's because," Danny Ray said softly, his voice shaking, "it's because the princess ain't really here. We were deceived from the very start, sir. That night at the Temple of the Dead, when we saw the vision of the princess surrounded by the three fantasms, we saw what we wanted to see. But what we were really seeing was four fantasms, not three!"

"If the princess is not here, then who," asked the king solemnly, "who is standing yonder beckoning to me?"

It was Cherry who first understood the awful implication of what the cowboy said. Her eyes went wide and her lower lip began to quiver.

Prince Blue looked first to the king, and then out toward Amber.

"Lord Red," commanded the king quietly, "you may release Danny Ray."

The cowboy rubbed feeling back into his arms and reached down, never taking his eyes off Princess Amber, and retrieved his cowboy hat.

"Father!" cried Amber as her eyes fastened on Arcile securely fastened about the king's neck. "What is that necklace you are wearing?"

"It is a gift, from Danny Ray," he responded, in a shaky voice.

"I told that detestable cowboy not to give it to you, Papa!" said Princess Amber, tears filling her eyes. She cast a hurt look at Danny Ray. "I wanted to give you my gift first, Father!"

"Oh, my dear!" he said, taking a feeble step toward her. "What gift do you have for me?"

"Something special, Papa," She wiped at her wet cheek. "But you must throw away that necklace!"

"But why?"

"Papa, please!"

King Krystal looked at her dreamily, her lovely eyes, her perfect nose, her lovely chin. But her eyes shifted to Prince Blue as he placed his hand on the king's arm, holding him back, his other hand resting on the hilt of his sword. Cherry peered out nervously from the radiant gold folds of the king's robe.

"Let me go to her!" breathed King Krystal.

"Stay right here with us, Your Majesty," said Danny Ray firmly, coming to stand on the other side of the king with Lord Red.

"Father?" cried Princess Amber, standing alone in the middle of the deck.

"Come to me, my darling daughter!" cried King Krystal, holding out his arms, his cane falling from his outstretched hand and clattering noisily to the deck.

"First, throw away that awful necklace!" she gasped.

"Don't do it, sir," Danny Ray cautioned.

The king's hand went to his neck, and hesitated. Princess Amber stood stock-still. Her eyes looked back and forth at the line of grim faces before her.

Danny Ray spit on the deck and said: "The game is up, Ikkus-Sark. We're on to you!"

A tongue appeared from Princess Amber's mouth and licked her lips. Her chin rose proudly. Hard lines appeared in that soft face. Her stern eyes followed the movement of the troublesome cowboy from the Otherworld as he unfastened his rope. Danny Ray heard the faint sound of grating metal as Prince Blue and Lord Red drew their swords and advanced toward her on one side, Captain Quigglewigg on the other. She nodded ever so slightly, ever so knowingly.

The princess smiled a terrible smile.

She raised her hand—*CRACKLE!* Bolts of lightning flashed through Danny Ray and the others. He sank to his knees in pain, his magical rope dropping lifelessly out of his hand. Lord Red and Quigglewigg cried out, "Ah!" as they fell back in a heap. Their swords flew from their grasps into the sky and exploded in a shower of sharp fragments.

THWAAAANK! Prince Blue's sword flew across the deck. It buried itself hilt deep in the gray stone of *Diamond*'s thick rim—only the handle showed.

"Amber!" repeated King Krystal, weeping outright.

Her eyes rolled back; they were now a blazing orange. Cherry screamed as the princess's dress ripped apart in a roar of hot wind. A dark form rose from the image of what once was Princess Amber.

"Ikkus-Sark!" muttered the cowboy, lying prone, feeling the rough deck against the side of his face. The charmed golden ring glowed sinisterly on his finger, its invisible iron bonds holding the cowboy down. Gosh! How could he have been so stupid? The White Lady had warned him that fair friends might be foul, and those who seemed foul, like the prince, would actually be fair!

Ikkus-Sark's black armor smoldered as if just taken from an oven. On his chest was fastened the Black Zazg, an ancient medal in the shape of a flying creature, its gems sparkling in hellish delight and marking him as a principal ruler of the Underworld. He exercised his skeleton fingers, closing them around the hilt of his sword, that ancient blade of abomination named of old Zazkamuzkûn, which in ages past slew the nobility of the

Varaldir. As he drew it forth, flames licked along the blade inscribed with runes of corruption, of perdition, of damnation.

The King of Fantasms looked about the bay, orange slits regarding the crowds as they fled in panic. Let them run. He would deal with all the rabble later, after he made King Krystal the fifth fantasm, when the Age of Stars would be ushered in!

Behind the dark ruler, outlined against a curtain of flames, stood the forms of the three slain fantasms, waiting eagerly for their redemption when King Krystal would embrace evil and complete their number. For eons upon eons had the King of Fantasms been held fast, waiting for this precise moment of triumph, of release from prisons of doom within the bounds of deep earth.

The eyes, flaming like coals, looked down on King Krystal, and the dread king's command sounded as if it came from beneath the earth: "Let us embrace, oh King of Elidor! Join now our brotherhood and let all bonds of light be cast aside! Embrace me and so regain your youth: reign with me, forever!"

Danny Ray was just able to turn his head. A dull shock went through him: the great horned shadow was the same demon that had accosted him in the storm on his journey from the magical doorway to Elidor.

This terrible moment was too much for frail King Krystal, standing alone, face turned upward toward Ikkus-Sark. His feeble hand found Arcile and gripped it firmly.

"Let all bonds of light be cast aside!" thundered the King of Fantasms.

The King of Elidor writhed in the vortex of a fire storm.

Ikkus-Sark's power was too great, and King Krystal's hand shook as he tore away the necklace and dashed it down on the deck. Arcile rolled free and came to rest a few paces from Danny Ray, flashing and glittering white. Prince Blue and Captain Quigglewigg along with Lord Red remained down. No help would be coming from the other rooks.

Danny Ray could just barely pull himself forward with his arms. It felt like an eternity to the cowboy just to move a few inches, as if a cannon were lashed to his back. At last! His hand closed around the precious gem, the same hand that wore the golden ring.

"Ahhhh!" He winced with pain, for as pure Arcile touched the evil golden band given to him by the fantasm, it blazed and burned. The cowboy cried out, an intense light streaming out from between his clenched fingers until the unholy ring was utterly consumed.

But it was then that the cowboy caught sight of someone so small and insignificant that she had been overlooked in the fiery moment, still hiding in the golden folds of the old king's robe.

"Cherry." Danny Ray was barely able to say her name. His mouth tasted like paste. "Cherry!"

Her mouth gaped wide, the sound of her weeping drowned out in the roaring flames.

"Here!" he croaked, from a desert-dry throat. With his last effort, with a burned, trembling hand, the cowboy raised Arcile and feebly tossed it Cherry's way. The gem sparkled wildly as it rolled, unnoticed, across the deck and beneath the king's robe. She looked back at the cowboy with terrified eyes.

"You can do it!" the cowboy mouthed. He knew they were doomed, unless—he could give Cherry a chance.

With the ring destroyed, Ikkus-Sark's binding will upon the cowboy was broken. Danny Ray found he could get to his knees, to his feet. Wearily, he trudged to the side, and just as feebly, waved his arms back and forth, trying to draw attention away from King Krystal. An anguished cry escaped his raw throat.

For that brief moment, that split second, Ikkus-Sark's binding gaze fell away from the King of Elidor. With venomous fury, an orange ball of flame shot from Ikkus-Sark's hand and bowled the cowboy over backward.

Danny Ray lay there, still as death. His strength was completely sapped. He rested his head on his arm and watched, with dull fascination, the towering black form of Ikkus-Sark looming overhead, as he began to extend his black-armored arms to King Krystal. Closer they drew to one another. Closer to an embrace.

And then it happened.

Out from the folds of the king's robe stepped a little blond girl with a slingshot fitted with Arcile, that ancient talisman, one of the great Stones of Audrehelm; and the slingshot was aimed high overhead directly at the King of Fantasms.

The great demon ruler of the underworld paused. Doubt clutched his proud heart, shaking his very soul. He had not bothered to charm the insignificant little girl as he had done the troublesome cowboy from the Otherworld.

He drew himself up, and his vast power spread out like dark wings. Fear, pure, unrefined fear would quell this little upstart, the last impediment to his dark empire. Cherry's hands shook, the slingshot still drawn fully back.

"You can do it, Cherry!" yelled the cowboy loudly, above the firestorm.

"I can't!" she cried finally, her hair blowing wildly with her dress. "He's too big to hit!"

"Cherry," called Danny Ray feebly. "He's too big to miss!"

And all of a sudden, her back straightened. Her eyes flashed with the light of revenge. Amid that torrent of flame, her hands grew calm, her arms as firm and strong as the slingshot itself.

TWAAAAANG!

Arcile blazed upward, meteorlike. It caught Ikkus-Sark square in the forehead, sinking in deep. With a loud shout that shook the foundations of Birdwhistle Bay, that caused the very towers to tremble, the King of the Fantasms fell straight down upon the deck, like a black tower collapsing within itself.

A wave of black ash engulfed the king and Cherry. It rolled like a tidal wave across the deck toward the cowboy, reaching out with grasping fingers and smothering him, and it sighed with the groan of a dying demon departing this world, heavy with the weight of doom.

And then darkness closed in on Danny Ray; darkness, nothing but darkness.

❧ 30 ❧

The Woolly Wulver

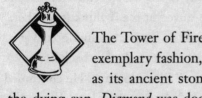The Tower of Fire was living up to its name in exemplary fashion, blazing like an orange finger as its ancient stonework reflected the fury of the dying sun. *Diamond* was docked near its foundation, her scorched and marred rim less noticeable in the growing darkness of approaching night.

The rodeo cowboy pushed his hat back and leaned against the Tree of Wisdom. A pitiful sigh passed through the old, gnarled branches, and a few despondent leaves flitted down to join their death-stricken fellows in a carpet of gold.

"We've come full circle, Danny Ray," said Prince Blue sadly, sitting in the exact place where King Krystal had seen them off aboard *Serpentine*. "It's not like last time when we ended at Grand Hall in broad daylight, me as the new Prince Blue and you holding the cage of the clabbernappers."

"And me being cast in to Dumbledown Dungeon!" barked Tûk, leaning against his pitchfork.

"At least I did my job back then, rescuing *Winter Queen* and all," commented the cowboy, his face becoming incredibly sad.

"She's very far away," said Prince Blue, shifting his gaze to the flaming sky. "Her song is growing fainter, like the sun fleeing to the west."

"Who is far away?" asked the cowboy.

"Princess Amber," he replied.

"I feel rotten about not rescuing her," replied Danny Ray heavily. "You know, come to think on it, it was the real Princess Amber that I saw in the graveyard at Dragonfly Bay riding her horse real slow like, on her way to the Vale of the Moon. The look in her eyes, the way she waved at me, I think it was her." He pulled a sparkling marble out of his pocket and looked at it. "Even with Arcile I couldn't get Princess Amber back home."

"We all failed her," said Prince Blue gloomily. He continued with great gravity in his voice. "Me in particular. I have been thinking a great deal about the terrible manner in which I be-haved on this quest." Prince Blue hung his head. "You should be king of Elidor, Danny Ray, not me."

"Don't know much about kinging," said the cowboy with a shrug. "All that throne-sittin' and parties and such. And besides, 'King Danny' would look downright goofy printed on my luggage—wouldn't it? Nah, something tells me you'll work things out."

"But Danny Ray, you solved the Riddle of the Fantasms. You have kingly intelligence!"

"I reckon the White Lady helped out there," said the cow-boy, scratching his chin. "She promised to give me Wisdom. I don't think I'd have figured it out elsewise."

"But I couldn't even defend Elidor, my own kingdom,"

remarked the prince. "I needed Cherry, a snippy little girl, to defeat the King of Fantasms!"

"Well, how do you think I feel?" said Danny Ray. "I'm supposed to be some big-shot Otherworld rodeo cowboy, and Cherry uses my slingshot to do the job that I was sent here to do. And don't forget that song I sang her on Sugarwood Island about boys being better than girls. Both of us got a lot of crow to eat!"

"Yes," mused the prince. "There's more to Cherry than meets the eye."

"I guess she upstaged us both, didn't she?"

"Yup!" Tûk snickered, champing his fangs together in a horrible smile.

They all fell silent, each of them deep in thought. "Well, don't fret too hard or your head might cave in! Yessir, or it might pop right off and go rolling down the road!" Danny Ray felt the edge of his singed hat and sighed. "Hey, Prince Blue, I was pretty rotten, too, you know. I jabbed you in the neck with the dagger, remember?"

"Yes, but I let you be whipped with the cat, Danny Ray."

"Yeah, but I stuck my foot in my mouth with the Queen of Dragonflies!"

"Yes, but I would have left Sugarwood Island without you," said the prince miserably.

"Yeah, but I knocked the daylights outta you just yesterday—"

"Yes, but I coveted the commodore's decorated and bejeweled watch with the gossip hidden inside that caused us so much trouble, remember?"

"Yeah, but I split up with all you guys twice, and took off on my own."

"Yes, but I was so proud and arrogant, Danny Ray, that I never said 'thank you' or 'please' just once to anyone for anything. It dawns on me now that you sprang me out of Dumbledown Dungeon. Thank you, Danny Ray."

All of the cowboy's attempts to get Prince Blue to smile had failed.

"Ah, shucks, Prince," he said cheerfully, "cheer up, for crying out loud! Just listening to you, I'd say you learned a whole lot already. Shoot! You'll make a great king!"

The hellwain devil cleared his throat and with an awful smile announced: "Maybe Tûk be King of Elidor, ha!"

Danny Ray slapped his knee and laughed as Tûk struck a kingly pose, holding his pitchfork like a scepter.

But then the hellwain devil stopped short, hissing menacingly at some small animal that had perched nearby on a rock. Its black, woolly hair could not entirely conceal its protruding belly and an oily, greasy hide beneath. Gnats and flies buzzed happily about its head. Its floppy ears tensed, sensing danger emanating from the devil, who had assumed a sneaky, crouching, hunting position. It sniffed with its black, runny nose, a bubble of mucus rising and falling as it breathed. In defiance of the devil, an awful snorting noise issued out of its open, gaping mouth.

Tûk hissed. The thing answered with a horrible blubbering noise from a wobbly throat, and spit a wad of white milky substance that splattered on the ground.

"Ah!" shouted Tûk and heaved his pitchfork. The animal disappeared in a flash, showing amazing agility for such a heavy, bloated, hairy thing, leaving behind a puddle of stinking slime on the rock.

"Wulver!" the devil growled in frustration, picking up his weapon.

"Wait," asked Danny Ray in a shaky voice. "What did you call that?"

"Wulver!" repeated Tûk.

"Oh," the cowboy said weakly. He thought back to that morning on Sugarwood Island when Tûk had been cooking meat over a fire—and Danny Ray had eaten hungrily of it. The cowboy broke out into a cold sweat. A sickly tremor ran up his spine and wiggled around in his stomach like a bowl of worms as he remembered what Tûk had called it: wulver.

Prince Blue's face split into a grin. Danny Ray wiped his mouth with the back of his sleeve and muttered, "I think I'm gonna be sick!"

❧ 31 ❧

Ghost Driver

 Clip-clip-clop! Clip-clip-clop! Clip-clip-clop! came the sound of horses' hooves along the circular roadway.

"Lookie there!" Danny Ray pointed. "Darnedest thing I ever saw!"

Here came a gold and white carriage drawn by six spotted unicorns. Sparks flashed from their silver heels as they pranced and danced along. The driver, a short fat man with no neck, and wearing a sack of a hat and a red suit, leaned back and puffed out his mouth as he reined them to a halt. The unicorns snorted and stamped on the brick roadway.

Out of the carriage stepped two figures the cowboy had come to love.

"King Krystal, sir!" This time Danny Ray remembered to bow respectfully.

The old king tapped over to them with his silver cane. The bottom half of his white beard had been burned away during the fiery confrontation with Ikkus-Sark. With him walked a serious little girl in a shimmering gown, twinkling and winkling with gems. Her beautiful yellow hair, singed so badly, had been cropped above her shoulders.

"Gosh, Cherry!" the cowboy exclaimed. "That sure is a pretty outfit."

"Don't you try to make up with me, Danny Ray!"

"Who put the spark in your furnace, girl?" asked the cowboy.

"My other dress is ruined forever!" She poked a finger in her ear. "Stinking soot!" she fumed, displaying a black finger.

Tûk stood off, studying his nails, his nose twitching to catch the scent of spiced tobacco wafting in the air as the carriage driver lit his pipe and sat back, smiling and satisfied.

"Approach me, my glorious prince!" said King Krystal. "And you, Danny Ray, my grand cowboy! Lord Red sends his congratulations from the hospital, while Lord Green is probably off to Cherrydale—confound him! Must be jealous of your success! Ah, there are certain proud people that not even a king may control!"

"We were just talking, Your Majesty," said Prince Blue frankly, "of how inglorious I am."

"And how I ain't so grand, neither," put in the cowboy sadly. "Seeing's how we failed to rescue your daughter, sir."

"You went out and tried your best, Danny Ray." The king sighed heavily, and his voice shook with emotion. "I say it with tears, but sometimes our loved ones depart this world and we cannot have them back." The hand that held the royal silver cane trembled. "Even though their time has ended unfairly soon, even though they are still young and full of light, of dancing, and of song, we simply cannot have them back."

King Krystal pointed across the bay to the top of the Tower of Fire, which had dimmed to a dull red as the sun disappeared below the western horizon. There, crowned by the newly awakened stars, stood a lonely figure looking out to sea. "Each day, Princess Ruby, my second daughter, stands there alone. But Lord Purple has been taken from her forever, and who may empty her cup of loneliness, of bitterness?"

Cherry began to weep, ever so softly, ever so pitifully. Her wet eyes looked out over the horizon where the barest sliver of a moon appeared. "The night of the new moon has passed," she said with a quivering lip. "Princess Amber's soul has traveled beyond the Vale of the Moon. It's too late to save her now."

Prince Blue said softly, "But you saved all of us, Cherry!"

Danny Ray came and knelt in front of her and added, "And you saved the whole doggone world!"

"Cherry is best!" exclaimed the hellwain devil, standing over the prince's shoulder.

"But I couldn't have done it without you, Danny Ray!" she said, weeping. "You made that awful king look away from me."

"And that twinkle of time was all you needed, Cherry!" put in Prince Blue.

"Made best of shot!" said Tûk.

But then she wiped away a tear and frowned. "What are you smiling about, Danny Ray?"

"Oh, there's this fellow back home, Hanky the Clown. He told me once that some days you're a cowboy, and some day's you're a clown." Danny Ray had this image of himself yelling and stomping and waving his arms around, just like a rodeo clown, distracting the horned demon, Ikkus-Sark, away from

Cherry long enough for her to aim the slingshot and take her shot. "I didn't know what he meant then, but I do now. Come to think on it, it *is* more honorable to be a clown."

"Bah!" snorted Tûk, rattling his pitchfork.

"Danny Ray," said King Krystal, "I see no lightning-filled magical door to take you home to the Otherworld. Consider staying with us here in Elidor. Once again I offer you your own castle!"

"Will you stay, Danny Ray?" cried Cherry with pleading eyes. "Will you? Will you?"

The cowboy scratched his chin and said: "Come to think on it, that ain't such a bad idea."

"And you, Prince Blue!" said the king. "When the days of mourning for Princess Amber are past, we shall celebrate your becoming the new Lord of Ironwood! I can hardly believe you were once a spoiled, bratty prince! No, rather, you are fast becoming the type of man to sit upon the throne of Elidor!"

"Wow!" said Danny Ray, looking at the red-faced prince with a twinkle in his eye.

There came a raucous commotion as the unicorns snorted, pulled violently against their reins, and stamped their hooves. The driver was jostled backward, his blue boots lifting up into the air, his white pipe popping out of his mouth and shattering on the roadway below. He grabbed the reins just as the frantic beasts lunged away.

"What the heck spooked them?" asked the cowboy, standing up and watching the carriage lurch away crazily down the roadway.

Tûk's nose twitched again, his yellow eyes paying no attention to the runaway carriage, but rather to the turbulent clouds boiling forth from the western horizon beyond the Tower of Fire. "There!" He pointed with his pitchfork.

They all looked to the west as the storm, glowing with an unnatural blue, swarmed against the clear sky and canceled out the slender sickle moon. And the flying carriage carried by that storm was unlike any other carriage that had ever been seen in Elidor or her environs, and the skeletonlike horses, unlike any that had ever graced the fair fields of Ironwood or of Cherrydale. And lo! the pale driver that kept those fell beasts in check was no less fearful, gripping the glowing reins with frightful hands, guiding them around the circle of Birdwhistle Bay in a thunderous rush of cold wind and dense fog. The ghostly carriage came to a halt before the Tree of Wisdom, which now sheltered a most astonished group of spectators.

Frost puffed from the horses' nostrils. Ice had formed on the corners of the windows, and from the roof railing of the carriage, icicles glittered over a faded line of words painted over the door: OVERLAND MAIL COMPANY.

"Gosh! A stagecoach!" Danny Ray said under his breath.

It creaked and groaned as the driver pulled the brake and slowly climbed down, leaving his breech-loading rifle propped in the front seat. His stovepipe hat shadowed a whitish face with dark eyes. Straggly white hair flowed down upon his shoulders, while his ground-length leather coat, buckskin gloves and britches, and knee boots flickered with frost fire.

The driver's mouth opened and said: "All stops! Siloam Springs, Wagoner, Muskogee . . . Tahlequah!"

Then the mouth closed. The vacant eyes looked directly at Danny Ray, and a spark of recognition flashed there. The haunting apparition rapped his whip against the stagecoach door, which began to waver in a watery blue color with lightning flashing over its surface—the magical door!

"I ain't going back!" Danny Ray called to him.

"Yeah! He ain't going back!" said Cherry, adopting her own Oklahoma accent.

"He's staying in Elidor with his friends," declared Prince Blue.

"And With Tûk!" snapped the hellwain devil.

"You may so inform the Lord Advocate for us!" announced King Krystal.

The gaunt face, shiny with ice and dusted with frost, gave them a terrible smile. Then, ever so slowly, it shook its head from side to side.

The cowboy rested his hand on his blue rope of thrillium. "I'm still a champion here in Elidor."

"That's right!" cried Cherry. Tûk nodded fiercely and gripped his pitchfork.

But the head only laughed, a jagged laugh like shattering ice. His coat wafted open to reveal a sawed-off double-barreled shotgun. He reached out his whip hand and opened the door. From the stagecoach stepped a lovely figure in a gray gown, her face hidden by a silver veil.

She left the stagecoach door open behind her.

"Who is that passenger woman standing there?" asked the king in a halting voice, afraid to even venture a guess.

But Danny Ray knew who she was. No wonder the driver was smiling. Danny Ray had no choice but to obey him.

Checkmate.

The cowboy turned to his friends and said, "Well, I guess I

was wrong about stayin' in Elidor for a while. I best be gettin' on home."

The cowboy reached out and shook Prince Blue by the hand. He handed him the glittering magical blue coil and his bag of treasure, saying with a smirk: "Try to take better care of my rope and my other stuff this time, just in case I ever come back."

Danny Ray grinned inside to see Tûk—big, red, hulking, unassailable Tûk, wiping away a tear. King Krystal gripped the cowboy by the shoulder and then let him go.

Lastly, the cowboy knelt down and hugged Cherry. Blue eyes looked into blue eyes.

"Don't go, Danny Ray!" she said in a shaky voice. "You promised!"

"I gotta go, Cherry," he said tenderly.

She began to cry again.

The cowboy, still on his knees, hugged her even more fiercely. And shucks! For the first time in his life he didn't care if anyone saw him hugging a girl, and his heart nearly busted in two to hear her sobbing. She held out a red object: the magical slingshot.

"You just keep that slingshot for yourself, Cherry," the cowboy said softly. "Truth is, you earned it! Make sure to tell your uncle Quigglewigg and Piper and Hoodie Crow good-bye for me."

"I love you, Danny Ray!" she said in a small voice.

"I love you, too, Cherry," he said, "but only when you're asleep and not causing me any trouble."

"You take that back, Danny Ray!"

But then her temper melted, and she giggled and hugged him one last time.

Danny Ray inhaled deeply and then took a step toward the stagecoach. The veiled woman took one step toward him. He took yet another step, and so she was allowed another step away from the carriage. In a few more strides Danny Ray stood opposite her.

She lowered her veil.

The cowboy's heart leaped into his throat. His eyes went moist.

"Been lookin' all over for you, ma'am," he said, taking off his hat.

"Princess Amber!" breathed Cherry.

"Oh, my daughter!" cried King Krystal.

The princess regarded the cowboy with those lovely gray eyes, and smiled. "I never thought I'd see you again, Danny Ray. Or anyone else in this world, for that matter." Her eyes circled around the bay, like someone who has just awakened from a long, troubling dream. "I was about to board that great ship for the Land of the Dead. The White Lady looked on me with mercy, and has returned me to Elidor along with her thanks for the spunkies, whatever that means."

Danny Ray's face broke into a grin. "Long story, ma'am."

Her eyes settled on her father, King Krystal, standing with Cherry, Prince Blue, and then on the hellwain devil.

"That's Tûk," offered the cowboy, answering her astonished expression. "He takes some gettin' used to. Don't be scared none by that scar on his face—just don't let him feed you nothing called a wulver."

From out of the driver's nose shot cold steam, like a locomotive. His shocking mouth opened again and repeated: "All stops!

Siloam Springs, Fort Smith, Muskogee, Wagoner . . . Tahle-quah—"

"Jest hold yer horses!" snapped the cowboy. "I may be deaf in one ear and blind in the other, but I can hear you, doggone it!" The cowboy turned to Princess Amber and grinned widely, saying, "Get it, ma'am—hold your horses?"

"What happened to your hat, la?"

"Another long story, ma'am." He smiled weakly, fingering his cowboy hat's singed edges, and wishing more than ever he could stay behind to tell her the whole tale.

"Someday, if you return to our kingdom, you can tell me some of these stories." She laughed lightly, and Danny Ray remembered how he loved the sound of it. "Once again the Lord Advocate has shown his wisdom by sending you, Danny Ray. Thank you."

"Well, I best be gettin' back home," he said at last, putting on his hat.

For a moment, as they stood suspended between two magical worlds, their eyes met again. A small blue bird flitted down and landed on her shoulder, chirping merrily, joined by another, and then another. She reached out her hand. It was warm, and Danny Ray kissed it lightly. She looked deeply into his eyes and smiled again. "Thank you, Lord Cowboy."

"No, ma'am," he said, "the name's Danny Ray, and I'm the best rodeo—well, I guess I'm just a regular rodeo cowboy this time!"

With that, Princess Amber turned and ran to receive her father's fierce hug while Cherry started crying all over again, but this time from joy, clutching Princess Amber desperately, afraid to let go of her.

The huge stagecoach swayed on its springs as the cowboy climbed up and took his seat.

"Sorry that you can't stay, Danny Ray," said the driver, a tone of sympathy in his voice. "Well, maybe I ain't sorry. The Lord Advocate—he knows it would be a tragedy for you, sooner or later. Staying on was a tragedy for me."

A look passed between them.

The cowboy nodded. "You didn't think I recognized you, huh, Mr. Tabbashavar?"

The mouth smiled. "I'm a century or so older since you last saw me! As soon as I left the island I began to age pretty quick."

Mr. Tabbashavar handed Danny Ray a Colt revolver. It felt cold and heavy in the cowboy's hand.

"What's this here gun for?"

"Hip howitzer—for guardin' the treasure box." Mr. Tabbashavar motioned. The cowboy tapped his boot against the green iron-bound box at his feet with the words WELLS FARGO & CO. printed in white. "Moved it from the front boot down to here. So, be on the lookout for robbers, Confederates more than likely, or Indians."

"Things have changed an awful lot back home," said Danny Ray, laying the firearm on the cushion next to him. "I won't be needin' no gun."

The cowboy's hand shot to his pocket. "Oh—I almost forgot! I got Arcile right here in my pocket! It came in real handy defeating the King of the Fantasms."

"Keep it!" responded Mr. Tabbashavar. "Come to think on it, take this." He opened his palm and handed the cowboy a yellow, marble-sized stone. "This is Aillel, sister stone to Arcile. Its magic built Sugarwood Island. I'm afraid all of its work'll be un-did, and the island will return to the way it was, but I guess it don't matter none." He looked straight at the cowboy. "I'm going home, now, thanks to you. I hope you're proud of me, Danny Ray—I sure do hope you're proud. It was a hard choice to leave Sugarwood Island, but the right one."

It must have taken a lot of courage for Mr. Tabbashavar to leave his island. And Danny Ray noticed that his face was healed—it no longer had that line down the middle dividing good from evil.

Before he closed the door, he paused and said to the cowboy, "Thanks for everything, Danny Ray."

The stagecoach leaned over slightly as, somewhere outside, Mr. Tabbashavar climbed up, took his seat, and gripped the reins. The cowboy pulled back the damask-lined leather curtain and peered out the window. Prince Blue was looking back at him, and they smiled a knowing smile at each other.

CRACK! came the sharp snap of a whip. Danny Ray was pressed back against the cushioned backrest as the stagecoach lurched forward and gathered speed. In a puff! Prince Blue and the others were lost in cloud and tingly mist.

Danny Ray pressed his nose against the cold glass. The stage-coach was flying! Far below he saw the deck of *Diamond* where Piper and Hoodie Crow paused from their chores to look up and wave. Abruptly they passed out of view as the stagecoach just cleared the Tower of the Rose and was swallowed up by that magical blanket of blue cloud: Danny Ray was headed home!

An unexpected urge welled up in the cowboy. He bit his lip as he looked down, hoping for a break in the clouds that he might catch a lucky sight of *Pearl* and of the sultana. But no, she was halfway to Port Palnacky by now.

The carriage rose even higher in the air. Danny Ray saw no sign of the Storm Demon that had assaulted him on his way in. Yup, Ikkus-Sark had been defeated. That didn't mean there weren't other villains to be conquered, but that one, at least, had been put to rest.

They rose up above the cloud cover, a vast cotton coverlet. The dying sun's rays silhouetted the stagecoach against a brilliant orange cloudbank. The cowboy grinned; the shadow of Mr. Tabbashavar was his own.

Danny Ray sighed and sat back. He was suddenly glad to be going home. He thought of everyone he was leaving behind— how proud he was of little Cherry and her slingshot, of Tûk coming straight out of prison to go on the quest, and Prince Blue too, and of Captain Quigglewigg and Piper and everyone else. When Elidor had needed them most, somehow they had come through again.

Funny, Mr. Tabbashavar had wanted to know if he was proud of him. Danny Ray was surprised to find that, out of everyone, he was proud of Mr. Tabbashavar most of all.

✦ Acknowledgments ✦

I must, first and foremost, acknowledge my young readers—how can I ever thank them enough? To Mitch and Marisa Stratelak, Sean Warmoth, and Anna and Maddy Preston. To Ryan Fadden, Alyssa Johnson, Rebecca Vickers and to my own precious but ornery niece, Brooke Bailey.

I am extremely grateful to Kathleen Doherty at Tor Books for her advice and excellent skill as an editor. To my exceptional agent, Tracy Grant of the Leona Literary Agency, and to Joy Wilcox for her hospitality, storyline insight, and sense of humor. To Dan Fulsang and Jose Medina for their friendship and technical support.

Last, but certainly not least, to my colleagues and friends with the Illinois chapter of the Society of Children's Book Writers and Illustrators (SCBWI).

Oh! And to Marsha Daudelin, a great organizer, planner, and fellow explorer!

✦ About the Author ✦

LEN BAILEY is a professional radio-commercial and voice-over actor and bagpipe player. He attended high school in Tahlequah, Oklahoma; college at Trinity College in Deerfield, Illinois, where he earned a B.A. in history. He also earned a journalism scholarship and was a member of the 1974 NCAA National Champion soccer team.

A sometime golfer who admits his best "wood" is his pencil, Len enjoys serenading the neighborhood with his bagpipe playing. He lives "quietly" with his wife and three sons in the western suburbs of Chicago.

Starscape

Award-Winning
Science Fiction and Fantasy
for Ages 10 and up

STARSCAPE

www.tor-forge.com/starscape